FACE DOWN
ACROSS THE
WESTERN SEA

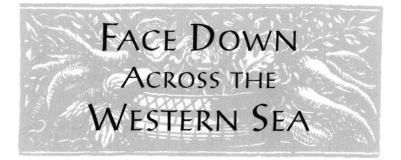

FACE DOWN ACROSS THE WESTERN SEA

Kathy Lynn Emerson

St. Martin's Minotaur
New York

www.minotaurbooks.com

Library of Congress Cataloging-in-Publication Data

Emerson, Kathy Lynn.
Face down across the Western sea / Kathy Lynn Emerson.—1st ed.
        p.   cm.
    ISBN 0-312-28823-9
    1. Appleton, Susanna, Lady (Fictitious character)—Fiction.   2. Great
Britain—History—Elizabeth, 1558–1603—Fiction.   3. America—Discovery and
exploration—Fiction.   4. Women detectives—England—Fiction.   5. Cornwall
    (England : County)—Fiction.   6. Herbalists—Fiction.   I. Title.

        PS3555.M414 F28   2002
            813'.54—dc21
            2001048881

    First Edition: April 2002

        10   9   8   7   6   5   4   3   2   1

Residents of and Guests at Priory House, Cornwall, 1571

Susanna, Lady Appleton, herbalist and sleuth
Sir Walter Pendennis, her host
Eleanor, Lady Pendennis, his wife
Rosamond, Eleanor's daughter, age eight
Jennet, Susanna's friend, companion, and former tiring-maid
Lionel and Fulke, Susanna's henchmen
Hester, Rosamond's maid
Melka, Eleanor's maid
Jacob, Walter's steward
The scholars: Martin Calthorpe, Bartholomew Fletcher, Samuel Gainsford, Owen Merrick, Sir Gregory Speake, and Adam Weller
Gwyn, Owen Merrick's daughter
Daniel, a clerk
Piers, a guard
David Ingram,* a sailor who had an adventure in the New World
Zachary Alday, son of John Alday,* manservant to Sebastian Cabot*
A visitor only: Tristram Pendennis, Walter's older brother
In Boscastle: Alexander Trewinard, a "ghost" from Walter's past
Elsewhere, but sending letters to Priory House: Dr. John Dee,* royal astronomer, and Nick Baldwin, merchant

---

*Indicates a real person.

v

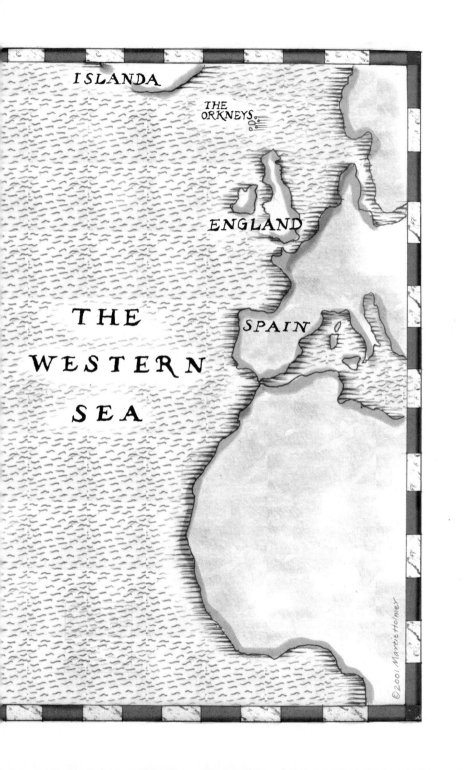

FACE DOWN
ACROSS THE
WESTERN SEA

1

To the boy on the pine-studded promontory, the English ship looked like a small island with strange and wonderful trees growing upon it.

He was big for his age, easily mistaken for a man full grown. His hair, black as midnight, grew to the middle of a back tanned to deep bronze.

"A stone canoe," his companion murmured in a tone filled with awe. "It is just as the legends describe it."

The boy said nothing for a long time. A variation of the same story claimed that men who came from the direction of the sun traveled the sea on the backs of whales. Only a few now living knew the truth behind the tales.

The ship bobbed at anchor in the bay. On deck, small figures garbed in colorful clothing set about launching a shallop in which to row to the rock-strewn shore. Friends or enemies? The boy remembered the last time men had come across what they called "the Western Sea." He remembered the killing.

"We must go back to the village," he said. "My father will know what to do."

2

SEVENTY YEARS LATER (JUNE 1571)
ACROSS THE WESTERN SEA, IN CORNWALL

Martin Calthorpe glowered at the sole occupant of what had once been a Cistercian abbey's chapter house. She was young enough to be his daughter. Indeed, she was the only surviving child of one of the greatest friends of his youth, Sir Amyas Leigh, a fact that made the pill Calthorpe was obliged to swallow taste more bitter still.

He should have been the one assigned to portion out the maps, manuscripts, and books at the heart of their research; but at her father's insistence, Susanna Leigh, now Lady Appleton and a widow, had been educated as if she were a boy. This was the unpalatable end result. A woman had been selected to supervise the work of Calthorpe and his fellow scholars at Priory House.

Alerted by some small sound from the doorway of the room Sir Walter Pendennis had converted into a library, Susanna glanced up from the letters she was cataloguing. "Master Calthorpe, good day to you. What have you to report?"

Enthusiasm shone in her intelligent, bright blue eyes. For a moment Calthorpe saw past her woman's clothing and the obviously female shape beneath it and glimpsed the quality he'd most admired in her father, his love of study. *"Amore ac studio,"* he mumbled under his breath.

Such a pity Susanna had not been born a boy. Amyas Leigh, he remembered, had sired only girls. The other had died young, and Leigh himself had gone to his reward when his remaining daughter was a mere lass of thirteen, four and twenty years ago. At her father's command, however, Susanna had already been taught Latin, Greek, mathematics, and philosophy. She had taken up the study of modern languages on her own and acquired some small skill at translating them into English. She'd also written two herbals and engaged in the study of cosmography, indulging herself with what Calthorpe considered to be a most unwomanly degree of interest in maps and geography.

"Master Calthorpe?" Susanna's voice had hardened at his silence. She had her father's sturdy build and above average height. When she looked stern, as she did now, she was an imposing, even intimidating figure.

"I have encountered several discrepancies." Calthorpe realized he was tugging at the end of his long, white beard and forced himself to let go. That he resented her position, she knew already, but he hoped she would not realize how uncomfortable the obligation to report to her made him feel.

"Discrepancies in one of the translations?"

Because of Calthorpe's expert knowledge of the Italian language, Susanna had assigned him to render into English several books published in Venice. At present he was working on a three-volume travel book, *Terzo Volume delle Navigationi et Viaggi,* but he'd also been given other tasks. He cleared his throat and decided to start with the most glaring difficulty.

"I was one of those who took down the statements of that sailor, David Ingram."

"Ah, yes. One of the survivors of a land journey from Spanish La Florida all the way to the northern part of the great land mass across the Western Sea. A remarkable feat. What of him?"

"As you say, he claims to have reached the area mapmakers now call Norombega, but I fear he tells a far different story from

3

that related by his companion, Richard Twide." Three scholars had questioned each man, but only Calthorpe had been present at both interviews.

"Go on." Parchment rustled as Susanna put aside the documents on which she'd been working, assuring Calthorpe that he now had her full attention.

"Twide gave his statement and was allowed to depart." He could not keep the irritation out of his voice.

"We had no authority to keep him here. Once we transcribed his account of the journey—"

"That is another problem. I cannot locate the transcript." Without the written testimony to consult, Calthorpe had found it difficult to compare his memory of Twide's story point by point with Ingram's tale.

"Do you mean it has been misplaced?"

"I mean it has been stolen."

The quill she'd been toying with stilled in her hand. "Borrowed, mayhap?" Her tone remained mild, but her gaze reminded Calthorpe of tempered steel. He bristled at the implied criticism. Unlike some people, he was not a man who leapt to unwarranted conclusions.

"May I remind you, madam, that not all those in residence here possess the same background or degree of ability. Furthermore, not having been to Oxford or Cambridge, you cannot appreciate the extent of the rivalry that exists among university scholars."

"Like my father, you studied at Christ College, Cambridge." Susanna pointed one finger in his direction then raised a second in preparation for ticking off the names of his colleagues.

Calthorpe found this habit, which she frequently employed to enumerate items on a list, annoying in the extreme. He gritted his teeth and forced a grim smile, but his patience had already worn thin.

"Masters Fletcher, Gainsford, and Weller are Oxford men, I grant you, but Sir Gregory Speake and Master Merrick also matriculated at Cambridge."

The sight of that upraised hand, little finger waggling at him, snapped Calthorpe's restraint. A quick temper had always been his greatest failing. Age had not made him less prone to blurt out a scathing remark, and he was long past the point of indulging Susanna because of her womanhood. "Merrick is a Bristol merchant's son. His understanding is that of a shopkeeper, not a scholar."

Susanna's palms slammed down flat on the worktable in front of her as she shot to her feet. Startled by her vehemence, Calthorpe took a step back, releasing the scent of bay leaves strewn among the rushes as he trod on them.

"Many clever and insightful men are merchants, Master Calthorpe, and we would be hard pressed to succeed in our task were it not for the careful records they keep. You discount their contributions at your peril and do them a great disservice, much like the disservice you do women by refusing to acknowledge that we have as great a capacity for intelligence as any man."

Uncertain what had provoked this passionate defense, Calthorpe nevertheless blundered on. "Academic competition is endemic among scholars, and few scruple to claim other men's work as their own. More to the point, Merrick's daughter is the only one who had access to my papers. Ask her what became of Twide's testimony!"

Susanna's eyes narrowed. "Have a care, Master Calthorpe. Theft of items valued at a shilling or more is a hanging offense."

"I do not make the charge without forethought." Calthorpe drew himself up straighter and glared back at her. "Consider, madam, that there was no reason for her to accompany her father here in the first place."

"Gwyn Merrick came to make herself useful. Had I not brought my own housekeeper from Leigh Abbey, I have no doubt she would have taken charge of those duties at Priory House." Susanna's voice was as cold as her stare, but it did nothing to cool Calthorpe's heated words.

"Useful!" He flung both hands into the air in frustration. Trust

5

one woman to defend another. "Merrick's daughter has pawed through my possessions, freed to examine each item by the excuse that she's been sent to clean and straighten."

"Unless you have proof to the contrary, I must insist we assume the missing document has been misplaced rather than stolen. We share our conclusions here, Master Calthorpe. Any of your colleagues had only to ask, and a copy of Twide's testimony would have been provided to him. There was no reason to steal it."

Calthorpe was marshaling a new argument to refute this conclusion when the unmistakable sounds of approaching horsemen reached him. Voices called out from the direction of the stables. Hooves thudded on hard-packed ground. Drawn by the commotion, Susanna crossed the library to a window that overlooked the stableyard and flung the shutters wide. Calthorpe joined her there in time to witness the arrival of several riders and a horse-borne litter.

Although the winter had been one of storms, floods, and landslides, the soil had long since lost its moisture. The dust stirred up by the horses swirled toward the window. Calthorpe pulled back, his eyes watering.

Even more irritating was what he'd seen. *Another gentlewoman,* he thought in disgust. *And worse, a girl-child mounted on one of the horses.* Turning to Susanna, complaints ready on his tongue, he bit back what he'd been about to say. She gripped the sill with white-knuckled force and was obliged to take several deep breaths before she regained her composure. Her face had gone as pale as a blanched almond.

Alarmed, Calthorpe forgot he was wroth with her. "Are you ill, Susanna? Shall I call someone?"

"I will recover." He heard a note of irony in her voice.

"Who are these people? How did they get past Sir Walter's guards? I thought he gave orders to send all visitors away."

"The girl on the roan is my foster daughter, Rosamond." She had to clear her throat before she could continue. "The litter transports Rosamond's mother, Eleanor Pendennis. She is Sir Walter's wife."

6

Sir Walter Pendennis, as the owner of Priory House, was their nominal host. While Calthorpe watched, Pendennis strode into the stableyard looking no more pleased at the sight of a woman and child than Calthorpe had been. Shoulders stiff, fists clenched at his sides, he advanced on the litter.

"I must go down!" Susanna was already moving toward the door. "We will have to continue our discussion at a later time, Master Calthorpe. After supper?"

"There is no great rush," he conceded. His temper, always quick to flare, was likewise fast to fade.

She took him at his word and hurried off, to interfere in Sir Walter's business, he surmised.

Calthorpe's pace was slower. He had no interest in the new-comers and made his way instead toward the former monk's cell he'd been assigned as a private study, determined to use this interval to write down all he remembered of Twide's account. He'd give that to Susanna this evening then go on to discuss the other matter he'd meant to bring to her attention. Another discrepancy, this one in records left by a certain gentleman of Mantua.

Lost in contemplation of how the two subjects might be linked, Calthorpe entered his cubicle and closed the door behind him. Only then did he realize someone was already in the small room.

"Put that back!" he ordered, outraged to recognize one of the most precious of his research materials in the intruder's hand. Protective as a doting father looking out for his child and without a thought for his own safety, Calthorpe advanced toward his writing table and the person cowering behind it.

The would-be thief came at him in a desperate rush. They collided heavily and Calthorpe fell, striking both knees on unyielding oak floorboards with enough force to rattle his bones. Too late, he perceived the extent of his danger, but before he could ward off the blow, pain lanced through his head.

His last thought, as he sank into unconsciousness, was that he wished he'd had time to tell Susanna Appleton everything.

3

Susanna knelt to embrace Rosamond, heedless of the prick of stones through the fabric of her kirtle and chemise. Tears welled in her eyes when the eight year old wrapped both arms around her waist and clung tight. Reveling in the scents of girl and horse, Susanna hugged her back.

After a moment, Rosamond squirmed free. "I missed you, Mama," she declared. "Did you miss me?"

"How could I not, my dearest?" She brushed Rosamond's soft cheek with her knuckles in an affectionate caress, pleased to see her own delight at their reunion reflected in Rosamond's dark brown eyes. "Now give me your hand to help me to my feet."

An old injury to her leg made her less nimble than she'd have liked, but Rosamond was prompt to oblige.

Over the top of the girl's dark head, through the tied-back curtains of the litter, Susanna met the cool, speculative gaze of Eleanor Pendennis. She had little choice but to remain inside. As the result of severe damage to both legs and one hip, she was crippled for life.

Susanna's joy fled, replaced by a growing sense of dread.

Standing next to the litter, ignoring Rosamond and Susanna as he spoke in low, earnest tones to his wife, was Sir Walter. He held himself stiff as a cadaver, but Susanna knew him well enough to be able to tell he was seething just beneath the surface.

When Eleanor had married him, almost six years ago, they had seemed perfectly suited. Susanna had been inclined to believe it might even be a love match. She had readily agreed to take charge of Rosamond while Eleanor accompanied Walter on various diplomatic missions.

Of its own volition, Susanna's arm slid around Rosamond's shoulders. In return, the little girl's fingers clenched on Susanna's hip, as if she sensed something amiss. Eleanor's child had lived at Leigh Abbey, Susanna's home in Kent, for more than half her life. It was only natural that she felt more comfortable with the woman she now called *Mama* than the one she referred to as *Mother.*

And Susanna loved her in return. She had not wanted to at first. Childless herself, she'd never had much to do with children, and Rosamond was difficult. But the bond that had formed between them was as unbreakable as it was inexplicable. Each time she'd had to leave the youngster behind at Leigh Abbey, their parting had been more wrenching. Now she felt physical pain at the thought that Eleanor intended to make their separation permanent.

"Go and see to your horse, Rosamond," she murmured, slipping free of the girl's grip. It was a great pity she could not as easily dislodge the emotional coils that bound her to Walter and Eleanor, but they shared too much history and too many secrets. Like a pall over them all hovered the shade of Sir Robert Appleton, Susanna's long-dead husband . . . and Rosamond's father.

Braced for unpleasantness, dreading the outcome of this unexpected turn of events, Susanna approached the litter. Eleanor, who reclined on soft cushions, traveled just at eye level, since the lightweight wooden framework was suspended by means of stout poles attached to the saddles of two horses, one fore and one aft. To protect her from the elements, a shell of shaved hide, which Eleanor had caused to be dyed bright yellow, stretched tight over her head, held in position by an abundance of polished brass nails.

The healer in Susanna assessed the other woman for signs her condition had been made worse by the arduous journey, but she saw nothing that could not be accounted for by simple fatigue.

9

Susanna could sympathize with that. Her own trip from Kent across the south of England to this eastern part of Cornwall had taken more than two weeks, most of it on surpassing bad roads.

Intent upon watching her husband stalk away, Eleanor did not look at Susanna. "He has lost weight since I saw him last. The change makes him look almost gaunt."

A slight reduction in girth, Susanna thought, glancing in the direction of the tall, retreating figure, *would not be amiss,* but the only difference she noticed was a more pronounced stoop of the shoulders. She attributed that to Eleanor's presence at Priory House. Since she had known Walter longer than Eleanor had, Susanna felt qualified to judge both his moods and his health. Once he had been Robert Appleton's closest friend and colleague. They'd had many shared interests; but while Robert's greatest weakness had been women, Walter's was ever fine food.

Turning back to the litter, Susanna addressed Eleanor. "You agreed to recuperate from your injuries at Leigh Abbey. I hope you have not done yourself irreparable harm with all this traveling."

"My place is at my husband's side." The sweet tone in Eleanor's voice rang false, the more so when she added, "After you left, I realized I had imposed upon your hospitality long enough. And you know it was always Walter's plan to bring me here upon our return from the Continent."

It was true that it had once been Walter's stated intention to retire to Cornwall and rusticate, but Susanna had always had difficulty imagining him as a simple gentleman farmer. Before he'd become a diplomat, he'd been an intelligence gatherer for the Crown.

"Some advance warning might have been helpful. There are several other . . . guests here now." Susanna was unsure how much she should say to Walter's wife. There would have to be some explanations made, but it was not her place to give them.

"Yes, I see that." Eleanor surveyed the others in the stableyard with a cursory glance then ignored them. "I had thought the place would be in better repair."

"You cannot see the new manor house from here. It is not yet complete, but I assure you that what there is contains all the necessities."

Walter had acquired the old priory from the Crown years before. As was the custom, he'd used stone from a dismantled church to construct his fine new house. Some of the original buildings remained, however, enough so that when the queen needed a remote location to accommodate a half-dozen guests, she had ordered Walter to make Priory House, and himself, available.

Eleanor turned her back on Susanna to speak in a low voice to her maidservant. Dismissed, Susanna looked around for Rosamond and located her foster daughter near the stable, still discussing the proper care of Courtier, her horse, with one of Walter's grooms.

The sight provoked a fleeting smile. How like her father she was, both in appearance and in nature. Strong-willed, self-centered, and quick-tempered, she could also be charming. Susanna had never been able to stop herself from responding to that aspect of her personality. Some said she spoiled the child, indulged Rosamond when she should be made to follow rules, but Susanna preferred to think she governed with love.

A woman moved in Rosamond's direction with hesitant steps, giving the clear impression that she'd not approach her at all were she not compelled to do so. Hester Peacock, once Rosamond's nurse, was now her tiring-maid.

The surname was misleading, Susanna thought. Hester Peacock was as plain and brown as a wren. She lacked that bird's delicate smallness, however, being tall and awkward and all but devoid of feminine grace. Still, she had a good heart and was loyal.

Seeing Hester made Susanna wonder who else had accompanied the entourage from Kent, but as she searched the milling crowd for other familiar faces, a tall man with the shambling walk of the short-sighted caught her eye—Master Owen Merrick, the scholar Master Calthorpe had so recently reviled. She noticed that he held a pair of bone-framed spectacles clutched tight in one hand while he rubbed his ear with the other. Mayhap, Susanna thought, the leather straps that held the spectacles in place had irritated his skin.

Merrick was in company with Master Bartholomew Fletcher, a plump, pleasant-faced individual with a ruddy complexion. Together, they were just leaving the stableyard, heading for what had once been the monks' dorter and now housed a private study for each scholar.

Susanna supposed that was where Martin Calthorpe had gone after leaving her, since she did not see him anywhere. A momentary sadness engulfed her. Master Calthorpe of Canterbury had been one of her father's great friends, and he'd assisted her with a certain delicate matter some four years earlier, but he was not happy here. He resented taking orders from a woman.

She had done little to mend the rift between them. In hindsight, she realized she had overreacted to his slighting remark about merchants. By his supercilious tone alone, it was obvious he knew nothing of her own intimate connection to a certain merchant.

That was a very good thing, too. Not that she was ashamed to have taken Nick Baldwin as her lover. He was a prominent member of the Merchant Adventurers, currently residing in Hamburg in order to advance the cause of English trade with that distant port. But as long as they did not intend to marry, discretion was essential. Both church and state disapproved of unsanctified unions. Nick and Susanna would both be universally condemned if their secret got out and probably be brought before the church courts and sentenced to public penance, and possibly even be forced into matrimony.

Susanna sighed. At the moment there was little danger of any of that coming to pass. It had been a year since she'd last seen Nick and another might well pass before his return to England. Indeed, a large part of the reason she'd agreed to accompany Walter to Cornwall two months earlier had been to take her mind off missing Nick.

Jerked back to the present by the sound of a restive horse,

Susanna forced herself to concentrate on the present. This was no time for daydreams.

She frowned as she caught sight of a man scuttling behind what remained of the rear wall of the old infirmary. David Ingram cast a furtive glance over his shoulder just before he disappeared from sight. Susanna could not imagine what he was up to, but then she knew little about him, save that he'd been a sailor all his life. She'd not yet had occasion to speak with him, although she had seen him often enough to take note of the odd fact that he carried a short, stout staff as a walking stick but never seemed to use it for getting about. He appeared to brandish it for show and, on occasion, jabbed one of the servants with it to get his attention.

The sound of her own name being called drew Susanna's attention to Lionel Hubble, the one manservant she'd brought with her to Cornwall. He came toward her in loping strides and with him was another big, strapping fellow, Fulke Rowley, head groom from Leigh Abbey.

Even though she was of unusual height for a woman, Susanna felt like an apple tree between two oaks when they stood one on either side of her. Fulke had dwarfed her since she'd known him, but she could well remember the scrawny boy Lionel had once been. He had grown into a handsome man, lean and well-muscled and prone to turn female heads wherever he went.

"I am glad you came along on this journey," she told Fulke, whose long, plain face resembled that of a mournful hound. "No one could better protect Rosamond from harm."

Although his expression brightened for a moment at her praise, it soon returned to its customary lugubriousness. Fulke was not much given to speech, either. Susanna had often wondered why he and Lionel remained such fast friends, especially when Fulke was so fond of Hester and she, in turn, suffered the pangs of unrequited passion for Lionel.

While Susanna questioned Fulke about the route they had taken and the difficulties encountered along the way, Lionel fidgeted. He seemed to be searching for something, or someone, for his gaze darted from stable to infirmary to chapter house.

Gwyn, Susanna thought, fighting an amused smile. She'd noticed on several occasions that Lionel watched Owen Merrick's pretty, black-haired daughter with deep admiration in his eyes. Nor was Gwyn immune to Lionel's masculine appeal. But Gwyn had not come out to the stableyard.

Neither had Jennet, the friend and companion who had come with Susanna from Leigh Abbey to act as temporary housekeeper at Priory House. The noise of arriving visitors had not, apparently, penetrated as far as the manor house. From where Susanna stood, she could not even see it. The ruins of the infirmary blocked her view.

All conversation came to an abrupt halt when Sir Walter Pendennis returned to order the grooms leading the litter horses to take Lady Pendennis through the narrow passage that led to the house.

"Come, Rosamond," Eleanor called, as she was jounced into motion.

Rosamond crossed her arms in front of her flat chest, sucked in her lower lip, and set one foot to tapping. The picture she presented was such a perfect imitation of Jennet in a fit of pique that Susanna could not hold back a muffled chuckle.

"I want to explore," Rosamond announced. "I have never been to a real monastery before."

"Certes, you have not." Eleanor sounded as petulant as her daughter. "They were all disbanded years before you were born. To me, girl, and at once! Will you never learn how to behave like a proper gentlewoman?"

No one who knew her was surprised when Rosamond disobeyed. She was a rebellious child, and it was second nature to her to resist any effort to guide her actions. She wanted to be the leader herself. At Leigh Abbey she bullied the other children unmercifully. And yet she was not impervious to criticism. The slow blink of her eyes, followed by a defiant toss of the head, told Susanna the harsh words had wounded Rosamond.

"Do as your mother tells you, dearest." Susanna made her voice as gentle as she could, but there was a thread of steel in the silk. Authority must not be flaunted with impunity. That led to anarchy. But Susanna meant to have a word with Eleanor on the subject of her daughter's discipline, in private.

Although Rosamond's face took on a sulky expression, she did not argue. Instead she bolted ahead. Susanna fell into step beside the litter.

Eleanor's first glimpse of the exterior of the new manor house produced a gasp of dismay. "It is so plain," she complained.

"You will find the interior well furnished and comfortable," Susanna assured her. "The exterior follows the precepts of Vitruvius." Walter had studied architecture in Italy as a young man and learned to appreciate an austere style of building, unencumbered with excess ornamentation.

"I will grow accustomed to it, no doubt," Eleanor muttered.

"You mean to stay, then?"

"This is my home." She sounded defensive.

"And Rosamond?" Susanna feared she already knew the answer. Eleanor would not have brought the girl all the way to Cornwall if she did not mean to keep her.

"It is time we were a family again—Walter and Rosamond and I." Eleanor's glittering gaze chilled Susanna to the bone. "My daughter will live here with me until she is old enough to marry, and then I will select a suitable husband for her. You need not trouble yourself about her future, Susanna. I have it well in hand."

4

nconsiderate," Jennet Jaffrey muttered under her breath. "Not a thought given to all the extra work there'll be now she's here." Most housekeepers would have bitten off their own tongues before they'd criticize their employers, even in private. When the lady of the manor arrived, with or without warning, it was the job of her husband's retainers to provide for her every need. But Jennet was no ordinary housekeeper. For one thing, Lady Pendennis was not her mistress. Lady Appleton employed her and had for many years. Sir Walter Pendennis had but borrowed Jennet's services to help put his country house in order.

With ill grace, Jennet ordered the unloading of baggage and the preparation of lodgings for the new arrivals. Then she followed the gentry into Sir Walter's great hall.

Under the supervision of her maidservant, Melka, Lady Pendennis had been transferred from her litter to the carrying chair she'd brought with her. Two stout fellows Jennet had never seen before had hoisted her up and conveyed her inside. Now they continued to support her weight, stoic expressions on their faces but quick to obey when Lady Pendennis gave them directions.

Melka, a short, stocky woman with small, wide-spaced eyes, followed orders more slowly. She had been hired in Poland during the time Sir Walter had spent in Cracow as Queen Elizabeth's ambassador to King Sigismund Augustus. If she spoke any English, no one had ever heard her. How well she understood the language was anybody's guess, but she was protective of her mistress. Someone had to be. Jennet had known only two or three others in her lifetime who would have been so little missed had they suffered a fatal accident.

Lady Pendennis leaned forward in her chair so that the light from an oriel window above the dais shone on the perfect oval of her pale face. The turned-up nose and wide, hazel eyes would have been accounted pleasing, had not livid scars slashed across one cheek.

Jennet exchanged a speaking glance with Jacob Littleton, Sir Walter's steward. Lady Pendennis appeared to be conducting an inspection of the premises, looking to find fault no doubt.

One bushy brow arched in a knowing fashion, Jacob watched his mistress's progress around the room. She had not acknowledged his presence in any way, but then he was a nondescript little man, easy to miss. He had been Sir Walter's manservant for years and was not only older than any of the other servants but more trusted. Jennet had always suspected Jacob knew far more than he'd say of what had passed between his master and mistress before their return from the Continent. Anyone with eyes to see knew there was now a rift between them that had not been there when they'd first wed and gone abroad. Doubtless it had to do with the accident that had crippled Lady Pendennis, an accident, Jennet had reason to know, that had been no accident at all.

Lady Pendennis had been fortunate to escape death, but she did not seem appreciative of her good luck. Jennet could remember feeling sorry for her when she'd first arrived at Leigh Abbey a year ago. Lady Pendennis had been very thin, almost emaciated, unable to walk, and horribly scarred. But she'd put on flesh since, and the scars had faded. She had potions and powders to dull her pain. Certes, she would never walk again unaided, but she could get about in that chair and, for short distances, on crutches. All in all, she ought to be grateful to God for her improvement.

Instead of gratitude for Lady Appleton's care, Lady Pendennis repaid her with resentment. The loss of mobility she'd suffered as a result of being trampled by horses and run over by the heavy wagon they'd been pulling had shortened her temper and made her intolerant of anyone she thought she could command.

She did not try to bully Jennet. Lady Appleton's housekeeper had never liked her, not even when she'd been whole, and she saw no point in yielding to a pampered gentlewoman's every whim just because she was crippled. They had clashed repeatedly during the last few months at Leigh Abbey. Jennet had been delighted to leave Lady Pendennis behind and set out on the journey to Cornwall. She had not been so pleased to abandon her husband and children, but that was the price of serving Lady Appleton and always had been. When the time came, her reunion with Mark, their son, Rob, and their daughters, Kate and Susan, would be all the sweeter for having been so long apart.

"This tapestry would look better on that far wall," Lady Pendennis declared.

Acting like some foreign pasha from one of Marco Polo's tales, carried around the room as she issued a string of orders, she did not seem to notice when Sir Walter and Lady Appleton went haring off in response to a message delivered by young Daniel, the scholars' clerk, or that Rosamond followed them. Jennet did not miss either departure, but her curiosity was not piqued until Jacob left a short time later, summoned by one of Sir Walter's guards.

The tapestry Lady Pendennis wanted moved was taken down and rehung. A chair also displeased her. She ordered it carried out of the room. Then she criticized the selection of wine—Canary, Rhenish, and Malmsey—set out on a serving table. She preferred Clary, hippocras, and sherry sack.

Typical, Jennet thought. *Intent on making changes just to prove she can.* She wondered how many more things would be shuffled about before Sir Walter's wife was satisfied.

"Let her have her way, then," Jennet muttered under her breath. "I'll hie myself back to Kent and leave her to it."

A soft chuckle behind her had Jennet whirling around to confront whatever person dared spy on her, but it was only Gwyn

Merrick. Jennet smiled at the younger woman, whose presence at Priory House had been a godsend.

Just twenty-one, still unimpaired by the agues and aches that came later in life, Gwyn had managed her father's household for several years and had offered to help in any way she could at Priory House, even lending a hand to the maids with the cleaning and laundry.

Willing hands and a strong back alone would have made her welcome, no matter the rest of her, but Gwyn also possessed a cheerful disposition and looks that were out of the ordinary. Her complexion would never achieve the paleness accounted beautiful by courtiers but had a pleasant, sun-warmed look to it. Her hair was a rich blue-black that somehow managed to reflect rather than absorb light. Her eyes, too, appeared black at first glance, but closer inspection showed them to be a deep, dark brown. Suppressed laughter danced in them as she spoke.

"I do not think you will go anywhere, Goodwife Jaffrey. If you leave, you'll never find out what happens next. Curiosity would drive you mad."

"I'd find out in time," Jennet muttered, "and 'twould serve you right if I did leave you here alone to deal with her. You've no idea what she's like."

"I have some inkling. Lionel has told me all about her and about the child." Gwyn nodded toward Rosamond, who had just reappeared at the screen end of the hall.

"Mother!" The girl raced toward Lady Pendennis at full tilt, kicking up freshly strewn rushes with every long stride.

"Stop that noise at once!"

Rosamond skidded to a stop, her mouth already open in protest.

Lady Pendennis silenced her with a glare. "How many times have I told you not to run in the house? You will grow up to be a hoyden, Rosamond, if you persist in such misbehavior."

"But, Mother, I—"

"Whatever you have to say can wait. I am too exhausted by our journey to listen to your ramblings."

With a peremptory signal to her chairmen and another gesture to command Melka, Lady Pendennis orchestrated her removal from the great hall. "You, girl!" she called to Gwyn. "Show me to my chamber and be quick about it."

"This way, madam." Gwyn gave a pert bob that scarce qualified as a curtsey before she led the entourage through a door at the dais end of the hall. It opened on a short passage to the family rooms—a parlor and Sir Walter's private study—and out one side of it was a narrow staircase.

Jennet relished the knowledge that there would not be room for both Lady Pendennis and her chair to be carried up. One of her henchmen would have to transport her in his arms. She'd not care for that. Neither would he, poor lout.

Not only dismissed but ignored, Rosamond sulked. Jennet might have felt sorry for Rosamond had the eight year old not caused her so much trouble over the years. While Sir Walter and Lady Pendennis traveled on the Continent and Rosamond lived at Leigh Abbey, she'd been educated in the company of Jennet's three children. Although Jennet was glad her offspring had the benefit of such schooling, it came at a cost. Rosamond was a troublemaker, a bad influence on anyone with a less forceful personality than her own.

Until Eleanor Pendennis took up residence at Leigh Abbey, Jennet had thought Rosamond much more her father's child than her mother's. She had Sir Robert Appleton's wavy, dark brown hair, his deep brown eyes, his narrow face, and his high forehead, although on Rosamond those features somehow combined to produce a prettiness that was decidedly feminine. She had also inherited a female version of his temperament. When she'd been younger, she'd been given to terrible tantrums. She was still prone to moodiness and to explosive bursts of temper, but as she grew older she'd learned there were more subtle ways to get what she wanted.

Jennet glanced at the door through which Lady Pendennis had exited the hall. A few distant thumps indicated she'd begun her progress upward. *How much of her mother's devious nature,*

Jennet wondered, *can also be found in Rosamond?*

A chill passed through her. If the child had inherited the worst traits of both her parents, the term "devil's spawn" would be no exaggeration.

Deprived of one audience, Rosamond sought another. "Goodwife Jaffrey!" she called, as she skipped across the floor toward the corner where Jennet lurked.

"Good day to you, Mistress Rosamond. Welcome to Priory House."

As she'd been taught, Rosamond's head bobbed in a perfunctory acknowledgment of the greeting, but the exchange of courtesies was not prolonged. "I know a se-cret!" she chanted, in an annoying, singsong voice.

"I have no doubt of it, but there are matters I must see to now. I have no time for idle chatter."

Rosamond heaved a great sigh and looked downcast. "It is because you do not like me that you will not listen?"

Arrested by the hitch in Rosamond's voice, as much as by the girl's words, Jennet hesitated. Had she hurt her feelings? Hard to believe, when Rosamond herself was so careless in her treatment of others. And yet . . .

Chewing thoughtfully on her lower lip, as was her habit when she considered a new idea, Jennet studied Rosamond's bowed head. Her cap was askew. A smudge of dirt decorated her nose.

Jennet placed a hand beneath Rosamond's chin and lifted her face until their eyes met. "You may have the right of it, Rosamond. There are a good many things about you that I do much dislike."

This blunt speaking seemed to shock the girl. Her dark eyes widened, and she burst into speech. "But I am pretty. And I am rich. And Mama says I am as charming as ever my father was."

Mama. Lady Appleton, she meant. She called Lady Pendennis *Mother* now, though once she'd used the same term for both women.

"That was not a compliment, Rosamond. Your father had charm, yes, but his flattery was often insincere. That is not a good quality in man or woman."

Lady Appleton encouraged plain speaking, Jennet told herself when Rosamond's eyes brimmed with moisture. Rosamond deserved to know the truth about the man who'd sired her out of wedlock.

"You did not like my father, either." Wiping away the incipient tears, Rosamond scowled up at Jennet.

"No, I did not. Moreover, I did not trust him."

"But you named Mole for him."

"His name is Rob." Jennet despised the ekename Rosamond had given her son, and Rosamond knew it.

"My father was Mole's godfather. Why did you name him for my father if you disliked him so much?" When Jennet did not answer at once, Rosamond looked thoughtful. "Godparents give gifts." Her tone turned accusing. "You named Susan for Mama and Kate for Lady Glenelg."

Jennet refused to be drawn. She'd done naught to be ashamed of. Any sensible parent chose the wealthiest person in the neighborhood to serve as one of the three godparents each child required. Life was uncertain at best. There was nothing wrong with providing for one's offspring.

"I have duties to attend to, Rosamond, now that you and your mother have come to stay. I cannot spend any more time talking to you."

"I will go back to Mama, then." Rosamond's eyes were bright and her face flushed. Remembering her talk of a secret, Jennet of a sudden felt uneasy.

"Where is Lady Appleton?"

"She went to inspect the body," Rosamond said, in a matter-of-fact voice. "I wanted to see it, too, but Mama sent me away."

"Body? What body?"

"I do not know who he was. Some white-haired old man sprawled face down on the floor of one of the little rooms in that other building. There was blood on the back of his head, so I suppose someone struck him from behind."

"*Another* murder?"

"Is it not exciting?" Rosamond asked. "Mama will have to find out who killed him, and I can help."

Jennet bit back a groan.

It had to be all those years Lady Appleton had spent experimenting with poisonous herbs. Somehow, in the process of decocting and distilling, she'd accidentally combined the ingredients that unleashed an evil spell. Nothing less than such a powerful curse could account for the frequency with which she encountered dead bodies.

5

Someone had tried to give Calthorpe's death the appearance of an accident. To Sir Walter Pendennis's trained eye, the evidence was unmistakable. He was meant to think Calthorpe had been reaching for a heavy, leather-bound book, strapped with decorative metal, and had lost his grip on the volume. It might have fallen from that high shelf with enough force for its sharp edge to cause a fatal wound. Certes, it had been the weapon used to strike the killing blow. But first Calthorpe had been knocked unconscious, or nearly so, by another weapon, something too blunt to break the skin.

"We must send for the coroner and justice of the peace," Susanna said.

"I hold both posts in this parish."

"That is . . . convenient."

With slow deliberation, Walter rose from his knees, his inspection of the body complete, and let her have her turn. As he had, she knelt to study Calthorpe's injuries. After a careful examination, she stood, regarded the single shelf, bracketed to the wall, on which the fallen volume, a specially bound copy of the Venice edition of Claudius Ptolemy's *La Geografia,* and several others, had been stacked.

She turned next to Calthorpe's writing table, covered with an array of books, papers, and rolls of parchment. Light from the window glinted off something on its surface.

It was a very small room, a former monk's cell. Susanna had difficulty maneuvering the bulk of her skirts around the table, chair, and Calthorpe's paraphernalia, but in the end she managed it and plucked up what appeared to be a shard of tinted glass.

"Odd," she murmured. "It is too small to identify with any certainty."

"A fragment of a dropped goblet?"

"It is thick enough; and if so, as he was not poisoned, it signifies nothing." She tucked the shard into a pocket hidden in a placket in her skirt, patting the dark red fabric with an absent gesture once she'd secured it there. In defiance of convention, she had put aside the widow's weeds she should have worn until her own death or remarriage, refusing to pretend to a grief she did not feel.

"Two blows to the head," Walter said. "One to knock him senseless; one to kill."

"Yes. No question about how he was killed. But who would want him dead? And why?"

Walter's thoughts went at once to the mission they had undertaken here at Priory House. The queen had insisted upon secrecy. He'd complied, but until now he'd not believed there was any need for it. Had he been wrong to discount the danger from foreign powers? Had he been careless in providing security because he'd decided guards inside the buildings were unnecessary?

"Calthorpe's death must be writ down an accident. That is the only way to keep the local authorities out of this business and maintain the secrecy the queen requires."

"You cannot let a murderer go unpunished."

"The queen demands secrecy," he reiterated.

Susanna gave him a sharp look.

"I will do all I can to discover who killed Calthorpe. With your help, it should be possible to learn if anyone saw a stranger on the premises." If Susanna questioned the other women and the servants, it could be done without the appearance of a murder investigation.

"You believe a spy killed him?" She sounded doubtful.

"I must consider that solution. I have no doubt that the Spanish ambassador in London has already heard rumors of a country estate turned into a clearinghouse for information relating to the land across the Western Sea."

King Philip would feel justifiable fury when word reached him of their attempt to prove Englishmen had reached the New World well before any ship sailing on behalf of Spain. And yet, how could anyone here in England have located Priory House? And why kill Calthorpe? Walter himself would have been a more sensible target.

"I concede you are more experienced than I at unmasking spies and thwarting treasonous plots, but how could a stranger get past your guards?" Susanna's frown deepened as she added, "How did Eleanor get past them?"

"How does Eleanor do anything? She attacked them with that sharp tongue of hers and left them bleeding by the side of the road."

Susanna looked at him askance.

"Eleanor told them who she was, and they let her in."

"Oh." Fabric rustled as Susanna sank into Calthorpe's chair. "We must search his possessions. There may be some clue."

"Let me have the body taken away first."

He stepped into the narrow passage to speak to Jacob, who had been waiting for instructions. Calthorpe's fellow scholars were all there, too, solemn faced but avid for news. So was Daniel, the young clerk who'd summoned Walter from the great hall, and Zachary Alday, who had discovered the body.

"Your colleague met with a fatal accident." Walter's brusque manner was meant to discourage questions.

It did not suffice. Anything less subtle than a cudgel blow would have failed. They clamored for details; and when he refused to satisfy their curiosity, Master Gainsford, bouncing on the balls of his feet as if that would bring them eye to eye, threatened to complain to the chancellor of the university.

"You agreed to defer to my authority when you came here," Walter reminded him.

The scholars had also vowed to keep silent about their undertaking and to complete their individual assignments with all due speed. The queen wanted results by Michaelmas, when all good husbandmen settled their accounts and presented the best of the harvest to their overlords.

That day could not come soon enough for Walter, even if the deadline passed without conclusive progress. It would be worth suffering Her Majesty's . . . disappointment as long as he could rid himself of the presence of his unwanted guests. Black robed, they looked like nothing so much as carrion crows as they hovered around the scene of Calthorpe's death.

"I claim his study," Master Weller of Oxford declared.

"By what right?" demanded Sir Gregory Speake, who was a fellow of Cambridge. He cleared his throat and gave a little cough. "I fancied moving into it myself."

Calthorpe's study was, Walter realized, a corner room, with two windows instead of only one. "No one is to enter that chamber until I give permission." Ignoring a chorus of protests, he sent them on their way, all but Alday; then he spoke quietly to Jacob. As soon as he'd given terse orders to his long-time servant, Walter faced the man who'd raised the hue and cry.

Alday was not a scholar, but rather one of a number of people invited to Priory House to share personal knowledge of the New World. He had not been there himself, but his late father had been personal manservant to Sebastian Cabot, one of the earliest explorers of the lands to the West.

"How is it you were in Master Calthorpe's study?" Walter asked him.

"We had an appointment. Master Calthorpe had asked me to stop by and talk with him."

"On what subject?"

"That I cannot tell you, Sir Walter. He did not say precisely what it was he wanted to discuss. I can only assume it had to do with Master Cabot's explorations. That is, after all, why I am here."

Walter considered questioning him further then decided to wait, the better to make Calthorpe's death seem an accident. He had no reason to suspect Alday of murder. The fellow was as bland as oatmeal pap. Thanking him for his help, Walter sent him on his way.

Susanna looked up from the documents scattered across the surface of Calthorpe's writing table when Walter returned to the study. She'd worked methodically through the bulk of them already, sorting the papers into stacks. "I will go and prepare the body for burial, Walter, as soon as I have finished here."

"There is no need. The servants can see to it."

"He was an old family friend. It is the least I can do."

He knew her well enough to realize the futility of argument. "We must talk first."

"Yes."

They were interrupted when Jacob came in with one of Walter's guards, carrying a plank upon which to bear Calthorpe's body away to a storeroom in the old, half-demolished infirmary.

"We will bury him quickly, with a minimum of fuss," Walter said when they'd gone. "How fortunate that our scholars in residence include a clergyman."

Susanna paused in the act of stacking books into another pile atop the writing table. "I doubt Master Calthorpe would agree with you. Now, explain yourself. How would his death benefit a spy?"

"It is possible he discovered something. . . ." Even to Walter, this sounded far-fetched. He shrugged. "When Dr. Dee relayed the queen's instructions to me, I got the impression he was more concerned about guarding the rare materials collected here than the scholars we would bring together to study them." The queen's royal astrologer, Dr. John Dee, had been their go-between in order to shroud the project in yet another layer of secrecy.

"The most valuable items are in the library," Susanna said, "not in the possession of any individual scholar. Some of the maps exist nowhere else. And there are other documents, too—letters and pipe rolls and transcripts of reports by those who have actually visited the New World. But these"—she indicated the books— "are not rare. Master Calthorpe's assignment was of no particular significance, either, only to translate them from Italian into English for the benefit of those who do not read both languages. Several others here are also fluent in Italian. Even I have some small skill at translating it."

"There may be something in these papers. Go through them with great care. Trust no one else to examine them."

She frowned. "How much do the scholars know about why they are at Priory House? How much did Master Calthorpe know?"

"Not as much as you do, my dear. They were invited to pursue three lines of inquiry but given the impression that Oxford and Cambridge were engaged in a joint academic project. They are unaware of the queen's interest or the political uses to which the results may be put."

"Three goals." She ticked them off on her fingers. "To investigate England's claim to the New World, to consider locations for possible colonization there, and to determine the best place from which to begin a new search for a northwest passage to Cathay."

"Yes. The latter is a subject in which Dr. Dee has been interested for a long time. You will remember, as far back as the years when you were a young woman in the duke of Northumberland's household, that he was involved with the opening of trade with Muscovy and the search for a northeast passage to Cathay."

She nodded. "He sought the duke's support and dedicated a book to the duchess to make her sweet."

"Now he feels a shorter route to the east may lie across the Western Sea, north of the lands claimed by Spain. Were it not for other duties, and the illness that laid him low at the time of my meeting with him, he would doubtless have taken a more active role in this project himself."

"He was ill when you visited him at Mortlake?" Susanna had left the worktable to inspect the contents of a small chest. Now she turned an inquiring look on him. "You did not mention that before."

"Calthorpe was not poisoned, my dear, and neither was Dee."

"How can you be so certain? Poisons are my area of expertise, not yours."

A slight bow acknowledged the truth of that. She had, after all, written a book on the herbal varieties. But Walter did not doubt his conclusion. "I am certain because the queen herself sent two of her personal physicians to examine Dee. Nor was it the plague," he added.

News had reached Priory House a week earlier that the colleges at Oxford had canceled lectures and sent their scholars away because of an exceeding virulent outbreak of that dread disease. No one was overmuch alarmed. Plague cropped up somewhere in England every summer, as regular as cases of swine pox in May, smallpox in June, and scurvy and putrid fever during the winter months.

"Why did Dr. Dee authorize you to tell me all?" Susanna's agile mind, discounting both poison and plague, had moved on.

"You must have made an impression on him all those years ago when he visited the duke. He remembered you well. He said anyone capable of compiling herbals should be able to make order of the materials we've gathered here." He'd said a great deal more, as well, but Walter had no intention of sharing that information with Susanna.

She dismissed the compliment with a flutter of one hand and closed the chest. "We must remove all these books and papers to a safer place."

"The library." It was in the same building, on the far side of a small parlor. "I will post a guard, someone to pose as your assistant during the day and sleep there at night." Piers Ludlow, he thought, the most promising of the new recruits among his henchmen.

"Does the queen mean to plant colonies? Is that why you think Spain may try to interfere with our work here?"

"She has, I do think, a keen interest in plantations. At present she keeps a close watch on those we have begun in Ireland. If she decides to expand into settlements in the New World, she must be certain that England's claims are as strong as or stronger than those of Spain, but Her Gracious Majesty began to consider the idea of such colonies almost a decade ago when French Huguenots tried to establish a base in La Florida and came to her for help to defend it against Spain."

"She did not give it."

"No." Walter did not need to add that Spanish troops had wiped out the French settlement, slaughtering men, women, and children. Susanna had studied the same accounts he had in preparation for their work here.

Her expression was troubled as she made a last circuit of the cramped study, looking for any clue she might have missed. "He must have come back here when I went out into the stableyard."

Walter straightened from his casual slouch against the door. "Do you mean to tell me you were with Calthorpe just before he was killed?"

"He wanted to talk to me about some discrepancies he'd found, but Eleanor's arrival interrupted us." There was a quaver in her voice. "I put him off. If I had not—"

"What happened to him is scarce your fault." He resisted the urge to offer comfort by taking her into his arms. She'd not appreciate the gesture.

"His attacker followed him. Or was already here."

And that attacker could have entered Priory House grounds in the confusion surrounding Eleanor's arrival. Walter's fists clenched. Pithy but silent curses filled his mind, distracting him. Only belatedly did he notice Susanna's hesitance. Her expression was not difficult to read. She'd thought of something she did not want to share with him.

"He said—" Susanna stopped in midsentence.

"He was murdered," Walter reminded her.

"He said that . . . someone . . . had stolen his notes on the interview with Twide. I was certain he'd only misplaced them, but . . ."

"Twide?" Walter prompted when her voice trailed off. He remembered the fellow. Twide had been at Priory House for a short while some two weeks back, but Walter had not dealt with him direct.

"Richard Twide. He stayed only long enough to give his statement. He was with David Ingram in the New World. After Master Calthorpe interviewed Ingram, he looked for the transcript of Twide's statement because the story Ingram told did not agree with what Calthorpe remembered Twide had said. Master Calthorpe did not say in what particulars." She shook her head, as if to unscramble her thoughts. "But I do not see how the matter could have anything to do with his death. You know as well as I do that there are always discrepancies when two witnesses give accounts of the same event."

"Then why are you so troubled?"

With a sigh, Susanna confessed the rest. "Master Calthorpe accused Gwyn Merrick of stealing Twide's testimony to give to her father. I discounted the claim. I still do not believe it."

"Why would he send her to steal? He could have asked to see any records he wanted." Merrick, he recalled, was the one who'd been at Cambridge during his own brief stint as a student there. As far as he knew, however, their paths had never crossed. No scholar, Walter had left without taking a degree.

"That is what I told Master Calthorpe, but he seemed to think academic rivalry sufficient motive for theft."

"Petty jealousies," Walter said in a dismissive tone of voice. "Such rivalries run rampant at Oxford and Cambridge both, but it is rare they lead to murder."

"I am relieved to hear you say so."

"Nor can I detect any reason for Merrick's daughter to have slain Calthorpe."

"Someone did, and that missing document appears to be the only clue we have."

"I will get Twide back, that we may question him. In the meantime, we will ask the other scholars who spoke with him to write down what they remember. We will tell them the truth—the statement is missing from Calthorpe's papers."

"But not that he was murdered?" Susanna's brow furrowed more deeply. "How are we to question suspects if everyone thinks Calthorpe's death was an accident?"

"Some inquiries should be possible. It is only natural to speak of what happened and wonder why no one heard him cry out when he was struck by that falling book." His gaze returned to the high shelf. Someone, he thought, should devise a better way to store books. Reaching overhead was awkward. Stooping to examine the contents of book chests was even more so.

"We must proceed in an orderly manner."

Walter saw with mild amusement that Susanna had reached for paper and taken up a quill to make a list. "Everyone will be at supper," he reminded her.

"Before that we must transfer all Calthorpe's possessions to the library and examine Calthorpe's bedchamber as well." She looked up from her scribbling. "I have not heard Ingram's story at first hand. I believe I will ask him to tell it." She tapped the top end of the pen against her chin and looked thoughtful. "I have it. I will suggest he entertain Rosamond with the tale. He can come to the library tomorrow morning and regale us both with his adventures. That should not rouse anyone's suspicion."

"What do you propose to do about the girl, Gwyn?"

"I will find some subtle way to question her concerning the missing papers. There is no reason for her to think I am accusing her of anything. Scholars are notorious for being absentminded. They misplace items all the time."

With a slow nod, Walter agreed to this agenda. He trusted Susanna to undertake the task of soliciting information. Furthermore, he suspected she'd have far greater success at getting answers without arousing suspicion than he would.

"Keep in mind the possibility that a Spanish agent may have infiltrated our company," he warned, "a servant, mayhap, or one of my guards. I investigated everyone, but even I can be deceived."

Susanna's quick, sympathetic smile made him bristle. The last thing he wanted was pity. She'd heard the bitterness that had leaked into that last statement and could guess he was thinking of Eleanor.

"It is a great relief to me that you are here to organize these matters."

"Sarcasm, Walter?"

"I can make inquiries about strangers in the area and order a search for a spy, even send word to the queen direct and influence the workings of Parliament, but I have not the least notion what to do about my own wife."

"I have told you before what I think, Walter. You did not want to hear it."

"I cannot forgive her."

"You married her, Walter." Susanna circled the writing table to stand right in front of him. He had no choice but to meet her eyes. "You are bound to each other for life. If you make no effort to settle your differences, you doom yourself to years of unhappiness. Propose a truce. Take it as a good sign that she's come here, a first step toward reconciliation."

"We both know why Eleanor followed us to Cornwall. She is jealous of you."

Susanna winced but did not back down. "You must convince her she has no reason to be." A brief smile appeared, a wry acknowledgment of their peculiar situation. "That she can feel jealousy may be a good sign—proof she still cares for you."

"She regrets losing her ability to influence me, nothing more." He tried to step away, but Susanna caught his arm, compelling him to stay.

"Speak to her in private now. There is time before supper to begin to mend this rift between you."

"You are the one I should have taken to wife, not Eleanor."

"I refused you, Walter. You are a dear friend, but I would never have agreed to a wedding between us."

Whether he believed that or not, he knew there was no escape from his impulsive marriage on this side of the grave.

Susanna's voice was quiet but forceful. "Talk to her, Walter."

A short time later, when they went their separate ways—Susanna to attend to Calthorpe's winding sheet and Walter to visit his spouse—Walter's jaw was set, his expression grim. Susanna had an unpleasant hour ahead of her, but by and large he thought he was the one who faced a more onerous task.

6

Eleanor Pendennis ached in every muscle, every bone, and she had no one but herself to blame. She might have remained comfortably ensconced at Leigh Abbey, waited on hand and foot, her every whim catered to.

But Susanna's servants felt only duty toward her, not respect and never affection. Eleanor had seized on the chance to leave, and in spite of the difficult journey, did not regret her impulsive decision.

Other regrets haunted her days and disrupted her nights.

She kept them at bay by dwelling on darker sentiments—resentment, distrust, and envy. At the core of them all was Susanna Appleton, and the worst of it was that Susanna refused to show anything but kindness toward Eleanor. The more Eleanor complained, the more Susanna tried to accommodate her.

The chamber she'd been given was a perfect example. The high, ornately carved and painted bedstead upon which she'd been placed was furnished with a featherbed and a mattress well stuffed with wool. Beneath her fingers she felt the smooth coolness of a silk coverlet. The plump bolster supporting her neck and back was covered with soft, tufted velvet.

She sighed. It was pleasant to be married to a wealthy man. Walter had always liked his comforts, and he was worse than any woman when it came to a desire for rich fabrics and bright colors.

But nothing made up for the inability to go where she wished, when she wished, without assistance.

Disconsolate, she watched Melka bustle about, stirring up the herbs strewn among the rushes as she unpacked Eleanor's belongings and stored them in a variety of chests and coffers. The distinctive scent of mint drifted up from the floor, together with a faint residue of burnt fleabane. Old rushes had been removed within the last few days and fresh brought in.

One of the doors of the livery cupboard on the opposite side of the room stood open. Eleanor stared at it, having nothing better to do. Inside she could see the ewer, basin, and chamber pot. There were toiletries, too, but not her perfumes and salves. She frowned. Had she displaced some other female guest?

As a different possibility struck her, she turned her head with a sharp jerk and attempted to see around the edge of the ash-colored hangings into the large, dome-topped wardrobe chest just to her right. Was Walter's clothing in this chamber? Had some woman also shared this room, this bed, with her husband?

A swath of decorative lace blocked her view of the chest, which she had noted when she'd been carried into the room. Frustrated, she examined the sections of the chamber that were in her range of vision, taking in an imported chair of Spanish make, pulled up close to the hearth, three stools of green Turkey-work with double rows of fringe, and a wall hanging that appeared to be a tapestry map—Cornwall, no doubt. In front of it sat a pedestal table covered with a Persian carpet and holding a pitcher of barley water and a tray of sweetmeats. She'd not felt inclined to sample either.

A door she had not noticed before, since it was located behind and to the left of the bed, abruptly swung open. Melka shrieked. Eleanor's heart raced, but she managed to contain any outcry.

"It is only Sir Walter, Melka."

"Send your woman away, wife. I would speak with you in private."

"As you wish." Eleanor signaled to the maidservant.

A deafening silence followed her departure. Walter finally broke it. "Why did you come here, Eleanor?"

"I am surprised you must ask." Hearing both distaste and a reluctance to be civil to her in his voice, Eleanor snapped at him. "There was a time when you were most insistent that we should make our home at Priory House."

"Do not play games. That was before you chose to deceive me."

Eleanor bit her lower lip to keep from crying out in dismay. His words confirmed her worst fear. Until now, since he'd avoided being alone with her, she'd only suspected that she had confessed to him when she'd thought herself at death's door.

Disjointed memories were all she had of the hours immediately after she'd been run down, but she supposed she must have told him she'd planned to leave him and, worse, let it slip that she'd turned traitor. For a man who had dedicated his life to serving his country, there could be no greater betrayal.

No one had expected her to live. Doubtless Walter had hoped she would die once she'd told him the terrible truth.

"And it was all for naught," she murmured. The plot had failed, and she had been well punished for her greed and deceitfulness. "I've paid for my sins," she said in a louder voice.

"Have you, Eleanor?"

"I suffer. You do not know—"

"I know you are not alone in your suffering. I am bound to you by law till death do us part."

When she'd first returned to England, unaware that he knew what she'd done, Eleanor had been confused by Walter's coldness. They had quarreled often during their marriage, but they had also loved. The most obvious conclusion had been that in the months they'd been apart, when he'd thought himself a widower, his feelings for Susanna Appleton had revived.

Eleanor still believed that might be true, which made her resent the other woman all the more, but she had gradually come to suspect that the real reason her husband had remained aloof during the last year was his abhorrence of what she had tried to do. He'd have found it easier to forgive infidelity than disloyalty to the queen.

She watched his face for some sign of emotion, but Walter had himself firmly under control. Not so much as a twitch gave away his thoughts. When he spoke, his words were uninflected. "You will leave here as soon I can make the arrangements."

"Not back to Leigh Abbey."

"Go to your mother, then."

She blanched, appalled by the thought. She'd be even less welcome in that house than she was here. Uncertain how much of her past Walter had uncovered, Eleanor hesitated. Had he cared enough to investigate or simply condemned her out of hand? It did not matter, she supposed. It remained a husband's responsibility to put a roof over his wife's head.

"The rooms you keep in London are too small for proper lodgings, and as far as I know, you own no property save Priory House. This is our home, Walter. I am here to stay."

"You mocked the idea of living in the country when I first told you I wanted to come here."

"I was capable of doing other things then." She made no effort to keep the bitterness out of her voice.

"You were overambitious and look where that led you." He gestured toward her useless limbs.

The cruel reminder hurt. She could only hope he did not realize how much. "I may be crippled, but I am capable of supervising my own household."

"Susanna—"

"Susanna tolerated my presence. She was no happier to have me living with her than I was to be there. Ask her, Walter. She's nothing if not truthful."

"She hoped to aid your recovery. She is a skilled herbalist."

"No herb can restore my shattered bones nor the full use of my legs." As if to emphasize her words, pain lanced through her again. She sucked in her breath and squeezed her eyes shut until it passed. "I am as well as I will ever be, Walter, and I am tired of being dependent upon your . . . friend."

He studied her with an enigmatic expression. "Why did you bring Rosamond here?"

"She is my daughter."

"She's more Susanna's than yours. When we were abroad, you had difficulty remembering how old she was."

"Her place is with me."

A dangerous smile contorted his mouth. He was not a man given to humor. "Susanna made the girl her heir. That gives her some rights."

Eleanor made a derisive sound. They both knew the facts. Before Eleanor married Walter, Susanna had decided that Rosamond, as her late husband's only child, was entitled to all he'd owned, even if the law did not agree that a bastard should inherit. Through a series of complicated legal maneuvers, she'd put several properties in Rosamond's name, to become hers absolutely when she reached her majority. Susanna would never take them back, even if she lost custody of Rosamond.

"Clever Eleanor. You brought her to bargain with." His gaze was so cold that she felt a chill. "Which of those properties do you covet? Appleton Manor? Or is that too far away? Mayhap you think to trade the girl for a splendid new dwelling house in London."

She had to clear her throat before she could continue. "I mean to make Priory House our permanent home." She was careful not to specify whether that "our" included Rosamond.

"You mean to make trouble. Why else follow me here uninvited?" His voice was rife with disapproval.

"Mayhap I missed your cheerful company."

"Do not use that sarcastic tone with me, Eleanor. I will not have it." He moved out of her range of vision.

Pushing at the bed with both hands, she lifted her upper body high enough to see where Walter had gone. He slouched against the window frame, gazing into the distance with an angry expression on his face. Satisfied, she levered herself back against the bolster and waited for his next move. Any emotion was better than none.

After a lengthy silence, Walter spoke. "There is one condition under which I will allow you to stay."

Eleanor contemplated a broken fingernail, wondering when

she'd snagged it. She told herself she'd known all along that he'd never force her to leave. Nor would he lock her up somewhere. To mistreat her now that she was an invalid would risk the loss of Susanna's high regard.

She waited for him to suggest that Rosamond accompany Susanna when the other woman returned to Leigh Abbey. Eleanor was prepared to allow herself to be coerced, after which she would try to persuade Susanna to leave Priory House sooner than she'd planned. But Walter had something else in mind.

"I have discussed your condition with the physicians and surgeons who visited you during your convalescence at Leigh Abbey." Walter approached the bed and jerked aside the light coverlet Melka had drawn over the lower half of Eleanor's body. "They tell me there was extensive damage to your hip and legs, but that in all other particulars your body functions as it should."

He scowled down at her misshapen limbs, then shifted his gaze to the scars on her face. When he reached out to touch them, she slapped his hand away.

"I have seen women worse disfigured by smallpox. They simply wear visors to hide the damage."

"If you do not like looking at me, close your eyes."

At the note of asperity in her voice, his lips twisted into another grim smile. "I plan to."

Of a sudden, Eleanor found it difficult to swallow. "I do not understand." But she was afraid she did, all too well. She knew that look in his eyes, but the last time she'd seen it had been under far happier circumstances.

"There is only one thing I want, Eleanor. Give it to me, and I will make certain you spend the rest of your life in luxury." Unspoken was the threat that if she failed him, he would do his best to make her miserable.

"What would have from me, Walter?"

"A son."

7

I need your eyes and ears, Jennet." Susanna stripped off the plain garments she'd donned to prepare Martin Calthorpe's body for burial.

"So it *was* murder." Jennet did not sound surprised. She helped Susanna into a clean chemise and held out the dark red bodice she had worn earlier.

"I fear so."

Martin Calthorpe's death was an affront, not only to all that was right and good in the world, but to Susanna's honor. She could not help but feel responsible for what had happened to him. If she had not rushed off to welcome Rosamond, he might still be alive. He'd not have . . . what? Returned to his study and surprised a thief? Met an old enemy who would have stalked him no matter where he'd been?

Or was Walter right? Did a Spanish spy walk among them?

"There's been no talk of murder," Jennet said, "save from Rosamond."

Susanna grimaced. "She is worse than you are, always listening from behind an arras or lurking outside a doorway. I will speak to her before I go down to sup." She'd have to lie to Rosamond, insist the dead man the girl had glimpsed when she'd followed Susanna and Walter from the great hall had been the victim of a tragic accident.

The huffing sound Jennet made hinted she was offended, but a quick grin betrayed her. She knew the true worth of her talent for overhearing what others said when they thought themselves private. "There's an excellent place to hide, I'll warrant." She pointed to the Flemish tapestry decorating one wall with a scene of an outdoor banquet. "Indeed, there are convenient hangings, suitable for concealment, in almost every room in the house."

As Susanna selected a heavily embroidered pair of sleeves and a larger ruff than she usually wore, to add elegance to her costume, and Jennet laced her into them, Susanna told her friend everything she knew about the murder and how Walter planned to proceed.

"I have already searched Master Calthorpe's bedchamber and found naught but an almost Spartan collection of necessities. He brought little with him save a change of smallclothes and a spare academic gown."

Jennet chewed thoughtfully on her lower lip. "So, one of this household killed him, or an intruder."

"So it seems. I rely upon you, Jennet, to determine where each of the servants was when Master Calthorpe died. Talk to the three women we employ, and to the cook, the two scullions, and all four grooms. And to Gwyn Merrick."

Dressed and ready for supper too early to go down to the great hall, Susanna went instead into the room that adjoined her bedchamber. Its windows overlooked the remains of the monks' herb garden, a soothing view. She took pleasure in imagining it as it must once have been.

Susanna's lodgings at Priory House took up most of one wing and were composed of three connecting rooms. Since Walter had yet to add a stillroom to his new manor house, she had converted the third to this purpose. It was unsatisfactory, being both makeshift and temporary, but it was better than nothing at all. She had the basic equipment to distill herbal waters and prepare medicinal salves.

From that room, Susanna could see the window of Master Merrick's study on the northwest corner of the old monks' dorter. She could pick out the window of Master Fletcher's study, next along that side of the building; but at this distance, and with the ruins of the old infirmary in between, she could not make out the exterior of the library at the far end of the same wing or catch even a glimpse of the stableyard.

"Keep close watch at supper," she told Jennet, returning to the outer chamber and taking the pomander ball the other woman offered her, "on everyone."

"You will be able to see them better than I will. The great hall is ill lit. The view from the dais exceeds that from below."

"I would cede my place with pleasure if I could." She did not expect sharing the high table with Walter and Eleanor to be pleasant. Walter's wife resented her, and Walter's resistance to mending fences and his foolish insistence that he had wed the wrong woman did not help matters.

An hour later, having spoken briefly with Rosamond, Susanna took her place at table. As she removed her little ivory-handled eating knife from its sheath and set it beside her trencher, she forced a smile for her supper companions.

Thunderclouds darkened Walter's expression. He gave her a curt nod. Eleanor, who looked even more unhappy, averted her eyes and did not look Susanna's way again. It appeared they'd failed to come to an understanding. Susanna wondered if Walter had even made the attempt.

"Ah, quinces," she remarked, hoping to coax them into conversation. Anything would be better than sullen silence. She tasted the fruit, which had been cored, roasted, and mixed with clarified honey. "Do you know why we eat quinces before a meal? It is because they are said to stimulate the appetite . . . and help keep drunkenness at bay."

Neither husband nor wife responded to the attempt at levity.

"These are last year's crop," she continued. "Well preserved, but come October, when they are gathered fresh, the taste will be even better."

No one troubled to comment.

Since meaningless remarks about the weather did not seem

worth her effort, Susanna held her tongue and turned her attention to assessing the five surviving scholars. They sat together at the table nearest the dais.

Plump and amiable, Bartholomew Fletcher, translator of Dutch and German, appeared to be engaged in a pleasant, soft-spoken dialogue with Adam Weller, who brought a knowledge of Portuguese and Spanish to their company. Both were Oxford men.

The prickly gnome with the bristly gray beard, seated on the other side of Weller, was Samuel Gainsford, also of Oxford, their specialist in Norse and Irish legends. Having quarreled with everyone present in the course of the last weeks, he disdained discussion to focus on his cup of ale.

Across from him at table was Sir Gregory Speake, the clergyman, at three and thirty the youngest of the scholars. Fluent in French, he had become expert in cosmography by virtue of a family connection to one of the great mapmakers of Antwerp. While he ate, he carried on a casual conversation with Owen Merrick, the rare prize of their group. Merrick had mastered two of the most difficult languages in the world, Welsh and Basque. Both Speake and Merrick represented Cambridge.

As Susanna watched, Merrick removed his gold-rimmed spectacles and rubbed his eyes. He looked years older than he was. Although his black hair was still unstreaked, a lifetime of squinting to see fine print had left deep wrinkles in his face. She made a mental note to recommend that he try distilled water of adder's-tongue to soothe his eyestrain or mayhap a wash of sweet-scented clary leaves infused in water.

All thought of herbal cures fled when Walter rose to speak, but Susanna's gaze remained fixed on the scholars' table. Would one of the five react when Walter confirmed that the death of Martin Calthorpe had been an accident? An expression of triumph would be too much to hope for, but it was possible simple relief might seep through.

8

Seated with the other upper servants at one of several trestle tables, Jennet sampled a bread pudding and considered how much information she could share with Lionel and Fulke, both of whom had assisted Lady Appleton to find murderers in the past. The pudding was rich with dates and currants but otherwise lacking in flavor. Sir Walter's cook had little imagination.

Fulke looked more woebegone than usual, doubtless because Hester was absent, obliged to attend Mistress Rosamond and take supper with the girl in her chamber. Lionel's face wore a puzzled expression, and he kept darting glances in Sir Walter Pendennis's direction. Their host occupied the seat of honor on the dais, his lady wife on one hand and Lady Appleton on the other.

"There is something rotten in Priory House," he muttered.

"Why do you say that?" Jennet asked.

"Never tell me you believe Master Calthorpe's death an accident? Lady Appleton had me move everything in his study to the library. And she put a lock on his bedchamber . . . after she searched it."

"Sir Walter said it was an accident." Fulke gestured toward the dais with a spoon. "Just now. Called it tragic, he did."

"And who would kill old Master Calthorpe? A more harmless sort you'd never have found. If someone was to be murdered,"

46

Jennet added, "there are more deserving candidates near at hand." Her gaze cut to Lady Pendennis.

Sir Walter's wife took dainty sips of her wine and picked at the supper set before her on the glossy elmwood surface of the head table. The trencher she shared with her husband contained slices of boiled mallard, bits of boiled mutton, and stewed pike, but she seemed to have no interest in food.

As if she felt Jennet's intent regard, Lady Pendennis looked up, sent her a quelling glare, then ignored her. Undaunted, Jennet continued to stare. Lady Pendennis looked exceeding pale, but that might just be the effect of the flickering illumination in the great hall. Iron candlesticks standing on tripods dotted the table-tops, allowing the company to distinguish one food from another but leaving great pools of darkness between the lights.

"Suspicious, I call it," Lionel insisted. "And why has no one from outside been called in? No justice of the peace. No crowner. Not even a clergyman. Sir Gregory Speake is to preside at the funeral."

"What is it Lady Appleton does here?" Fulke asked, without looking up from a hare pie.

"She runs the place," Jennet said with a smile.

"That fellow, Ingram, told me this is a den of treasure hunters." Again, Fulke used his spoon to point. "Met him in the stables. He says there's gold and jewels in the New World across the sea. Plenty for everyone."

Jennet turned her attention to Davy Ingram, deep in conversation with Zachary Alday, a middle-aged man whose most distinguishing feature was a mole on one cheek. Ingram, younger but more grizzled, showed no outward trappings of newfound wealth. From his clothing to his table manners, he looked what he was—a sailor who was out of his element in a gentleman's country house and drinking heavily to make himself feel less alien.

"What did he do with his share?" Jennet asked. "Certes, he did not spend it on himself."

"Wasted it all on drink and dalliance?" Lionel suggested.

"He was put ashore in Spanish territory," Fulke told them. "He had to walk hundreds of miles to the north before he was rescued by a French ship."

"Is that where he says he found treasure?" Jennet did not bother to hide her skepticism. Everyone knew the Spanish controlled all the emerald and gold mines of the New World. English privateers relieved them of their shipments home on a regular basis. But those riches were in the southern part of the lands called America.

"Aye," Fulke insisted, "a whole city full of it."

"Then those wenches he dallied with must be wearing silk and lace and drinking their wine out of golden goblets." For someone who'd worked for Lady Appleton for so many years, Fulke was surpassing credulous. Jennet abandoned her portion of hare to bite into an herb tart.

Lionel chuckled. Fulke's usual ruddy color went even darker as he fell upon his meal and tried to ignore their teasing.

Replete, since the food was filling even if it did want seasoning, Jennet leaned back from her trencher and absorbed the conversation flowing around her in the hall. The company was a mixed lot—antiquaries and scholars, merchants and seamen. Even without Lady Appleton's assignment, she'd have listened with considerable interest to the strange and wonderful matters they discussed.

"If the conquest of Gelindia could be proven," Master Bartholomew Fletcher declared, steepling his fingers as was his wont when about to deliver a lecture, "it would give England undisputed prior claim to all of the New World."

"No one, as yet, has found proof of the existence of King Arthur," argued his supper companion, Master Weller, who was notable for being bald as a plucked chicken. "That he's said to have sent colonists to Gelindia would be even more difficult to establish."

"Arthur was real," Fletcher insisted.

"And Merlin, too?" another scholar demanded. Gainsford. The quarrelsome one.

"Why not?" Fletcher's nostrils flared as he glared at both his detractors.

"No doubt you think there was a real Robin Hood, too. Lord save us from ghosts—men who persist in legend but leave no tangible record behind."

Jennet frowned. She did not understand Master Gainsford's attitude. Every person with any sense knew both Robin Hood and Merlin were real, even if they had lived a very long time ago. Merlin had been a great sorcerer who served his king, just as Lady Appleton's old friend Dr. Dee was a great sorcerer who served Queen Elizabeth.

"Norombega is real," Davy Ingram said loudly, following his statement with a resounding belch. "Seen it for myself, I have."

"Goodman Ingram," Lady Appleton called, "I would speak with you of this anon."

"At your pleasure, madam. After supper, mayhap?"

"On the morrow, I do think. So that my foster daughter, Rosamond, may also hear the tale."

"Saw it with me own eyes," Ingram boasted, "and I'll tell ye every detail, madam." He belched again. "On the morrow."

"Nine of the clock," Lady Appleton said, "in the library." Then she skillfully turned the conversation to reports of the recent outbreak of plague at Oxford.

Jennet had to admire her skill. Although casual conversation was not Lady Appleton's best suit, she had agreed to keep all the scholars sitting over their supper long enough for Sir Walter to conduct a search of their chambers. Jennet had seen him slip out of the hall, as if to visit the privy, just before the last course was served.

"What do you mean to do with Calthorpe's papers?" Sir Gregory Speake asked into a lull in the conversation. He gave the little cough that began most of his sentences. "How will you reapportion the tasks assigned to him?"

The other scholars listened just as intently for Lady Appleton's answer.

"I will take charge of them myself, good sirs." She bestowed an impartial and serene smile upon them all. "You gentlemen have your own work to do. I would not burden you with more."

"You are no scholar, madam," Master Gainsford protested.

"I am, however, qualified to organize Master Calthorpe's notes and finish the translations he began." Her voice was mild, but Jennet saw the warning sparks in her eyes.

"We are well aware of your abilities, Lady Appleton," Master Weller said, "but you have other duties here."

"As do you, and since there will be few new materials arriving, I have fewer responsibilities remaining than the rest of you."

Diplomacy having failed, Master Weller went to the crux of the matter. "You are a woman, Lady Appleton."

"Do you mean to imply, Master Weller, that a woman's mind is inferior to a man's?"

Jennet watched with interest as the scholar struggled for words. His colleagues had wisely retreated from the battle, though Jennet was certain at least one or two of the others shared his views. Few men could accept the concept of a learned woman. Lady Appleton's father had been an exception. He'd had all the servants at Leigh Abbey taught to read and write, too.

"You must know, Lady Appleton, that women are not permitted at the universities nor to practice law. Wiser men than I have decreed it should be so."

"And yet women can and do earn respect for their intellectual accomplishments. I have heard, for example, that men travel great distances to consult with the widowed Lady Hoby on the subject of mathematics, even university scholars. Any number of learned ladies have translated religious texts, sermons in particular. The queen herself—"

Sir Gregory Speake's soft cough interrupted her. "Have a care, madam. Remember that the Act for the Advancement of True Religion, passed in the reign of King Henry, forbids reading the Bible to women, artificers, apprentices, journeymen—"

"Reading the Bible in English, Sir Gregory. And a very good argument that makes for a woman to learn Latin. You cannot suppose that the queen, who is, by law, head of the Church of

England, lets her councilors interpret Holy Scripture for her. I have heard that a book written by Her Majesty's one-time tutor, Roger Ascham, has been published of late. I will obtain a copy for you. Perhaps his arguments will convince you of the importance of education for women, since mine appear to fall upon deaf ears."

Sir Gregory acknowledged the offer with a slight inclination of his head, but Master Gainsford bounced to his feet, sputtering with indignation. "I need no book to instruct me, madam. Nor do I oppose all learning for women. I have found it most useful for them to read and write in English and to cipher, to know enough of sums to tell when a merchant is trying to cheat them and keep their own accounts. But that is enough. Women should concentrate on the skills they need to run a household and no more."

Master Merrick spoke for the first time. "It is good for women to have knowledge, and kind of Lady Appleton to ease our burden by taking over Martin's work." He rose slowly from his stool. "We have too little time to complete our tasks as it is, but should you need assistance in translating from the Italian, madam, I beg you call upon me."

With that, he made his shambling way toward the exit at the lower end of the hall. Still arguing among themselves, the others followed. Only moments later, Jennet found herself alone with Lady Appleton.

"Well, Jennet?"

"Nothing, madam. I cannot say I care for any of them, but neither did I see any evidence of guilt or remorse."

"Nor triumph, nor relief, nor even simple grief over the loss of a colleague." Lady Appleton sighed. "And I fear I have cut off my nose to spite my face. It will be impossible to ask any of them for help with the translating after the stand I took here tonight."

9

Walter was in the last bedchamber, that assigned to Gwyn Merrick, when he heard a sudden babble of voices through the open window. One quick glance outside confirmed supper was over. That Priory House's two guests, Alday and Ingram, were in company with the scholars meant most of them would convene in the old lay brothers' frater, there to spend several more hours in conversation. Or rather, in debate. Walter did not think he'd ever encountered such a contentious group.

Taking care to place it just as he'd found it, he returned a very old volume of household accounts and recipes, written in Latin, to Gwyn's bedside table. He'd not realized she was literate in any language but English, but he was not surprised. Like Susanna, she was a scholar's daughter.

He'd found oddities in every room, but nothing to rouse dire suspicions. No stolen papers shared space with Gwyn's spare shifts and handkerchiefs. Indeed, Merrick and his daughter seemed to have less to hide than the others. Merrick's interest in their project at Priory House appeared to dominate his every waking hour. Books and papers were piled high on every surface, as if he could not bear to leave them in his study at day's end.

Walter slipped into the old monk's cloister and blended into the shadows. What would Susanna say, he wondered, when he told her that Gainsford was keeping an account of his fellow scholars' most foolish comments, his apparent intent to write a satire for the popular market?

His other discoveries paled in comparison. Under the spectacles Speake used for close work, an ornate German-made pair with colored lenses made of beryl, Walter had found a codebook; but since the fellow had lately been employed by the French ambassador as a messenger, he could infer nothing nefarious from that. Had Weller been in possession of such a thing, Walter would have worried, for Weller was the one with Spanish connections. His only vice, however, appeared to be a liking for that potent Welsh drink, metheglin.

Fletcher had hidden something, too, an ugly little statue. That had puzzled Walter when he first came upon it in Fletcher's clothes chest; but once he hefted it and realized it was made of gold, he decided it was the scholar's nest egg, an object that could be melted down and sold to a jeweler if a pressing need for money ever arose.

Unseen, Walter slipped into the small parlor next to the library.

"Who goes there?" came the expected challenge from the guard he'd left on duty.

"Sir Walter Pendennis." He was pleased to see that Piers identified him by sight before he lowered his arquebus.

After a brief conversation, Walter went on alone. Careful to shield his light, he made a swift but thorough search of each scholar's study. As had been the case with the bedchambers, he found nothing that struck him as significant. Only Merrick appeared to take all the material he worked on during the day back to his chamber at night. Either he was less trusting than his fellow scholars or so dedicated that he returned to his labors every evening after supper.

A quick examination of the guest rooms came next. What had once been lodgings for the priory's infirmarian were situated on the far side of an open space that would in time become Walter's pleasure garden. For the most part this structure was in ruins and had been slated to be torn down for building stone, but one end had been sound enough to salvage for extra bedchambers when the need arose—more than good enough for a simple sailor like Ingram and adequate for Alday, who was a merchant but had not made any great success of himself.

Walter unearthed nothing of interest and did not tarry. Before long either Ingram or Alday, or both, would seek their beds. He did not want to be caught rifling their possessions. Neither did he wish to be late for the appointment he had made with Eleanor.

As soon as he stood once again in the open air, Walter's gaze slid to the light that marked his wife's chamber. He stared at the glowing window with narrowed eyes. She must have ordered every taper in the room to be lit.

Only when he caught himself wiping them on his trunk hose did Walter realize his palms were damp. He could play the part of a thief in the night without turning a hair, but the mere thought of entering his wife's chamber made him sweat. He shook his head at his own foolish hesitation, then continued on toward the house, toward Eleanor. A curious mixture of reluctance and anticipation stirred in his soul.

10

'

Susanna heard Rosamond's approach well before she saw her. The child was capable of being quiet. She was as skilled as Jennet at going unnoticed when she wanted to listen in on other people's conversations, but more often she liked to make people aware of her presence.

In haste, Susanna put away the lists she had been making. She had added a great many items since the previous night.

Calthorpe's papers now sat on her own writing table, together with a stack of books that included the three volume *Navigationi et Viaggi*, the deadly *La Geografia*, the 1534 Venice edition of the *Summario* of Peter Martyr d'Anghiera, dean of Granada, and a smaller and less impressively bound publication that at first appeared to be the account of a visit to Persia but also contained another travel narrative whose title Susanna translated as *The Discovery of the Islands of Frislanda, Eslanda, Egronelanda, Estotilanda, and Icaria, Made by Two Brothers of the Zeno Family.*

Unfortunately, her command of Italian was limited. She had begun to teach herself the language some years back by reading Machiavelli, but making sense of these books would be a slow and arduous process. She wished, and not for the first time, that Nick Baldwin could be here at her side. He'd have comforted and encouraged her. And since he was also fluent in Italian, he'd have been able to help her with her self-imposed task. The truth of the matter was that she did not trust anyone here to do the job. Any one of them could be Calthorpe's murderer.

"Good morrow to you, Mama!" Rosamond danced into the room, eyes bright and dark tresses flying.

"Good morrow, Rosamond. What do you think of Sir Walter's library?"

As Rosamond explored the spacious room, Susanna tried to see it though her eyes. Most of the books and papers were stored in chests, but a few, the ones scholars needed to refer to most often, were stacked on a single shelf suspended at eye level by brackets. As was the custom in most private libraries, these volumes were placed with their spines facing the wall. The titles had been written on the fore-edges for ease of identification.

Rosamond ignored the books in favor of the maps hung like tapestries on the walls. "This is bigger than the *mappa mundi* in your study at Leigh Abbey," she said of the largest.

"That is Master Mercator's rendering of the world."

It consisted of more than a dozen separate sheets of copper-plate engraving, hand colored with a patterned border and mounted together on a length of canvas more than four feet in height and six in length. It was a magnificent work of art and one of the most accurate representations of known geography. It endeavored to show unknown regions as well.

"Look just above the image of the giant dolphin," Susanna suggested.

Rosamond dragged a stool over to the map and stood on it. "Norombega," she read, tracing the fine italic lettering with one finger.

"That name is used for the entire region. Now look for an unnamed river and a red dot and towers."

"That means a city. It is labeled Norombega, too."

"That is the place Goodman Ingram says he visited." Susanna rose from the Glastonbury chair that was the library's most comfortable place to sit and crossed the room to another wall map, one of Spanish origin. "Look here, Rosamond. This is the same river."

56

"Rio de Gamas," Rosamond read when she had repositioned her stool and clambered up to stand eye level with the spot in question.

"That means Deer River. Now look closer. There is no city on this map. Nor is it shown on Master Sebastian Cabot's map of the world."

"Does that mean it does not exist?"

"It may mean that."

"What is on other maps?"

With an approving smile, Susanna led her foster daughter back to the writing table and reached for *La Geografia*. The moment she lifted the heavy volume, she remembered how it had last been used. A shudder passed through her. In her mind she could still see the terrible injury to Master Calthorpe's unprotected head.

"What is wrong, Mama?"

"Nothing, Rosamond. A sudden chill."

Her forced smile turned grim as she began to leaf through the book. Why had Master Calthorpe been bareheaded? All the scholars at Priory House followed the academic tradition of wearing hooded, ankle-length woolen gowns and square caps.

More proof he had been murdered? she wondered. If, as Walter surmised, he'd been knocked unconscious first, his headgear must have been dislodged when he fell, allowing the murderer to strike a killing blow on Calthorpe's unprotected pate.

"There are many maps in this book," Rosamond observed.

Recalled to the lesson she meant to give, Susanna found the one she'd been searching for and held the volume so that Rosamond could see the open page. This map showed the Oceano Occidentale on the right, La Florida at the lower left, and an area between it and Tierra del Laborador labeled Tierra de Nurumberg.

"What do you think, Rosamond? Could this place in the New World have been named after the German city of Nuremberg?"

Rosamond stared at the engraving. "Why would they do that? This map is Italian." She thought a moment longer. "Mayhap the

57

man who made the map did not know the proper spelling of the name."

Chuckling, Susanna closed *La Geografia* and returned it to the writing table. "You may have the right of it."

Selecting one of the volumes of the *Navigationi et Viaggi,* she opened it to a map of La Nuova Francia. Here the name was spelled Terra de Nurumbega and shown just to the left of a cape labeled Breton, doubtless after sailors from the French province of Brittany. No city appeared in this rendering, but there were small pictures of natives clad like ancient Greeks or Romans.

"There are other possible explanations for the name," Susanna continued. Although she'd not yet had the opportunity to hear Master Ingram's tale in its entirety, she was no stranger to the idea of a place called Norombega. It appeared regularly in stories about the New World. "It could have been named for a Seville map printer, Lararo Noremberger. Or, since the Spanish name for Norway is Noruega, one of the Spanish cartographers may have named the region in honor of those raiders from Norway who first set foot on the other side of the Western Sea. Norombega may also be a place name used by native inhabitants."

"You could write to one of the mapmakers and ask where the name came from," Rosamond suggested.

"An excellent thought, but most mapmakers simply copy what they are told by those who have been to the places on the maps. What I have done is list all the various names that have been used for certain areas, and all the different spellings, too, and cross-reference them. That makes it possible to discuss geographical locations in a sensible manner."

Although she looked doubtful, Rosamond did not pursue the subject. "Where is the storyteller?"

"A good question, Rosamond." She suspected Ingram was still sleeping off the previous night's overindulgence in drink. "He should have been here by now. I will send someone to fetch him."

"You tell me a story while we wait. Something with pixies or fairy folk." Rosamond was fond of hearing the adventures of these

58

little people, who could be benign or malevolent as it suited them but were always magical.

Susanna hesitated, giving herself time to think by sending her new "assistant," a stalwart individual named Piers, in search of Ingram. She did not want to shatter Rosamond's childish beliefs, but she had seen far too many people, Jennet included, grow to adulthood convinced that, if they were not careful, they could fall prey to supernatural maladies. A short lecture on the impossibility of becoming elf-shot or fairy-taken seemed in order.

When she had finished, Rosamond nodded, her expression solemn. "Yes, Mama. I understand."

"There are no ghosts, either."

"Yes, Mama." Rosamond settled herself at Susanna's side on the window seat. "Now will you tell me a story, even if the characters are not real?"

How could she resist?

"Here in Cornwall," she began, "the little people who live in mines and give warnings of cave-ins are called tommy-knockers."

11

"He's gone, Walter."

Startled out of his brooding, Walter stared blankly at Susanna. Framed in the door, she'd have been a sight to lift a man's spirits . . . if she'd not looked so distraught. Belatedly, her words sank in. "Who?"

"Ingram. He vanished during the night. I intended to question him this morning, but he did not keep his appointment with me. When I sent Piers to look for him, he was nowhere to be found."

Walter blinked slowly. "Well, that seems straightforward. There is only one logical reason why the fellow should run away. He must have killed Calthorpe. Would that all murders were so simple to solve."

"Too simple."

"Why, Susanna, never tell me you've become cynical."

"Sarcasm does not become you, Walter. Why should David Ingram kill Martin Calthorpe?"

"To prevent Calthorpe exposing him as a liar? If, as you believe, Calthorpe knew his tale did not match Twide's."

"That seems a trifling reason to kill."

"Far less can lead to murder. We will discover the motive when we locate Ingram. I will send men after him. How hard can it be to capture a man who walks with a stick?"

Several hours later, he had the answer to that question: passing difficult. Although he'd instructed his henchmen to pursue the fugitive at all speed, his orders yielded only negative results as the day wore on. Ingram had not stolen a horse, indicating that he was on foot, but no one had seen him walking any of the local byways.

"Our men have been all the way to Launceston, on the one hand, and Boscastle, on the other," Jacob reported. "No one has seen any sign of him."

Walter frowned. If Ingram had chosen to avoid the main roads and follow the country lanes that connected scattered homesteads and hamlets, he could be anywhere. Hidden? A possibility, although not in the open. The terrain was virtually treeless, and for the most part, hill and wasteland covered with nothing more substantial than scrub and furze. Like Priory House, however, which was nestled in a narrow but fertile valley where bearded French wheat could be planted on the best soil and rye on the worst, there were a few other prosperous estates in the vicinity. Walter's brother Tristram owned one such. Did another house a traitor, someone conspiring with Ingram to learn the queen's business by spying on those at Priory House?

"The harbor at Boscastle is said to be a smugglers' haven," Jacob said.

Searching his memory, Walter called the place to mind, for he'd been there once or twice in his youth. They'd kept prisoners in the old castle, called the Court by the locals, even though the structure had been crumbling to ruin for years. "The harbor is a poor one," he said, "affording uncertain protection from storms on the Severn Sea."

"But a harbor all the same, and Ingram is a sailor."

"Aye. It makes sense he'd head for a port. Send more men to Boscastle, Jacob, and expand the search. As I recall, there is no noteworthy place or building northeast of Boscastle until Stratton, twelve miles away and a mile inland. If they do not apprehend Ingram in Boscastle, order the men to range that far before they return here."

"Ingram's talk was all of Plymouth, Sir Walter, whence his ship set sail for the New World."

If he was headed there, Walter thought, there should have been a sighting between Priory House and Launceston, where Launceston Castle looked out over the valley of the Tamar and commanded the only passable road into Devonshire. The only other way for Ingram to reach Plymouth would be by a circuitous and inhospitable route that would take him across Bodmin Moor.

"Expand the hunt in that direction as well," he instructed. "Send men along the great highway from Launceston across the moor and dispatch other searchers to the branch road to Camelford and Padstow and the smaller road that links Padstow and Stratton."

Narrow tracks led down to small harbors all along the north coast of Cornwall, but Walter vowed to leave no stone unturned. When maps had been consulted and more orders given, Jacob hesitated, his thick eyebrows almost knit together in an expression of concern.

"Is there aught else?"

"One of the houses where the men stopped to ask questions was your brother's, Sir Walter. Afterward, Master Tristram Pendennis came to the Priory House gate. He was most insistent that he speak with you."

"He was turned away, I trust?"

"Aye, Sir Walter, as you instructed. But he left this." After handing over a note, Jacob fled.

Walter eyed the folded bit of paper with a jaundiced eye. He knew what Tris wanted. Not so long ago, he'd thought he desired the same thing—reconciliation with his family, a new beginning in the land of his ancestors.

That had been before Eleanor's betrayal.

He'd put off contacting any of his brothers since he'd been back. To maintain security, he'd told himself.

A pitiful lie. The real reason was much simpler. He did not want to face his family until he had something splendid to show for all his time away. A grand house, complete with rich furnishings. A wife he could trust not to undermine his position in the household. Children.

He wanted it all—wealth, power, home, and family. When he'd told Eleanor he intended to exercise his rights as her husband and beget an heir, the demand had been meant as a ploy to make her leave and take her brat with her. But the moment the words were out, he'd realized that he *did* want a son, even if Eleanor must be the boy's mother. All he'd once desired remained within his grasp . . . if he was willing to compromise on the issue of his wife's loyalty.

Swearing softly, he ripped open the missive from his older brother. His eyebrows lifted as he read the warning scribbled on the page.

12

Gwyn Merrick was lying.

Susanna was certain of it but could think of no reason why that young woman should dissemble. She wondered what Jennet, in concealment behind a tapestry showing the siege of Troy, made of the young woman's denials.

"I scarce spoke with Master Calthorpe in all the time he was here," Gwyn insisted, "and never about his work. He was a most secretive man."

"He told me you were the only one besides himself who ever touched his books and papers."

"Never, madam. I never went into Master Calthorpe's study. Never."

"Are you certain of that, Gwyn? I know you lend a hand with the housework here at Priory House." There were not enough women servants, leaving both Gwyn and Jennet to do tasks that should have been performed by the maids.

"Not in Master Calthorpe's study."

The clink of glass and the slosh of liquid were the only sounds in the stillroom as Susanna collected the distilled borage water she'd prepared for Master Merrick. "Poor Martin Calthorpe is dead. I cannot question him about this matter. But I have compiled a list of all the documents I assigned to him. One is missing."

"I know nothing about it, Lady Appleton."

"Mayhap he lent it to another scholar." Susanna let the suggestion hang in the air between them.

Gwyn was a clever girl. Susanna hoped that if she knew where the transcript of Twide's testimony was, she would take the hint and "find" it in some obscure corner. She could always claim that Calthorpe himself had misplaced it, or that one of the others had borrowed it and forgotten to return it. If either of those alternatives occurred to Gwyn, however, she gave no sign. Looking even more downcast, she did not respond to Susanna's suggestion.

"Very well, Gwyn. That is all."

The young woman started to leave.

"Wait. Take this with you."

"What is it?"

"Something to ease the inflammation in your father's eyes."

Stifling a small gasp, Gwyn backed away, putting both hands behind her as if she had some reason to be afraid of the medicine Susanna offered.

"It is a simple preparation of borage you can make for him yourself. Only remember to use the green herb. It loses potency when it dries out."

"This is not necessary, Lady Appleton."

"I believe it is. I have seen how often your father rubs at his eyes. This will soothe them. Take it."

With unflattering reluctance, Gwyn did.

"Tell him to wash his eyes at night and again upon rising."

"Yes, madam." Once more she started toward the door.

"Oh—one other thing."

"Yes, madam?" She turned, the container of borage water clasped tight between her hands.

"Where were you yesterday when Lady Pendennis arrived? I did not see you out in the stableyard with the others."

No one with Gwyn's dark complexion could be said to blanch, but she did change color. Her eyes bulged, and she had difficulty getting any words out. The glass container fell from her trembling fingers and shattered on the wooden floor, spilling out its contents.

"Never mind the mess." Susanna's sharp tone made Gwyn jump. "Speak up, girl! I asked you a question."

The young woman managed to stammer an answer. "I was in the lodgings I share with my father, lying down. I felt unwell."

That this, too, was untrue, could not have been more obvious. Everything about Gwyn's manner and voice screamed falsehood. Most telling of all, she took pains to avoid meeting Susanna's eyes.

13

Behind the tapestry, Jennet wiped damp palms on her apron
and prepared to follow Gwyn when she left Lady Appleton's
presence. As usual, Lady Appleton's instincts had been
sound. She'd been wise to take the precaution of providing a second questioner, foreseen that her own interrogation might frighten
the young woman.

The sound of a door closing brought Jennet out of hiding to
exchange an unhappy glance with her mistress.

"Give her a moment, then follow." Lady Appleton waved Jennet
away when she would have tried to help clean up the broken glass
and spilled medicine.

Lady Appleton's rooms at Priory House gave onto a narrow
passage that led to a staircase. At its foot, one door led to the wing
that contained the buttery, pantry, and kitchen. Another went directly into an overgrown garden. Jennet caught up with her quarry
there, after a brief detour—Priory House had a great many
doors—to make it appear as if she had just come through the
bakehouse.

"A word with you, Gwyn," she called.

A hart pursued by a hunter could not have looked more cor-
nered, but Gwyn came to a stumbling halt in the middle of what
had once been the priory's herb garden.

"Whither were you bound in such a hurry?"

"Nowhere." The denial came with suspicious swiftness.

Jennet pasted a concerned smile on her face and advanced. She would lend a sympathetic ear, encourage Gwyn to confide in her. "You seem passing nervous, Gwyn. What troubles you?"

"Nothing."

Inspiration struck. "It is Lionel, is it not?" She'd seen the way he looked at Gwyn each time she spoke to him—he all but drooled with doglike devotion. A genuine smile replaced the false one. If Jennet learned naught else, she intended to discover how Merrick's daughter felt about that young man.

"Lionel?" Color shot into Gwyn's face. "What of Lionel?"

With a soft chuckle, Jennet led Gwyn to a stone bench and sat her down. "Do not encourage him, Gwyn. He borders on the arrogant as it is. At all cost, avoid paying him compliments."

"He is most handsome," Gwyn murmured. "His eyes sparkle when he is merry."

"I pray you, do not praise that cleft in his chin. He is too vain about it already."

"You mock me." Gwyn started to rise.

"I envy you." Jennet tugged her down again. "A matron with three children I may be, but there is naught wrong with my memory. I, too, loved a handsome lad." She exaggerated only a little. Mark was far from ugly, but his ears were overlarge. "They must be brought to heel with great care, else they slip away."

"I do not seek to trap him."

"I have known Lionel since he was a stripling and seen him break far too many hearts during the last few years." Hester, for one, would never be the same. "The first rule to remember is that you cannot trust a thing he says. On more than one occasion even I have been cozened by the wretch. Why, once he'd had me convinced I'd been cursed by a witch, and it was months before I learned she was naught but an ill-tempered old woman." Jennet could smile at the memory now, but at the time she'd been in a sorry state, convinced she was doomed.

"You do not understand. Lionel would never deceive me."

"Has he persuaded you to meet him alone? Have you let him

kiss you?" Certain she understood now why Gwyn had lied to Lady Appleton, Jennet forged ahead. "Has he promised to marry you, Gwyn? If he has, then you may be sure Lady Appleton will oblige him to keep his word."

"You must say nothing to her!" Panic flared in Gwyn's dark eyes. "My father would be furious if he found out."

"Found out what, Gwyn?"

"That I was with Lionel in the warming house."

Jennet frowned. "When?"

"Yesterday. After I told Jacob I was not feeling well and meant to lie down in my chamber."

"You looked most fit on your return to the manor house." Dallying with a handsome young man did that for a woman.

The warming house was situated between the old monks' dorter, where Master Calthorpe had been murdered, and an unused hall. It was a private place, but one from which Lionel could reach the stableyard within moments of Lady Pendennis's arrival and from which Gwyn might have crept into Calthorpe's study unseen.

"I lied to Lady Appleton," Gwyn blurted.

Jennet waited.

"She asked me where I was when Lady Pendennis arrived, and I said I was in my bedchamber."

"You were with Lionel."

Misery etched in every feature, Gwyn nodded.

Jennet patted her arm. "You make too much of this. Did you go along to your chamber after?"

"Aye. But I did not stay long. Father came in and told me there were guests and sent me to the manor house to make myself useful."

Jennet visualized the floor plan of the old priory. Beyond the warming house and the old monks' hall was a disused kitchen and then what had once been the lay brothers' frater, with their dorter above. It was in the latter building that the scholars lodged. Merrick and his daughter occupied the suite of rooms at its north end.

"There is only one thing I do not understand, Gwyn. Why was Lady Appleton asking you questions?" Jennet was careful not to mention any missing papers. She was not supposed to know anything about the matter.

Gwyn's head bowed in shame. Her hands clenched and unclenched in her lap. "I did not do it on purpose," she whispered. "It was an accident."

"What was?"

Gwyn sniffed. "Some papers fell from Master Calthorpe's writing table while I was cleaning his study. They landed on the brazier and caught fire."

A brazier burning at this time of year? Jennet thought it odd, but she'd seen stranger things. Master Calthorpe had been near sixty years old. No doubt he'd felt even a slight chill down to his bones. "Did Master Calthorpe know this happened?"

Gwyn shook her head. A tear dropped onto her clenched fists. "I feel so wretched. When he died without having complained that the papers were missing, I thought I was safe, that no one else would care. I was relieved to hear he was dead."

"Only natural." Jennet would have given her a comforting pat on the knee, but Gwyn, too agitated to remain seated, sprang to her feet.

"When Lady Appleton asked me about the papers, I was afraid to tell her the truth." A little sob escaped her. "When she finds out she will send me away, and my father needs me here."

Jennet studied the young woman as she moved in fits and starts along the sanded paths. How many more questions could she ask without making Gwyn suspicious? Something in the young woman's thinking was already askew if she believed Lady Appleton would make a fuss about a bit of burnt paper. She'd lied when she'd had no need to.

Instead of further interrogation, Jennet offered consoling words, but Gwyn was too distraught to listen. "I've an errand to run for my father," she blurted, and fled.

"She is nervous as a flushed gamebird," Jennet said, when she rejoined Lady Appleton a short time later.

"I could see that much from the window. What upset her?"

Jennet recounted the entire conversation. When she finished the tale, Lady Appleton sent for Lionel.

"Why do you suppose Gwyn was so reluctant to take the potion for her father?" Jennet asked, while they waited for him to arrive. True to her word, Lady Appleton had cleaned up the mess herself.

"In truth, I do not know. My offering should not have upset her. Unless . . . Sir Walter did say she has an old book of recipes in her chamber. I wonder if Master Merrick has been keeping a secret from us?"

"That he is the murderer?" Jennet felt her eyes go wide at the possibility.

Lady Appleton's soft chuckle told her she was on the wrong track. "Consider what we know, Jennet. Gwyn is protective of her father. She is afraid of being sent away. He rubs his eyes and wears those spectacles."

"There is something wrong with his eyes?"

"I think he may be losing his sight. It is possible Gwyn came with him because he requires a scribe."

There would be little work for a blind scholar, Jennet realized. And if Master Merrick was dependent upon his daughter, he would object to losing her to a husband. That explained, at least in part, why Gwyn would lie about Lionel.

A few minutes later, Lionel himself appeared, cap in hand and an anxious look on his clean-shaven face.

"Has Gwyn Merrick spoken to you in the last hour?" The look Jennet sent him was rife with suspicion.

"I have not seen her all day."

"Liar. You are leading that girl on."

"She's scarce a child. And what is between us is none of your affair."

"Enough." Lady Appleton took her turn to play the sympathetic role. "We do but seek to sort out a few troubling contradictions."

She gestured for him to sit on a stool while she took the room's only chair. Jennet perched on the window seat, her avid gaze on the other two.

71

"Now, then, Lionel," Lady Appleton continued. "Papers are missing from Master Calthorpe's belongings. Do you know what happened to them?"

"No, madam."

"And when Calthorpe died—where were you?"

"I do not know when he died, madam."

"At about the same time Lady Pendennis arrived."

"I was in the stableyard."

"You were in the stableyard before they came?"

Only the slightest shifting of his weight betrayed his disquiet. "Just after."

"And where were you just before?"

"I . . . do not remember, madam."

"Hmmm. Well, I doubt this will come as a surprise to you, Lionel, since I have been told of the comments you made on the subject last night at supper. Master Calthorpe's death was not an accident."

Lionel looked daggers at Jennet, then returned his attention to their mistress. "I did not think so." He started to say more, then broke off with a look of slowly dawning horror on his face. He sprang to his feet so quickly that he overset the stool. "You cannot mean to suggest I killed him, madam! I would never do such a thing!"

"Fool!" Since he'd moved within reach, Jennet smacked him on the arm. "You know better than to believe she would think that."

"I do not suspect you, Lionel. Indeed, I trust you not to say a word about what passes between us in this chamber." Lady Appleton's severe look had him swallowing hard and nodding. "Sir Walter knows the truth but everyone else must believe Master Calthorpe's death an accident."

"Yes, madam." Cap crushed in one hand, he used the other to right the stool and obeyed her silent command to resume his seat.

"At the same time," Lady Appleton went on, "neither Sir Walter nor I mean to allow a killer to go unpunished. To discover the murderer's identity, we must determine what each person at Priory House was doing at the time of Calthorpe's death and find out what other individuals he or she might have seen. Thus will we eliminate suspects."

Although Lionel nodded to signal he understood, his brow puckered in confusion.

"Can anyone vouch for your whereabouts?" Lady Appleton leaned forward, the better to see his eyes.

Lionel's inner struggle showed plainly on his open face. After a moment, he drew in a deep breath and lifted his head to meet his mistress's inquiring gaze. "For some time before Lady Pendennis arrived, I was in the warming house with Gwyn Merrick. We were . . . talking."

"And when you heard the commotion in the courtyard?"

"We went to see what it was about."

"Together?"

"Yes. Together." But Lionel broke eye contact and sounded as if he were strangling on the words.

"She says she went back to her lodgings," Jennet told him. Lionel had surprised her. He never had difficulty telling lies when he tried to cozen her.

"Were you together, Lionel?" Lady Appleton asked. "Or did you leave the warming house in opposite directions?"

"It would not have been seemly to . . . that is, I did not wish—" He broke off to rake agitated fingers through his hair. "We separated that no scandal should attach itself to her name."

"So, you do not know where she went?"

"You cannot believe Gwyn murdered Master Calthorpe!" He bounced up again.

"I do not know what to think, Lionel." This time Lady Appleton also rose to her feet.

"She is innocent! I swear it. She is the sweetest, most—"

"Enough!" Lady Appleton lifted one hand to stop the flow of praise. "I am inclined to agree with you, but I must have the truth."

Lionel's words came out in a rush. "I went to the stableyard, and Gwyn said she would go to a window to see what was going on."

"What window? Where?"

Common sense told Jennet it would have been in the parlor or the dorter, but she did not interrupt.

"I do not know, but she'd never have gone into Master Calthorpe's study. His room looks out on the wrong side of the building."

A *telling point,* Jennet thought.

"And how do you know that, Lionel?" Lady Appleton seemed amused by his vehemence. Jennet supposed that meant she approved of Gwyn as a prospective wife.

"We, uh, had to be careful that we did not make any noise when we entered the warming house. Master Calthorpe was wont to leave his window open. If he'd heard anything and looked out to see us go in through that door, he might have told Gwyn's father."

"Well, that explains all," Lady Appleton said. "No doubt Gwyn saw that a gentlewoman had arrived and circled back to the house."

The mildness of her mistress's voice did not deceive Jennet. She was surprised Lionel accepted the remark at face value.

"Yes, madam. That must be what happened." A pathetic eagerness laced Lionel's words.

"Still, I will have your oath that you will say nothing of this matter to anyone, not even Gwyn. Do you swear silence?"

"Yes, madam."

"Very well, then." With a consoling pat on the same arm Jennet had earlier struck, Lady Appleton dismissed him.

"He'll tell her the first chance he gets," Jennet predicted when Lionel had left the room.

"I hope not. I would like to think I can still trust my faithful band of retainers."

Jennet sniggered. "Lionel, of all people! Pierced by cupid's arrow at last." Abruptly, she sobered. "It will be hard on him if Gwyn killed Master Calthorpe."

"I do not think she did."

Lady Appleton produced a piece of parchment from a pocket

and studied what was written there. A list of some sort, Jennet imagined.

"Gwyn lied," Jennet reminded her, "again. Unless she changed her mind after leaving Lionel, she went to look out a window, not direct to her chamber."

"Some people are quick to deny guilt, even before they are accused of anything."

"Most often because they are guilty of something else. The children do it all the time." In particular, Mistress Rosamond, but Jennet did not say that aloud.

"Yes. And it is a habit some carry into adulthood." Lady Appleton folded the paper and tucked it away without Jennet having gotten a close look at it. "Be that as it may, I do much doubt Gwyn Merrick is a murderer. It took strength to fell Master Calthorpe."

"She's strong enough. Scrubbing builds fine muscles, madam." Jennet was not sure why she continued to argue for Gwyn's guilt. She did not, in truth, think the young woman capable of violence. Gwyn was not even very good at lying.

A faint smile flickered across Lady Appleton's face. "Unless Gwyn stood on a stool, she'd have been hard pressed to deliver the downward blow that knocked Master Calthorpe to his knees. Besides, she had no reason to want him dead."

"Not even if she feared he'd denounce her as a thief?"

Lady Appleton gave Jennet a sharp look. "You do not believe the destruction of the document was an accident?"

"What if the missing papers were not burnt, as Gwyn claims?"

"If they did not fall into the flames by accident, I'll warrant they've been consigned to the fire by now. We have found no trace of them." Deep in thought, Lady Appleton made her way to the window that overlooked the herb garden. "And yet, what Gwyn told you may well be the truth. The papers could have been burnt by accident. She might have lied to me for fear of being turned out. Add to that a sense of guilt over her dalliance with Lionel, of which her father would disapprove . . ."

That must be the answer, Jennet decided, as Lady Appleton

fell to silent musing. And that meant the missing transcript had naught to do with the murder. Perhaps Sir Walter had the right of it. Davy Ingram had killed Master Calthorpe and run off to avoid being questioned.

Satisfied with this conclusion, Jennet dismissed the murder of Martin Calthorpe from her thoughts. Instead, she contemplated the courtship of Lionel and Gwyn and the pleasant prospect of a wedding in the near future.

14

Eleanor was in no mood to deal with Susanna Appleton. She had not slept well, she was in pain, and her emotions had an annoying tendency to plunge from peak to valley without any warning. "I do not need your advice on how to deal with my daughter," she told her uninvited visitor.

"She only wants to please you, Eleanor." Susanna sat, hands folded in her lap, on the cushioned window seat, but there was nothing subservient about her. Her very presence challenged Eleanor's authority.

"The child has an odd way of showing it! She disobeys me at every turn. She is still abed, lazy creature, having ignored my summons. I meant to begin her instruction in needlework an hour ago. It is an area of her training that you have sore neglected."

"I have no talent for it myself."

The words were soft, like the early morning sunlight streaming in through the window behind her. The two women occupied the small chamber Eleanor had claimed for herself on her first full day at Priory House. Although the term was out of fashion now, she thought of it privily as "my lady's solar."

"If you will not teach her all she needs to know," Eleanor insisted, "then you are in no position to criticize me for making up your lack."

"I must object to your efforts to destroy Rosamond's confidence in herself. Did you tell her she was slothful, Eleanor?"

Eleanor's silence gave Susanna her answer.

"Is it any wonder, then, that she resists your commands? You expect her to do your bidding, but all the while you stab at her with words. Have you ever once offered her praise?"

"I will do so when she's earned it." Stung by the criticism, Eleanor bolstered her defenses. It would never do to appear weak, not before Susanna Appleton. Eleanor dared not show any doubt about the wisdom of her actions.

"I applaud your desire to instruct her in needlework," Susanna continued, "and it is long past time you attempted to know your own child. But if you mean to do naught but criticize her, then you defeat your own purpose."

"What do you know of my purpose? Mayhap I intend to do to her what my own mother did to me, send her off into some wealthy household as an unpaid servant." Eleanor had endured many unpleasant years as a waiting gentlewoman to an elderly cousin, who had treated her more like a slave than a poor relation.

"I am certain you want better than that for Rosamond."

"Are you?" Glaring at her rival, Eleanor reached for the beaker on the table next to her chair.

Ignoring the lifted brow her action provoked, she poured a generous libation of sherry sack into a goblet and drank it down. The strong, sweet wine eased her far better than any of Susanna's herbal remedies and smelled better than most of them.

"Bristol milk," she said, refilling the glass.

"Aye. I have heard it called that, since it can be made in Bristol for far less than the cost of importing sack from Xeres." Disapproval tinged the words, but Susanna was not diverted from her purpose. "You said you meant Rosamond to remain here until you found a husband for her. You claim you wish to teach her wifely arts. All that is well and good. I can scarce object. But there could be much more, Eleanor. It pains me to think there might not be, for either of you."

"What is it you babble about now?"

"Love, Eleanor. Affection between mother and daughter. A

78

bond that is surpassed by no other." In an agitated movement, Susanna surged to her feet. A few steps brought her to Eleanor's side.

"That is as much a falsehood as the idea of lasting devotion between a man and his wife." Eleanor did not look up. Let the woman loom over her if she must. Susanna Appleton was not worth getting a crick in the neck for.

"No, it is not." Stooping, Susanna brought her face level with Eleanor's. "I grant you Rosamond can be difficult, but she is not beyond redemption. She requires patient handling. And caring. You were abandoned by your own mother at a tender age, Eleanor, and you left Rosamond with me when she was still a toddler; but if you make the effort now, you can still win her trust."

Eleanor's fingers clenched around her goblet, wishing she could stand to confront Susanna eye to eye. Or, better yet, stalk out of the room. But although she had been working with a pair of cumbersome crutches for the last few months, she could do no more than shuffle, awkward and slow as a beached mermaid.

Biting back the urge to scream in frustration, Eleanor strove for calm. She was not at all sure she wanted anything to do with Rosamond, but her stated intention to keep the child did seem to bother Susanna. That gave Eleanor a pleasing sense of power. Time enough later, she decided, to pretend to change her mind and send the girl back to Leigh Abbey.

"If Rosamond wants my love," she said aloud, "she must learn to obey me."

Susanna's eyes flashed with irritation. After a short silence, she tried again. "Would it not have been useful, Eleanor, to speak the languages of the countries you and Walter visited in your travels?"

The question took Eleanor back to splendid palaces and glittering receptions. It had been galling to stand by Walter's side at those foreign courts, first in Poland, then in Sweden, unable to follow conversations. She and Walter had spent many months in Cracow, and Melka had been with her ever since; but even now she could understand only a few words of Polish.

"French is the most useful language for diplomats."

Eleanor said nothing. Susanna knew she'd once hoped for the post of ambassador to France for Walter. She'd have liked to live in Paris even if she'd not have understood the language there, either.

"I have asked one of the scholars in residence here to tutor Rosamond in French," Susanna said. "If you were to share those lessons, it might create a bond between you. You could practice conversation with one another."

"And you, Susanna? Do you plan to join these discussions?"

"It would be well if I could, for I fear my own ability to read foreign languages far exceeds my ability to pronounce their words correctly. But I have no time to indulge myself in the pleasures of learning."

It salved Eleanor's ego to hear the other woman admit a short-coming. She almost smiled. "What? You are not expert at everything you undertake?"

A rueful laugh answered her. "I know herbs, and scarce all about them. I believed I could do more to improve your condition. It is plain I failed."

The goblet halfway to her lips, Eleanor froze. Whatever else she believed about Susanna Appleton, she had no doubt the other woman had done all she could to effect a cure. That thought led to another.

"If I am to attempt to win my daughter's affection, then I will have something from you in return."

"What is it you want?" A note of caution underscored the question.

"Some of that knowledge of herbs."

"You seek to relieve your pain?"

"Nothing so simple."

"I will not provide you with poison." Susanna Appleton was famous for her expertise on the subject of poisonous herbs. She had even written a book on the subject.

Eleanor laughed. "Do you imagine I mean to take my own life? Think, Susanna, you'd have it all if I died—the girl and Walter in your bed as well."

"I do not *want* Walter in my bed." Susanna had gone very still, stopping her restless pacing to stare at Eleanor.

"Neither, as it happens, did I; but my wishes are of little concern to him."

"I will not help you to widowhood, either, Eleanor."

"Oh, I am willing enough to give him the son he desires above all else, but in my own time."

At last Susanna understood. She knelt beside Eleanor's chair, once more bringing their eyes level. "You want to prevent conception."

"I miscarried once, in Poland, and came close to death afterward. Rosamond's birth was also difficult. Is it so wrong to wish to rekindle Walter's passion for me before I risk my life in childbed? I want again what I once had, before I so foolishly sacrificed it to my own ambition."

Eleanor waited, counting on Susanna's well-known disdain for the law that gave the male head of a household absolute control over its women and children. Why should she balk at the notion of protecting a wife, even Walter's wife, from the risks of bearing a child? It was not as if Eleanor meant to deny Walter progeny forever.

Susanna drew in a shuddering breath and leaned even closer to grasp Eleanor's hands. Her grip was painful. "Hear me well, Eleanor. Such measures fail as often as they succeed. And if a child should quicken, I will not give you potions to rid yourself of it."

"Help me prevent any quickening for as long as you are in residence here, and you may direct Rosamond's studies as you will. I will even agree to join her language lessons, if that will please you."

"That will please *her*." A sound of exasperation accompanied Susanna's withdrawal. She rocked back onto her heels and loosed her hold. "Is it so much to ask that you make an effort to appreciate your own daughter?"

"Do we have a bargain?"

Their eyes locked. For a long moment they stared at each other, measuring, weighing. "The empty chamber in my wing would make an excellent schoolroom," Susanna said.

"Done." Eleanor knew Walter would give Susanna permission to use the room even if Eleanor herself objected to the idea. Far better to agree.

Susanna sighed and stood. "I will teach you to make a potion that should serve."

"You have a stillroom here?"

"It is only a room in my lodgings, but you are welcome to use it at any time. This is the proper season to make conserve of roses and to begin to distill rose water, too. You are most skilled, as I recall, in preparing both."

Eleanor frowned at the reminder of long-ago days when she and Susanna had worked in harmony in the stillroom at Appleton Manor. Did the woman think they could reestablish that sense of ease between them? Impossible! Too much had happened in the interim.

And grow close to Rosamond? That, too, seemed unlikely. Every time Eleanor looked at her daughter, she saw Robert Appleton, the greatest mistake of her life.

Aloud she said only, "I have a most excellent recipe for rose water."

15

This will be your schoolroom, Rosamond."

Once she'd won Eleanor's approval, Susanna lost no time equipping the chamber with the necessities. The furnishings were sparse, only a chair and writing table and a chest for storing books, but the books themselves had been brought in, together with a supply of paper, sharpened goose quills shaved of feathers to make pens, and an excellent ink composed of oak galls and green vitriol.

There was also a globe, one of Master Behaim's. It was not a very accurate representation of the world, since it had been made before much exploration had been done across the Western Sea, but it was richly decorated in beautiful colors and Susanna thought it would appeal to her foster daughter. She gave it a spin as she passed by. Illuminated manuscript vellum gores had been applied to a plaster sphere twenty inches in diameter, and the whole was mounted to metal meridian and horizon rings in a tripod stand.

"I want to work in the library with you."

Startled, Susanna turned to find Rosamond watching her with a sulky expression on her pretty face. "I fear you would distract me, dear one. But we will spend many hours together here, and I will bring you books from the library if you wish. You will spend your morning translating, as I will. Did you know that the queen herself exercises her mind each morning by turning Latin into English and then back into Latin?"

"Do you translate Latin, too?"

Biting back a sigh, Susanna shook her head. "No. It is Italian I must master, and believe me when I say that I will find it every bit as challenging as you do your assignment."

Thank goodness she would not have to speak the language. As she'd told Eleanor, she had a sad history when it came to mispronouncing foreign words. Robert had been wont to laugh at her for this failing.

"Let me help," Rosamond begged. "I will learn Italian, too."

"Mayhap someone here will instruct you." It was a good thought. Master Merrick had already offered to help with Susanna's translations, although she had no intention of accepting his offer. Of all the scholars, he was the one who could least spare the time from other tasks, for he was the only one among them able to understand the language of the Basques, who had whaling ports in the New World.

Several people, however, read Italian, including Walter. She wondered how he would react if she asked him to tutor his stepdaughter.

"But, Mama, I want *you* to teach me." Rosamond's whine grated on Susanna's nerves.

"That is not possible, dear one; and you must stay here, or if that does not suit, you may go to your mother for instruction in embroidery." Susanna meant that Rosamond do so in any case, but she'd intended to lead up to that subject with more tact.

"I do not like to sew." Rosamond seized her Latin dictionary. "I will come with you."

"No, Rosamond."

"But, Mama—"

"Enough. And if you persist, there will be no lessons in Italian."

The girl stamped her foot. "I do not want to learn Italian. I want to learn . . . French!"

"Very well, Rosamond," Susanna told her, holding back the information that she'd already made arrangements for both mother and daughter to share a French tutor. "So you shall. But that does not alter the fact that I must go now and tend to my own duties." She started toward the door. "I will return in a few hours. Until then, study your Latin verbs."

Susanna hoped her tone brooked no disobedience. If she had to spend any more time placating Rosamond, she would be late for an appointment.

"Abandon me, then!" Rosamond flung herself into the chair and assumed a dramatic pose she must often have seen her mother strike.

Susanna ignored her, turning instead to Hester, who had been hovering in the background. "Make certain she stays here."

With a long-suffering sigh, Hester promised to do her best.

Rosamond was a clever mimic, Susanna thought, as she made her way to the library. But such performances were not convincing even with Eleanor in the leading role. As a bid for sympathy, Rosamond's imitation fell far short.

Under the watchful eyes of the ever-vigilant Piers, Zachary Alday waited for Susanna to arrive. He rose when she entered the room, inclining his head toward her in deference to her position in the household. Piers retreated to the adjoining parlor.

"Sit, please, Goodman Alday. You must forgive me for keeping you waiting. I know you are anxious to be on your way."

"I have pressing business in Bristol."

"I will not keep you long. I have copies here of the anecdotes you related to Masters Gainsford, Weller, and Speake."

It was the policy of the Priory House project for three scholars to interview each of the men brought in to share their memories of the New World. In this case, Alday's accounts were at third hand, having been told first to his father by the great explorer Sebastian Cabot.

"It was good to reminisce about those old times." Alday scratched at the mole on his cheek. "Hard to believe old Cabot's been gone near fifteen years."

Studying the notes before her on the writing table, Susanna grew thoughtful. "A pity he left no account of his own."

"Oh, I expect his executor has possession of his papers."

Had Dr. Dee overlooked that possibility? Making a mental note to ask Walter about it later, Susanna focused on the man before her. "As you know, Goodman Alday, I have been given Martin Calthorpe's notes. I see nothing to indicate why he wanted to talk to you on the day he died." It might have had naught to do with his death, but Susanna did not want to overlook any possibility.

Alday's cheerful smile faded. "Nor do I know for certain, madam. And the poor fellow seemed a bit confused the last time I talked to him. Thought it was Master Sebastian Cabot who sailed to the New World for old King Henry."

Brows knit in confusion, Susanna blinked at him. "I thought Master Sebastian Cabot did sail for King Henry."

"Aye. Well, so he did, but only once. For the queen's grandfather, that is, Henry VII not Henry VIII. 'Twas a disastrous voyage. Afterward, young Sebastian left England and went to work for the king of Spain. But this Italian book Master Calthorpe had made the claim that Master Sebastian Cabot led the earlier expeditions, too. Master Calthorpe said a gentleman of Mantua told its author that Sebastian Cabot had told him, the Mantuan gentleman, that his father, that is John Cabot, Sebastian's father, died in England at about the time Master Columbus reached the New World in Spanish ships, and that Sebastian was the one who sailed west to discover other lands for England to claim. A lot of nonsense, that is! John Cabot made two voyages before Sebastian was old enough to go with him. On the first he claimed the north part of the lands across the Western Sea for England."

"And on the second?"

"May, in the year of our Lord 1498, John Cabot set out with five ships. Four of them were never heard of again. That's what my father told me, and I'll stake his word against what's in some Italian book any day."

Susanna was certain he had the right of it. She could remember, years ago in her own schoolroom, reading in Polydore Vergil's *Angelicae Historicae,* a book she would have to see about acquiring for Rosamond, that John Cabot had never returned to England from that voyage. Even then, she'd been captivated by stories of faraway lands.

"Had you already told Master Calthorpe this?"

"Oh, aye, madam."

"Then why do you suppose he wanted you to meet him in his study?"

Alday hesitated, then ventured a guess. "To show me the text, mayhap? But I fear I cannot say with any certainty, for by the time I arrived, he was no longer in any condition to explain himself."

"If only Goodman Alday had gone a bit earlier to his appointment with Master Calthorpe," Susanna lamented a short time later.

"Alday was with my man, Piers Ludlow, when Eleanor arrived. He left him to meet with Calthorpe only after we escorted my lady wife to the manor house."

Walter's afternoon visit to the library appeared to be for the sole purpose of collecting any information Susanna had for him. She fought the urge to question him about the demands he'd made of his wife and asked instead what he meant to do about Zachery Alday.

"I've sent a man with him to Bristol. His orders are to return and report if Alday reached his destination in safety. I would be assured Alday is engaged upon the exact business he says he has there."

"You think he lied?" She felt her forehead crease as she stared at the pattern on the pillow she'd plucked from beside her on the window seat.

"I think everyone lies, unless I can prove otherwise. More to the point, I have no desire to lose track of any more former guests. At least Richard Twide has been accounted for, but he's on a ship bound for the Canary Islands and will not be available for questioning until it returns to England."

"Will you send for the papers Alday mentioned? Master Cabot's effects?"

"I'll ask Dee to secure them for us from Cabot's executor when I write to tell him of Calthorpe's murder."

Susanna rose, tossing the cushion aside, and crossed to her writing table. "I do not think Master Calthorpe's death had any direct connection to our mission here. I have examined all of his possessions and found nothing missing save Twide's testimony, and we have an explanation for that." She gave him a brief account of Gwyn Merrick's accident with the brazier.

"Have you been able to recreate Twide's testimony?" Walter asked.

"I had Weller, Fletcher, and young Daniel, the clerk who took down the interview, depose all they could remember of what Twide said, but it had been two full weeks since they heard him, and they'd dealt with a great deal else in the interim."

"I've glanced at the transcript of Ingram's interview with Calthorpe, Gainsford, and Merrick myself, but I've scarce had time to do more. Did it differ greatly from Twide's account?"

With a rueful smile, Susanna handed him a roll of parchment. "I have made a list of all Ingram said and to whom."

He gave it back to her. "Tell me your conclusions."

"The start of the story is the same and agrees with the book Master Hawkins wrote about his voyage. In early August of 1568, a small squadron of English ships out of Plymouth was buffeted by two storms in succession and forced into harbor in a Spanish port in the New World. Shortly thereafter, a Spanish fleet arrived, sank one ship, and captured two more. The remaining English fled, but the *Minion* had some two hundred men aboard, far more than she could safely carry. About three weeks later, half of them volunteered to be set ashore at the bottom of the Gulf of Mexico. The *Minion* left them there and returned to England."

"I know that much," Walter said, "and that John Hawkins tried to mount a rescue mission. The queen forbade it. To be blown off course into Spanish territory is acceptable. To return there with deliberate intent is not."

Susanna nodded. Hawkins claimed he'd given the volunteers money and cloth for barter but no weapons, to avoid trouble with the Spaniards. They'd set out toward the south, hoping to find a settlement. "Both Ingram and Twide reported they were attacked by natives, who killed some of their fellows and took all of the cloth. After that, the survivors split into two groups. The largest party continued on toward Spanish territory, where they meant to surrender. I do not know what happened to them."

"I imagine they were imprisoned and sent to Spain," Walter said. "That was the fate of the crewmen on the captured ships. And now Hawkins, so I am reliably informed, will go to any lengths to regain their freedom."

"Even treason?"

"So some at court believe."

"And Ingram was Hawkins's man."

"He could be spying for his old master. I want him back, Susanna. Murder or no, I've questions to ask the fellow."

"I cannot believe he would spy for Spain, not after all he suffered trying to avoid capture by the Spaniards. According to him, he and a small number of others chose to go north, thinking that they would find English fishing vessels in Newfoundland. They had little notion, it appears, of how far away their destination was. They followed native trails for the best part of a year before they reached the area claimed by France. Most of them did not survive the long and arduous journey. Ingram deposed that the few who did were half starved and clothed in naught but animal skins by the time they came upon a French ship at anchor and secured passage to Le Havre. They arrived back in England at the end of 1569, shortly after Master Hawkins published his account of the venture."

"And how does Ingram's story differ from Twide's?" Walter asked.

For a brief moment, Susanna fought a smile. "It changed every time he told it. It is all here." Once again, she handed him the parchment.

With a resigned sigh, Walter unrolled it. His eyes widened as he read, making Susanna's lips twitch again. In the official interview with Masters Calthorpe, Gainsford, and Merrick, Ingram had maintained he'd visited a town half a mile long with many streets far broader than any street in London; that the inhabitants had much resembled the ancient Greeks, fair of face and limb; and that the women had worn plates of gold over their bodies, much like armor. To Daniel, the clerk, in private, Ingram had added pillars of gold, silver, and crystal to his city.

Walter looked up from his reading. "There is no large city in New France. We would have heard of it if there were."

"The Spaniards found great cities to the south."

Ignoring the reminder, Walter read on. Susanna watched his eyebrows climb.

"A beast almost as big as an ox with ears of a great bigness like the ears of a bloodhound?" he read. "What nonsense is this?"

"Evidence that Ingram has a good imagination, I do think. As you can see, at various times he added red sheep, white-skinned natives, and elephants. He also told Fulke that the scholars here are all treasure hunters."

"Better he believe that than know the truth."

"David Ingram would not know the truth if it bit him." Susanna selected another document from her writing table. "Weller, Fletcher, and Daniel say Twide made no mention of any city. He reported only small native settlements, not even any large encampments. And the only treasure was a broken and rusty sword, no doubt left behind by one of the French expeditions."

"Twide and Ingram were the only survivors?"

"Their numbers had dwindled to three by the time they stumbled upon that French ship." Leading the way to one of the maps that decorated the walls of the library, Susanna pointed to a jut of land. "It must have been about here. Cape Breton, it is called on another depiction of La Nuova Francia."

"What happened to the third man?"

"I have no idea and neither did Twide. His name was Richard Browne. Ingram said he was ill when they returned to England. He may be dead."

"I will have my men look for him, though with a name as common as Browne I do not hold out much hope of finding him."

"Unless he is the sort to boast of his adventures in taverns."

"Like Ingram?" They shared a smile. "This may mean the discrepancies Calthorpe spoke of can be accounted for by Ingram's tendency to . . . exaggerate."

"I begin to think most of those who have written accounts of Norombega were afflicted with Ingram's disease—a tendency to embroider upon the facts. Master Calthorpe was translating an Italian book that contains an entire section on that area of the New World. Included are a number of French documents, rendered into Italian before Calthorpe transcribed them in English. I wish you had more time to help me with the remaining translations," she lamented. "Your Italian is much better than mine."

"You will do well enough on your own, and I have little interest in travelers' tales."

"I proceed at a much slower pace than Master Calthorpe. Still, I have already located the source of the Mantuan gentleman Goodman Alday mentioned and discovered that Master Calthorpe had also translated a later section of the same work in which Master John Cabot's voyages are not confused with those of his son. It may be that this second account is what he wished to show Goodman Alday to resolve the discrepancy."

"I do not understand why Calthorpe should have bothered, but then I am the first to admit I have difficulty comprehending most of what motivates scholars. Have you much of Calthorpe's work still to complete?"

"Too much. Best leave me to it, my dear, and write your letters. As things stand now, only one thing is certain: We need more answers and as soon as may be."

16

Three days after they buried Calthorpe, Walter still had no clue to Ingram's whereabouts. Further, he'd had letters from John Dee and from the queen herself, both demanding results. Find a murderer. Prove England's claim to the New World predated Spain's. And guard the remaining scholars well. As suspects or as potential victims? Walter wondered.

The weather, as if in sympathy with his mood, had been unrelentingly foul ever since Alday's departure. Rain, heavy at times, had fallen every day, making it even more difficult for Walter's men to track the fugitive Ingram. Only this morning had the sun at last returned. It shone through the library windows, bathing Susanna in a golden glow. Walter's spirits lifted the moment he entered the room.

They plunged again when she asked for news.

"If I did not know better," he told her, "I would think the fellow had vanished off the face of the earth. No one has seen him."

"Has language been a problem for your searchers?" Susanna asked.

"In this part of Cornwall, most people can speak English."

"Can, but *will* they? Fulke tells me that when he asked one of the locals for directions to this place, he was answered in the Cornish dialect." She scrunched up her face and attempted to reproduce the sounds: "Meea navidna cowzasawzneck. What does that mean?"

Walter fought a smile. Cornowok, a Celtic dialect similar to Welsh and Breton, was a pleasant-sounding tongue, but not the way Susanna mangled it. "I can speak no Saxonage," he translated. "That is what they will say to a stranger, but they understand well enough."

"A pity you cannot borrow Dr. Dee's magic glass. I have heard he has a crystal ball and can scry the answers to all manner of questions with it. Locate things that are lost. Predict the future."

"Unfounded rumor." Walter appreciated her effort to lighten his mood and attempted to match her teasing tone. "Dee himself laughs at the idea of crystalomancy, but he does own several unusual mirrors, including one that can be used for signaling and another that he calls a speculum. It is made of a dense, dark, vitreous stone."

As was her wont, Susanna sat on the cushioned window seat, one leg tucked beneath her. The misty morning sunlight created a halo around her head. When she glanced down at the book on her lap, in order to mark her place, the gauzy fabric attached to the back of her French hood drifted forward against her cheek. She shoved it away with an impatient gesture that left the entire headdress slightly askew. She did not notice. Nor was she aware that a lock of hair had worked its way free of confinement to dip across her brow in a most enticing manner. The smile she sent Walter's way was that of an old friend and nothing more.

"I should like to see such a thing. I warrant Rosamond would enjoy it, too."

For a moment, he could not think what she was talking about. Then he remembered. "Ah, yes. Dr. Dee's mirror."

She gave him an odd look. "You are distracted today. Is anything wrong?"

"Other than the fact there is a murderer still loose?" He lifted the Glastonbury chair and moved it closer to her perch, then sat, fussing with the bottom of his heavily embroidered doublet as he did so. Rich fabrics had a soothing effect on his temper. So did wearing baubles crafted by skilled jewelers.

"That is sufficient, I agree." Susanna set the closed book aside to give their discussion her full attention.

Walter abruptly changed direction. He was sick to death of talk of Ingram, spies, murder, and treason. "What is that you have been reading?"

"I have been translating the record of a voyage by one Antonio Zeno." She ran her fingers over the soft leather cover of the small volume resting on her knees. "There is also a second narrative contained herein, the account of travels in Persia by another member of the Zeno family. By a curious coincidence, Nick met a man named Zeno when he visited that distant land."

Another subject he did not wish to discuss, especially when he could hear the longing in Susanna's voice when she spoke Nick Baldwin's name. The merchant's return to Hamburg for an indefinite stay should have been enough to make her forget all about him. Instead, the fellow's prolonged absence seemed to have strengthened the bond between them.

"I have a letter ready to send to Nick," she added, apparently unaware she was pouring salt into Walter's wounds. "I understand the need for secrecy about our project, but I would like to ask him if his friend ever spoke of an old family story about a New World voyage."

For once, Walter failed to hide his reaction. Her sharp eyes caught his flinch. "Walter? What is it you have not told me?"

Disgusted with himself for giving so much away, he bowed to the inevitable. "Your merchant was once an intelligence gatherer for John Dee. Baldwin traveled to Muscovy and Persia as a spy."

She dipped her head, hiding her expression. "That explains a great deal."

So, she had not known.

He had been suspicious of Baldwin for a long time, certain he was in the service of some powerful court figure. Nothing less could explain how he'd managed to circumvent certain trade regulations. But if Dee himself had not revealed their connection,

Walter would never have guessed that Baldwin reported to him, sending information to the queen's Merlin in return for a favorable word in Her Majesty's ear.

"Baldwin has already been authorized," Walter reluctantly admitted. "You may tell him what you will of our work here." His name had come up during Walter's visit to Mortlake, in connection with Susanna. John Dee's sources were as good as Walter's own. He even knew of Susanna's visit to Hamburg two years earlier.

"Excellent. Then I will add a note to my letter and you can send it by special courier, since this is now official business. How long do you think it will take to get an answer?"

"A month, at the least. As much as three would not be cause for concern."

"Poor Walter."

Susanna reached out to stroke his cheek with her knuckles, as he'd seen her do with Rosamond. Was that how she thought of him? Another child to be cosseted? It was painfully obvious to him that she was unaware of the elemental male response her touch provoked.

"A pity you must be saddled with the responsibility for running what amounts to a small university here when all you want to do is build your dream house. Cheer up, my dear. Research advances apace. We will be done and out of your hair in no time."

"Research," he answered, his voice glum, "in my experience is never done. But, in truth, Susanna, I am in no rush to have you go back to Kent."

If he remained at Priory House and she stayed at Leigh Abbey, they might as well be on opposite sides of the Western Sea. Once their project was complete, he doubted she'd return to Cornwall . . . unless Rosamond remained here to lure her back for visits.

What a pass! To keep the woman he loved in his life, he was forced to rely upon two most unfortunate circumstances—Susanna's love for Eleanor's brat and her penchant for stumbling upon murders.

An awkward silence had fallen between them by the time Jacob entered the library. One look at his face told Walter there was new trouble.

"What is it?"

"Your brother, Sir Walter."

Ignoring the curiosity in Susanna's expression, Walter excused himself. He did not demand information until the library door was tightly closed and he and his long-time servant stood in the stairwell leading from the parlor to the stableyard. "Well, Jacob?"

"Master Tristram Pendennis is here, Sir Walter."

"I left orders not to let him in to see me."

"He did not ask for you, Sir Walter. He asked for Lady Pendennis."

One or more of the guards, Walter thought with growing irritation, was about to be sent away without the promised bonus. "What fool told him she was here?"

"That I cannot say, but when word was brought to her that he had come to visit, she instructed that he be admitted at once. He's been shown into her solar."

Walter realized he was grinding his teeth and forced himself to stop. Between Susanna and Eleanor, his legendary ability to conceal his emotions had become sadly tarnished. "Her solar?" he repeated in a soft, dangerous tone.

"The room above your private study, Sir Walter."

By the time he'd stalked across the open space behind his new manor house, climbed to the upper floor, and stormed though his own chamber and Eleanor's and along the narrow passage outside Rosamond's bedchamber to the "solar," Walter's chest was heaving and he was thoroughly incensed. He was also grimly aware that the last time he'd felt this out of control, he'd attempted to kill Nick Baldwin by pushing him off a castle's curtain wall.

17

So Nick Baldwin was an intelligence gatherer for John Dee. *Had* been. She must remember that. Susanna doubted Nick still engaged in such activities. She hoped he did not. During her marriage to Robert Appleton she'd had quite enough of the complications that sort of thing caused.

When Susanna examined her feelings, she realized she had not been surprised by Walter's revelation. Nick had always avoided answering when she'd asked him who had been his source of information about those at Leigh Abbey. For a long time, Susanna had assumed Walter was the one who'd told Nick she could be trusted; but when Nick and Walter had first come face-to-face in her presence, she'd been obliged to introduce them.

Shaking her head, Susanna took out the letter she'd already written to Nick. Was it some peculiar masculine tendency, she wondered, to plot and scheme and spy and send messages in code or invisible ink when direct dealing would suffice? She understood the need for such machinations as little as she did the dislike that had blossomed between Walter and Nick as soon as they met. Simple jealousy, according to Jennet. Susanna doubted it. Both men might have proposed marriage to her, but she'd also refused them both.

She'd written at the top of the page: "1571, 18 June, at Priory House," and then: "Beloved friend, I commend me unto you, thanking you for your gentle letter unto me." Susanna skimmed the rest of what she'd said, a careful account of her journey to Walter's Cornish estate. Until now, she'd not been permitted to divulge the real reason for the visit.

Susanna sharpened her quill, dipped it in the ink bottle, and penned an addition, telling Nick that her trip to Cornwall had been made at the behest of an old friend of his, the sponsor of his Persian adventure. Sponsor? She considered the word. Was it clear enough? Instigator would not be correct. Nor master. Scratching out "sponsor of your Persian adventure," she substituted "recipient of your tidings from Persia."

"Now, dear friend," she continued, "I must be a suitor unto you, desiring you to do a charitable deed, and my trust is, good Nick, you will do it the sooner at this my request." She tapped the top of the quill against her teeth. If there were spies everywhere, she must be cautious in her wording, but she refused to put the letter in code. She'd had enough of such nonsense when she was Robert's wife.

When she'd expressed her need for information on the Zeno family, Susanna considered telling Nick about Calthorpe's murder but thought better of it. He'd only worry that she might have placed herself in danger by asking questions. *Little chance of that*, she thought ruefully. No one here, save her own servants, had shown the least sign they even knew there had been a murder, let alone that she and Walter were investigating. Instead, she penned the salutation she was accustomed to use on letters to Nick: "I commit you to the protection of the Highest. Your loving friend, Susanna Appleton."

She sanded the ink and blew the excess away, missing Nick more than ever. No matter how many letters they exchanged, nothing made up for his prolonged absence.

After folding the page, she heated her wax, used the signet ring she'd had made in her widowhood, which showed a tiny mortar and pestle above an open book, and sealed the missive. She ran her finger over the wax imprint when it had cooled. Nick would touch it just so before he broke the seal and read what she had written.

A tear splashed onto the letter.

Appalled, Susanna blotted it, then dashed the moisture from her face with the back of her hand. Enough of such foolishness. It was time to return to work.

She had a murder to solve and a translation to finish. She collected Master Zeno's book and carried it with her to the window seat, determined to remain optimistic. Why, with any luck at all, by the time she'd rendered it all into English, she might also have come upon some clue, some tiny detail that would help her understand the reason Martin Calthorpe had been slain.

18

Tristram Pendennis was ten years older than Walter and had about him an air of solid respectability. Eleanor found him delightful. He flattered her, flirted with her, and if her scars repulsed him, he was courteous enough to hide his reaction.

"Would that I had met you first, sir," she declared, running her fingertips along his sleeve.

The fabric was not as soft as she'd anticipated. Her face puckered into a small frown, but before she could say more, an all-too-familiar voice shattered the peace of her solar.

"I stopped sharing women with my brother when I was fifteen," Walter announced. As usual, he wore an enigmatic expression, but his tone dripped ice pellets.

"Curious you should choose to remind me of that." Tristram Pendennis stood. For size and for formidable self-control, the two men were well matched, but the older brother lacked the younger's years of experience as a courtier. Eleanor had already discovered he was accustomed to plainspeaking, and he did not let her presence deter him now.

"Tamesin's brother wants you dead, Walter."

"So you said in the note you sent." The slow lift of one eyebrow his only reaction, Walter appeared unconcerned.

"God's teeth, man! It will be your own fault if you end up with a stake through your heart."

Startled, Eleanor gasped. It was no news to her that Walter had enemies, but most would have settled for shooting him with a pistol. "What do you mean? What villain would do such a thing?"

"This does not concern you, Eleanor."

"I am your wife. How can it not?"

It was Tristram who came to kneel beside her chair, concern writ large on his features. "You must guard yourself well, dear lady."

"Why?"

"Go ahead." Walter's taunting voice egged his brother on. "Tell her."

After one disgruntled glance over his shoulder, Tristram rocked back on his heels. He did not touch Eleanor, but he held her gaze as he began the tale. "When your husband was a lad of fourteen, madam, he took his first mistress, a maidservant in our household."

"Tamesin," she murmured.

"Aye. She was ambitious. She'd already been in my bed. But when she found herself to be with child, our father forbade either of us to marry her."

"You never considered it," Walter broke in.

Surprised, Eleanor twisted around to look at him. He stood in shadow. She could not see his face.

"Be that as it may, she grew desperate and tried to rid herself of the child. Whatever potion she took, it was too powerful." Eleanor felt herself pale. "She died," Tristram continued, "and the babe with her. The church declared it a suicide, and she was denied burial in holy ground."

"She was interred at a crossroads, a stake through her heart to prevent her returning from the dead." Walter's voice was uninflected, but Eleanor sensed anger beneath the words. Had he loved this girl? Had he wanted to marry her?

Tristram finished the tale, his gaze never leaving Eleanor's pale face. "Alexander Trewinard vowed revenge. It would not surprise me if he tried to hurt you in order to get at my brother."

"He was a lad of eight or nine at the time," Walter objected. "You exaggerate the danger."

Leaving Eleanor's side at last, Tristram went to stand close to Walter. She had to strain to hear their exchange.

"It has been more than twenty-five years," Walter said.

"Do you think he ever forgot what was done to his sister? Or that you foolishly accepted the blame for her condition?"

"You would not."

"I do not know if it was my child or yours or the goatherd's. That scarce signifies. You were the one who tried to persuade the vicar that Tamesin's attempt to kill her unborn baby was a lesser sin than killing herself."

"I have heard this all before," Walter interrupted, impatience and anger at war in his demeanor. "Father made it most clear that there was no need for anyone outside the family to know our business."

"He was right. Certes, young Trewinard did not need to hear such a story bandied about. Is it any wonder he still feels honor bound to punish you for what happened to his sister? He once vowed to kill you, Walter, and the moment he learned you'd returned to Cornwall, he vanished from hearth and home. He has not been seen since."

"When?" Walter demanded. "When did he go missing?"

"The day you sent your men door-to-door inquiring about that sailor, Ingram."

Watching closely, Eleanor thought the tension in her husband's big body eased a bit at Tristram's words, but it was difficult to tell. His posture was still rigid.

"There has been no sign of him here, Tris. I thank you for your concern, but we are well guarded."

"Walter's life is often threatened," Eleanor observed.

Tristram caught Walter's arm. "Even if you have no care for yourself, think of your wife. Trewinard could try to harm her."

Eleanor's laughter echoed Walter's. "He would do my husband good service to eliminate me, dear brother."

Bewildered, Tristram Pendennis's gaze came to rest first on Walter then shifted to Eleanor. "I do not understand the ways of the court," he muttered, "but I have done all I can to warn you."

His glower moved back to his brother. "On your head be it if Trewinard takes his vengeance on innocents."

For a few minutes after Tristram's departure, neither Walter nor Eleanor spoke. Then she forced a soft, ironic chuckle. "Once upon a time, you spoke with loving fondness of your family, of a reunion with your brothers."

There were three of them, she recalled, all older than Walter: Carew, Tristram, and Armigal. And three sisters: Grace, Honor, and Temperance. His father, Sir Benet Pendennis, had died while she and Walter were in Cracow. His mother—Eleanor did a quick calculation in her head—would have died shortly before Walter became intimate with Tamesin Trewinard.

"Who was she?"

To Eleanor's surprise, Walter answered. "Her father was one of the Trewinards of St. Erth. She was a bastard. So is her brother."

Like Rosamond, Eleanor thought.

A shudder coursed through her. If Rosamond, at the age she was now, the same age young Alexander Trewinard had been then, were to vow revenge on someone, Eleanor had not a doubt in the world that she'd be capable of nursing it for decades. And when the opportunity arose at last to carry it out, no matter how many years later, she would exact that vengeance with devastating effect.

19

Walter left Eleanor's solar as abruptly as he'd entered it. It was well he'd given himself time to calm down before he'd confronted Tris. Nothing had changed between them. He still resented his older brother.

When he'd walked in on them it had looked for all the world as if Tris intended to seduce Eleanor. Or the other way around.

How could he have believed he could mend the past? They'd all turned against him when Tamesin died. He'd been sent away to the household of John Dudley, an important government official who had later become duke of Northumberland and had been, for a short time, the most powerful man in England.

Walter saw now that he'd been a fool to think he could return to his roots. His father might be dead, but the past lingered on to haunt and torment.

He rubbed his throbbing forehead. Susanna would suggest something to ease the ache. Of their own volition, his feet carried him toward the library. He wondered if she had a remedy for confusion.

Walter found her, once again, at her favorite perch on the window seat. She sat with both feet curled beneath her, shoes discarded on the floor nearby.

"I was about to solicit your opinion on the search for David Ingram when we were interrupted." Responding to the questions in her eyes, he added, "Ingram is the only subject I want to discuss."

"As you wish." Unspoken were the words "for now."

Walter cleared his throat and gathered his thoughts. "Ingram's complete disappearance may have the same explanation as Twide's. Both are seamen. It is logical to suppose Ingram also shipped out, even though the inquiries my men have made in every port within a hundred miles of here could unearth no proof of it."

"Do not be so hard on yourself, Walter. Unless he made a point of telling someone where he was bound, it is possible no amount of questioning would reveal his whereabouts."

"If your intent is to cheer me, madam, I must tell you that you have missed your mark." The chair was where he'd left it, facing the window, and he sank into it, leaning toward Susanna.

Contrite, she reached across the short distance between them to give his hand a reassuring squeeze. He grasped her fingers before she could pull back and lifted them to his lips.

She tugged and he set her free. As soon as she'd reclaimed her hand, she seized a cushion, hugging it to her bosom as if she sought to put a physical barrier between them.

"I would like you to help me review all we know, from the beginning. You agree Calthorpe was struck first with some blunt object, to stun him?"

Solemn eyed, she nodded. "When I prepared Calthorpe's body for burial, I noted abrasions on his knees, as if he had landed hard on them just before he was killed. There was also a bruise on his right arm."

"And while he was down, someone clouted him, striking a killing blow with the sharp edge of the book."

"That part troubles me, Walter."

"That he was killed with a book?"

"The fact he was hit twice, both times on the head but with two different weapons."

"He was not a young man, Susanna. If he surprised a thief, he'd have tried to go for help. Desperate to stop him, the thief landed

105

the first blow, sending him to his knees. Mayhap he crumpled to the floor, stunned."

Setting aside the cushion, she stood and locked both hands together, lifting them above her head. "Someone struck him, thus."

Of a sudden, she brought her arms down, hard, aiming at Walter's face. He flinched, but she pulled the blow. He felt only a rush of air.

"Calthorpe was of average height. I do not recall that Ingram was any taller."

"If Ingram struck Calthorpe down, it was not with his fists. There is a more obvious weapon."

"His walking stick?" Susanna looked thoughtful. "I did notice that although he was wont to carry it everywhere, he did not seem to need its assistance to get about."

"A good stout weapon."

"But what was Ingram looking for in Calthorpe's study? And after he'd knocked Calthorpe unconscious, why not flee at once, leaving him still alive? No one would have stopped him."

Now it was Walter's turn to nod. Her thinking agreed with his. "Consider this, too," he said, after a bit more pondering. "If he was driven to kill in the first rush of panic, why not finish the job with the same weapon?"

"Never tell me there were two attackers!"

"No, only one. Driven by panic or anger, mayhap, to strike the first blow; but then, in full possession of his wits, this villain considered the situation and decided he wanted the man he'd merely rendered unconscious to be dead. With malice aforethought, he did deliberate murder, but in such a way as to make Calthorpe's killing appear to have been no crime at all."

"And for all anyone knows, he succeeded. You gave out it was mischance. Why, then, should he feel obliged to disappear?" Fabric rustled as Susanna paced. "Why not stay on another day or two? That way, when he left, no suspicion could attach itself to his departure."

"There was no reason for him to flee," Walter agreed, "which means we must consider an alternative explanation, that Ingram himself has been the victim of foul play."

"Dead?" She turned to stare at him, eyes wide. "But then where is his body?"

"Somewhere on Bodmin Moor, or so I suspect."

"I believe I prefer the theory that he shipped out; but if Ingram did not kill Martin Calthorpe, who did?"

"Aye, there's the problem. No clear suspect has emerged. In my capacity as justice of the peace, I questioned all the scholars, letting them think it a mere formality, that I was required by law to ask about the circumstances since the death was unattended."

Susanna nodded. "The simple truth, in point of fact. Meanwhile, Jennet and I took advantage of the urge people always feel to talk about a tragedy after the event. We gathered the same information, or rather lack of it, from the rest of the household. We were unable to learn anything useful. Only Gwyn and Lionel were nearby, and they account for each other."

Walter was willing to take Susanna's word for that . . . for the moment. Neither he nor Susanna had undertaken a simple task, Walter thought. Only the guards could be asked pointed questions, and even then he'd had to caution them to speak of their interrogations to no one else.

"As you know," he said, "Calthorpe had the end study on the northeast corner. Merrick, who occupies the room opposite, claims he'd already gone out to see what all the noise in the stableyard was about and was therefore well away from the scene before Calthorpe dislodged the book that caused his death."

"I saw both Merrick and Fletcher in the stableyard just after Eleanor arrived. But their presence there exonerates neither. It would not have taken long to kill Calthorpe." She frowned. "*Could* Merrick hear Eleanor's arrival from his study?"

"Better than from Calthorpe's. Fletcher, in the room that adjoins Merrick's on that side, also claimed to have heard the uproar."

"Did they go out together?"

"They say not, but both appear to have been there in time to

107

witness my reunion with my lady wife." He grimaced, remembering how angry he'd been, far too furious to have noticed anything else. Murder and mayhem could have been committed right in front of him, and he'd have remained oblivious to everything but Eleanor's false smile.

"Calthorpe was still with me at that point," Susanna murmured. "When I saw you cross the stableyard toward the litter, I realized I must go down at once."

"To keep me from killing her?" Thoughts of strangling Eleanor had been running through his mind at the time.

"What of the others?"

Susanna's question forced Walter to focus on the matter at hand. "Gregory Speake, our clergyman, says he was engrossed in translating French into English until after you and I were summoned to examine the body. Likewise, in the study across from him, the irritable and irritating Master Gainsford claims he continued to work through Eleanor's arrival and Calthorpe's death. He did much resent being interrupted when the hue and cry was raised and was even more put out by what he termed my 'foolish questions.' "

A faint smile slid into place on Susanna's face. "He resents a great many things. Have you noticed that when he is surpassing agitated he bounces on the balls of his feet?"

Walter came close to smiling back. "He was out of his chair within moments of my arrival, and by the time I was ready to move on to my next suspect he did much resemble a rabbit."

"All that hopping up and down?" Her smile turned into a grin. "What of Master Weller? His study is right next to Master Calthorpe's."

"He says he'd nodded off, having been up late the previous night. He was sound asleep and heard nothing." Walter was inclined to believe the bald scholar.

Susanna's humor vanished. "A pity none of the grooms, or the cook, or a maid were in the vicinity at the right time." She bent over a piece of paper, quill moving rapidly. "I wonder . . . if Ingram is not the murderer, is it possible *he* saw something?"

108

"Not that he'd admit, for I questioned him, too, and Alday, and Daniel, the clerk. Alday, as you know, found the body. He rushed out and all but collided with young Daniel, who'd been sent by Gainsford to borrow a book from Merrick and was on his way back with it."

"The lad's overworked. With six scholars, we should have had at least as many clerks."

"Secrecy prohibits it," Walter reminded her. "Daniel also claims to have been drawn to the stableyard by the arrival of newcomers and to have stayed overlong and been scolded for it by Gainsford when he returned to his duties."

"And Ingram?"

Ingram told me he was already in the stableyard when Eleanor arrived. No one remembers seeing him until later, but no one had reason to pay attention to who was where. Not then."

Susanna had made a rough sketch of the Priory House buildings and marked with x the location of each of the scholars, Ingram, Gwyn Merrick, and Lionel. "Someone is lying." She sounded discouraged.

"We will expose him, and discover who killed Calthorpe, but for the present we must continue as we have been and call no undue attention to our efforts. If we wait and watch, the villain is bound to betray himself." Walter spoke with a confidence he was far from feeling, hoping his words would bolster Susanna's flagging spirits.

"Can we rule anyone out?" she wondered aloud.

"Only those you could see from this window when Calthorpe stood here beside you."

"Eleanor. Rosamond. You."

Walter's lips twisted into a wry smile. He could also eliminate his brother and Alexander Trewinard as suspects. Neither had known then that Walter was back in Cornwall.

20

Susanna was roused from sleep by loud alarums outside her window. By the time she and Jennet reached the old herb garden, Bartholomew Fletcher was in a rage, his normally ruddy complexion bright red in the lantern light and his usually pleasant facial expression conspicuously absent.

"You baboon! You imbecile. Lady Appleton, tell this great ape to unhand me at once!"

Biting back the impulse to inform him she was no ape leader, Susanna laid a hand on Piers Ludlow's arm. "I've sent for Sir Walter. He will not flee. Release him into my custody if you please."

With obvious reluctance, Piers complied.

"Good man." She drew her night robe more tightly about her, for she wore nothing beneath, and looked Master Fletcher straight in the eye. "How is it, sir, that you were here to have Piers apprehend you?"

"What? Do you say he had a right to accost me?"

"Answer the question, if you please. Sir Walter's men are charged with keeping Priory House safe at night. They had no reason to expect one of the household to be out and about this late."

Huffing indignantly, Fletcher's ire waged a visible war with the need for calmness. He had not quite succeeded in getting himself in hand before Walter and Jennet arrived on the scene.

To Susanna's surprise, Walter's first sharp reprimand was directed at Piers. "I left you in charge of the library. How come you here?"

"Time enough to question Piers later," Susanna interrupted. "Here's Master Fletcher, out in the middle of the night. He was about to explain what he was doing in the old herb garden."

When Walter turned toward them, into the flickering light, Susanna's eyes widened. That Jennet would have found him in his bed she knew, but she'd not expected such obvious signs of just how he'd spent the earlier hours of the night. There were teeth marks on the side of his throat and a fresh scratch on his cheek, and even from two feet away, she could detect Eleanor's distinctive perfume. The aroma of sweet marjoram wafted toward her on a gentle breeze, together with an even more telling scent. Startled and cautiously pleased, she avoided meeting Walter's gaze, but she could not fail to hear Jennet's snicker.

"Why am I treated like a criminal?" Fletcher demanded. "I did but go outside to clear my head. A breath of fresh air in the garden, that is all I wanted."

"You've a cloister near your lodgings," Walter pointed out. "Why come here?"

"Such a to-do over nothing," Fletcher complained. "I needed exercise and tired of walking 'round and 'round in one place. Where is the harm in that, I ask you?"

"Piers?"

A nervous shuffling of feet preceded the guard's answer. To Susanna's sharp eyes, he looked more guilty now than Fletcher did. "I saw someone outside the wall," he mumbled. "When I came to investigate, I found Master Fletcher. I thought he was the intruder, Sir Walter, for when I challenged him, he ran."

"As would any sensible unarmed man in the middle of the night," Fletcher grumbled.

"Did you see anyone else about, Master Fletcher?" Susanna asked. She wished she could see his face more clearly when he answered, but he had moved back a bit from the lantern's glow.

He hesitated, then shrugged. " 'Tis possible I did, now that you mention it." He pointed, glancing back at Piers. "Just over there?"

Piers nodded and everyone looked toward the wall that ran around the entire estate. If someone had clambered over it at that spot, his movements toward Priory House would have been masked by trees and bushes for most of the distance in between.

"Have that field cleared in the morning," Walter ordered. "And see to any repairs to the wall."

"Aye, sir."

"What need?" Fletcher asked. "Are we in danger of attack, Sir Walter, that you take these precautions?"

"You know our work is of a delicate nature, Master Fletcher. Before you came here, you swore to speak of it to no one."

Fletcher's snort told them what he thought of that. He dusted himself off—he appeared to have gotten quite dirty when Piers apprehended him—and made a stiff bow. "If you've quite done with me, I will retire now. I've no mind to listen to more of this nonsense."

The answering dip of Walter's head was barely civil. "Confine your midnight rambles to the cloister, Master Fletcher, and we'll all sleep better."

Susanna watched the scholar go, taking Jennet's candle with him to light his way, then turned her attention to those remaining. The scuffle had woken her, and perforce Jennet, who slept with her; but if any of the servants who lodged in this wing of the house had heard it, they'd stayed in their beds.

In quiet, deadly tones, Walter berated Piers and the reason for his guilty look tumbled out. Piers, assigned to guard the library, had been bored by his duties. He'd convinced another of Walter's men to trade places with him.

"And he, no doubt, is sound asleep among the tomes. Go and take up the duties you were given, Piers, and report to me at once if there is anything amiss there. And henceforth, when you are given orders, do not think to alter them without permission."

Piers went.

Jennet had faded into the background, although Susanna could

112

sense her presence nearby. She turned to face Walter. "You were hard on him."

"With spies and murderers at large, I cannot afford to be lenient."

"Was there someone outside the walls? Ingram come back? Another enemy?"

Walter peered into the surrounding darkness. "It is possible Ingram has been hidden in the area all this time, that he came back to steal other papers, or sent someone in his stead. I will call out the rest of my men and search the grounds just to be certain there's no one here now."

It seemed a futile effort until morning should provide sufficient light to see by, and Susanna supposed the intruder, if there had been one, was long gone now, frightened off when Piers sounded the alarm.

She glanced at Walter. His face was in shadow, but she could see the tenseness of his jaw and at his sides his fingers flexed, betraying the strong emotions he sought to hide. She shared his frustration. There had been a guard posted, no doubt more than one, but this was not a fortress, and Walter did not have enough men to watch every inch of the wall every minute of the day and night. Someone determined to get in could manage it, and there were a great many places on the premises to hide. She shivered.

Walter noticed. "You are cold. Go back to bed, Susanna. There's no more for you to do tonight."

Although she was reluctant to admit it, she knew he was right. She turned to go and trod on something slippery, nearly losing her footing on the uneven cobbles. Puzzled, she stooped and felt for what she'd stepped on. The texture was familiar to her, the briny smell more so—rock samphire. For its tangy taste, it was much used in pickling.

"Seaweed," she murmured.

Walter went still at her side. "We are at least eight miles from the coast."

"Ingram is a sailor."

Walter said nothing.

"Have you another suggestion? An unknown Spanish spy?" She huffed out an exasperated breath. "But what are they *after?*"

"There is another possibility," Walter said. "A former . . . acquaintance of mine named Alexander Trewinard."

"Why should this Trewinard invade Priory House?" Susanna asked.

Walter did not answer her, but as he walked away, distracted by his own thoughts, she heard him mutter to himself, "I suppose I must deal with the fellow after all," he said, "if only to rule out any connection between old business and new."

21

The brewery was on the north side of the domestic buildings and had been situated next to the bakehouse, so that both brewing furnace and bread ovens could take fuel from the same supply. In two months as housekeeper at Priory House, Jennet had, one by one, assumed most of the responsibilities of the lady of the manor. Lady Appleton had been too busy with Sir Walter's secret project to spend time supervising the servants.

Once Lady Pendennis arrived, Jennet would have stepped aside, but Sir Walter's wife had shown no inclination to exert herself. Had she been able to get about more easily, Jennet supposed she would have demanded the keys. As it was, they still jangled in cheerful discord from Jennet's waist. Therefore it fell to her to discover what had made the last batch of beer so bitter.

"It is a most excellent brewhouse," said Gwyn Merrick, who had accompanied her.

If she knew of the previous night's uproar, she gave no sign of it. Serene and bright with approval, the young woman's gaze moved from the high ceiling, designed to allow steam to dispel, to the louvered windows on the north side, to the purpose-built brewing vessels set into the paved and cobbled floor. In many households, the laundry copper and washtubs did double duty as brewing tun and underbucks. It was not unheard of for a trace of soap left in one of the wooden tubs to spoil the beer. This equipment, however, was reserved for use in brewing.

They reached the massive, brick-cased copper, in which water was boiled up, by climbing a short flight of six steps. A shallow, rectangular, lead-lined cooling tray stood on spaced joists below the plug cock at its base. "I have never seen better in Bristol," Gwyn declared.

"Is that your home?" Jennet had thought Merrick and his daughter lived in Cambridge, since she'd most often heard him referred to as a fellow of that university.

"We have lived many places, but my father was born in Bristol, as was his father before him."

"And your mother?"

"She was the daughter of a Cambridge innkeeper. She died when I was born."

If Gwyn felt any embarrassment that her father had married beneath him, she did not show it. Indeed, she seemed most knowledgeable about the workings of the brewery, indicating that she might have spent considerable time in the household of her maternal grandfather.

Jennet addressed the woman in charge of brewing. "Do you allow the water to cool until you can see your face through the steam on the surface of the liquid?" That was the test Lady Appleton always applied to make certain the temperature was right.

The brewer nodded.

Step by step, Jennet reviewed the process, checking the woman's answers. The water in the copper had to be run off into the mash tun, where mash was added. After several hours, if it had been well stirred all the while with a mash paddle, a sweet extract called wort was the result.

"We draw it off from the barrel in buckets and replace it in the copper," the brewer said, "then boil it up again with hops and sugar."

But the hops were inferior, Jennet saw. Those which were fresh, bright yellow in color and pungent of scent, gave the best

116

flavor. "Can better be had in Bristol?" she asked Gwyn.

"No doubt in the world of it."

"The spree should be at blood heat before it is drained from the cooling tray into the fermenting tun," Jennet continued, turning to inspect the broad-based oaken barrel where yeast, saved from an earlier brewing, was added to the hopped wort and the whole was left for a few days to ferment before the yeast was skimmed off the surface and the beer strained into casks.

"I do use my elbow to test it," the brewer assured her.

Jennet gave the woman's arms, bared almost to the shoulder by her rolled-up sleeves, a pointed glance. "In future, wash that elbow first."

Oblivious to the criticism, the brewer declared, "Needs to be left longer afore 'tis drunk."

"That will not help," Gwyn put in. "Not at this time of year. To produce strong beer, brewing must be done in the cool months."

"And we have too many thirsty men in this house to delay drinking what we make," Jennet agreed. The beer cellar had a number of casks as yet unbreeched, but that supply would not last long if the brewery did not continue to produce an appreciable amount of drink to augment it.

The brewer, who also had charge of the bakehouse, heaved a sigh but made no objection. As one of the three women servants employed by Sir Walter, she was well paid to follow instructions.

"Proceed with the brewing," Jennet told her. "Next month you will have better hops."

"Do you think inferior hops alone caused the beer to be bitter?" Gwyn asked as the two women emerged into the open space to the south of the brewery. Ahead was the new stable, its construction suspended when Sir Walter had been obliged to turn his house into an enclave for scholars. Some fifty feet beyond, off to the southeast, were the ruins of the old infirmarian's lodgings and beyond that the yard of the old infirmary, also a ruin, and the stable and stableyard that were still in use.

"What else could have spoilt the batch?"

"A rat or a mouse could have fallen into the copper."

Jennet grimaced. "If that did happen, we'll never get the brewer to admit it."

"Serve the good beer to Sir Walter and the gentlewomen, or give them wine," Gwyn suggested. "No one else will complain. I vow, my father and his fellow scholars scarce notice. There are times Father forgets about meals altogether."

"Is that why he keeps you close? To remind him?"

Making certain first that they were not downwind of the sand-ridge, a compost heap composed of sea sand and manure intended for use as fertilizer, they found seats on some of the building blocks brought to the site of the future stable. It was pleasant there in the warmth of the sun, and the fresh air soon dissipated any lingering fumes from the brewhouse.

"That is one reason," Gwyn said.

"Lady Appleton thinks his eyesight is failing." Gwyn opened her mouth to deny it, but Jennet rushed on. "She does not think any less of his contribution for that. Indeed, I have heard her say he's the most highly valued of all the scholars here."

"He has mastered two of the most difficult languages," Gwyn agreed.

"As, I think, have you."

"No." A wistful look came over Gwyn's face. "I would I could read and write in other languages than English and Latin. I would be much more help to him then."

"But you do more than fetch and carry."

"I have been hostess and housekeeper for him for several years, but as you have guessed, I also take down dictation and organize his notes for him."

"When you marry, he will have to hire a clerk to replace you."

Gwyn seemed startled by the thought.

"You must mean to marry one day," Jennet continued. "Indeed, I do think you have a most avid suitor even now." With or without her father's approval, Gwyn had spent a great deal of time in Lionel's company. She appeared to be as smitten with him as he was with her.

The young woman would not meet Jennet's eyes. Shifting her position on the makeshift seat, she stared unseeing at the open field to the west. Jennet likewise turned until she was once more side by side with Gwyn.

"You could do worse than Lionel, for all that you seem to have little in common."

"And well I know it." The words were so soft Jennet could scarce hear them. Then a faint smile blossomed. "I've never met anyone who knows so much about crops. He says that Sir Walter does much neglect this land. On any normal manor, the order would have been given by now to begin to carry dung to the sandridge. Dozens of loads a day."

"Ah, to be young and in love," Jennet murmured. "I remember the feeling passing well." Nothing less would make a discussion of the manure pile seem romantic! 'Twas plain it did not matter to Lionel that Gwyn could read Latin or to her that he'd first come to Leigh Abbey as a laborer in the herb garden.

"Lionel says you and your husband are the most devoted couple he's ever met."

Her mind flooded with fond memories, Jennet spoke without thinking. "I knew how much I cared for Mark when I almost lost him." She chuckled. "There is something to be said for a courtship spiced with murder."

Gwyn's head jerked up, her dark eyes wide and startled. "Murder?"

Her reaction made Jennet wonder if Lionel had broken his promise to Lady Appleton and told Gwyn that Calthorpe's death was no accident. Resolving to take greater care with her words and alert for Gwyn's slightest reaction, Jennet elaborated. "Some years ago, the steward at Appleton Manor was found dead, face down in a marrow-bone pie. Poisoned. Lady Appleton had to go all the way to Lancashire to discover who killed him. Mark and I went with her. Fulke and Lionel, too."

She gave Gwyn an abbreviated account of their adventures, in which her own role became much larger than it had been in reality. To Jennet's mind, it was the prerogative of the storyteller to

119

embroider upon the truth, so long as doing so enhanced the telling. "Mark and I were married soon after," she confided, when she came to the end of the tale. "Odd, is it not, that a murder should lead to marriage?"

"Mayhap it has to do with facing danger together," Gwyn mused. "There is an old story in my family, one my great-grandfather told me when I was very small, that has a similar outcome."

"Will you tell it to me?" Jennet loved to hear a good tale almost as much as she enjoyed recounting one.

Gwyn seemed happy enough to oblige. "Many, many generations ago, two of my ancestors met and married because she was accused of murder. It was in the time of King Henry IV, on the border between England and Scotland. He was a Scot. She was one of the twelve daughters of an English baron."

"Twelve! That seems excessive."

Gwyn giggled. "He kept trying for a son. He married four times."

"And none of them—"

"No. And his widow, who was barren, was the one who was murdered. My ancestress, Alison, was accused of the crime, but the Scot, Sir Gavin Dunnett, proved her innocent and carried her off into Scotland and married her. He was in the service of a great prince in that land, the ruler of all the Orkneys."

Jennet had no notion what or where the Orkneys were, but this talk of the border with Scotland, a most inhospitable place that she had, in fact, once visited, sparked her curiosity. "I thought Merrick was a Welsh name."

"Oh, it is indeed. From Ap Meryk." Suddenly flustered, Gwyn stared down at her clasped hands. "I told you," she mumbled, "this courtship, and the murder, were a long, long time ago."

"Gwyn!"

She jumped at the sound of her father's voice. So did Jennet. Soundless, Owen Merrick had crossed the open space between the building that housed his study and the place where they sat sunning themselves. Jennet wondered how much he had heard of their conversation, for he was now at Gwyn's elbow.

"I need your assistance, Daughter."

"Your pardon, Father, I lost track of the time." Gwyn rose and dusted off the back of her skirt, ready to follow him wherever he led.

"My thanks for your advice in the brewhouse," Jennet told her, then turned to Master Merrick. "Your daughter suggested we send to Bristol for hops."

He blinked behind his spectacles, putting Jennet in mind of a befuddled owl, and absently rubbed his abdomen with one hand, as if his ribs ached . . . or he suffered from an empty belly.

"Hops? What have hops to do with our mission here?"

A soft sigh escaped Gwyn as she took his free arm to guide him back to his study. "I know you will not believe this, Father, but to most people, food and drink are as necessary as books."

22

On the first Monday of each month, the scholars at Priory House met formally to compare their results. At the two previous meetings, Susanna had been more observer than participant. This time, she took Martin Calthorpe's place at the table they set up in the parlor next to the library.

Calthorpe would have been dismayed by this usurpation, Walter thought. No. Appalled. But there was no help for it. And if men could accept a woman ruler, it only made sense that they should further adjust their thinking and admit that a woman's mind, properly trained, could be just as sharp as a man's.

Susanna did not give anyone an opportunity to protest. She simply presented herself as their equal and ignored the raised eyebrows and low murmurs of disapproval.

She seemed oblivious to the startling contrast she presented, sitting there with the others, but Walter was not. They were all in somber black—long robes and academic caps. She wore deep gold tones, with a falling band instead of a ruff, and cuffs that had been freshly laundered to remove the ink stains that so often decorated her attire. Her dark brown hair was hidden by a French hood, but it was anyone's guess how long the unruly locks would stay put. Did they ever notice such details, these scholars? Walter wondered. If they did not, they missed a good deal of the pleasure the world around them had to offer.

Adam Weller spoke first, summarizing all he'd discovered in Spanish and Portuguese documents about what cosmographers called the "indrawing seas." As Walter understood the term, it referred to the area across the Oceanus Atlanticus from England and to the north of the great new continent explorers had found there. The indrawing seas, or so explorers hoped, were the entrance to a northwest passage to the riches of Asia.

"A pity we cannot gain access to the Spanish archives at Simancas," Weller lamented.

"We have a great deal of material here," Susanna reminded him. "This is the first time so much on the subject has been gathered in a single location. And we have what Spain lacks—English manuscripts."

"I am not so sure about that," Weller argued. "There are many Portuguese records that contain information on Bristol's trade with Lisbon and the Azores and the attempts by English merchants from that city to locate the place they call the Isle of Brasil."

"Brasil is naught but another name for Brendan's Fortunate Isles," Samuel Gainsford objected.

"What addlepated logic brings you to that conclusion?" Owen Merrick demanded.

"Translate the Celtic word *breas-i*. It means fortunate."

"Some say Brasil is a corruption of Bristol," Bartholomew Fletcher offered.

"You play word games!" Gainsford complained. "I am the expert on the Celtic tongue."

"There is a place called Brazil on several of the maps," Susanna said. "It is located near the area the Spaniards named Peru."

Gainsford made a derisive snorting noise.

"Spain uses the name Brazil for part of the mainland," Weller explained. "It is not the same location at all."

"There never was such a place!" Speake glowered at his colleagues over the rims of his spectacles.

"Nor was there ever an Island of the Seven Cities," Merrick said in far quieter tones. He removed his spectacles, which had much thicker lenses than Speake's, to rub bloodshot eyes.

"There we differ, sir." As Weller drew himself up straighter, his cap slipped from his shiny, bald head. With an impatient gesture, he retrieved it from the floor and tossed it onto the table. "Portuguese legend tells us such a place was settled some eight hundred years ago by Portuguese Christians fleeing from the Moors."

"Is that the same legend that speaks of silver in the sand, just waiting to be plucked up and turned into ingots?" Disdain laced Merrick's voice.

As the argument continued, with Gainsford dropping the names of Irish monks and Norse sagas and Fletcher chiming in with his pet theory concerning King Arthur, Walter's mind wandered.

Was there a killer at this table? Weller? He was fluent in Spanish, familiar with the location of its archives. Could he be in the pay of King Philip?

His gaze shifted to Fletcher and narrowed. There had been no further nocturnal alarums, but the more he'd thought about it, the more he wondered at Fletcher's presence in the herb garden that night. Had he lied to them? Had he gone to meet Ingram? Or had he, mayhap, encountered someone else? By chance? By design? Walter was no closer to answers now than he had been then, just as he was no closer to discovering where Ingram was. He could not even locate Trewinard, although he had discovered something of the fellow's doings. Tamesin's brother was a smuggler, operating out of Boscastle. Walter had a man there waiting for the return of Trewinard's ship.

He'd also had reports on Gainsford. He studied the small man. Gainsford was getting on in years, but he was fierce when it came to defending his opinions, quick to anger, judgmental. And according to the information Walter had received two days earlier, he'd wed the woman Calthorpe had once planned to marry.

That seemed a possible reason for Calthorpe to kill Gainsford, not the other way around, but Mistress Gainsford had died the previous year. Who knew what she'd been up to at the last. Had she regretted her choice?

Walter could not help but think of his own situation. What if Gainsford had learned something on his wife's deathbed about her past with Calthorpe? She'd given Gainsford children. Had the eldest been Calthorpe's? Anything was possible. Add to a personal rivalry the competition between men of Oxford and those from Cambridge, and you had a volatile situation indeed.

Ingram's name, spoken with contempt, pulled Walter's attention back to the ongoing discussion.

"This may be the source of his tale," Sir Gregory Speake said. "I do not think the fellow clever enough to have invented it on his own."

"Your pardon, Sir Gregory," Walter cut in. "*What* may be the source?"

"*Les Voyages Aventureux* of Jean Alfonce de Saintonge. He recounts a legend of a white tribe at the headwaters of the Riviere de Norenbegue, some fifteen leagues from the sea. Saintonge visited that spot when he was a pilot sailing to the Saint Lawrence with the colonizing fleet of the Sieur de Roberval. He had been in the area with Roberval and Cartier the previous year as well. Cartier, however, says naught of any city in his writings, nor does he mention any white tribe."

"And so you believe Saintonge made up the tale?"

"Mayhap. 'Twould increase sales of his travel book to do so. Just as Ingram's story pleases the crowds in the alehouses he frequents."

Fletcher's eyes glinted with sudden malice, making him look like a malevolent cherub. "I warrant members of this 'white tribe' are descended from Brendan the Navigator."

"He was celibate!" Weller snapped. "A holy man."

"Madoc's people, more like," Gainsford declared.

They all turned to look at Owen Merrick, since he was responsible for translating the Welsh documents.

Walter consulted the list Susanna had made after the last of these sessions. The earliest tale of settlement in the New World concerned King Arthur sending colonists out from Scotland, but no one knew precisely when Arthur had lived or even if he *had* lived. The Irish monk, Brendan, was said to have sailed to the Promised Land a thousand years ago, even before the Norsemen, whose sagas had not been written down until hundreds of years after the actual voyages. Walter remembered that the library here at Priory House contained a copy of *Navigationi Sancti Brendani*, as well as one of the rare manuscript copies of *Inventio Fortunatae*, which recounted several stories of voyages westward from Britain.

"*Circa anno 560*," Susanna had written. "Brendan, Irish monk, discovered western parts. *Circa anno* 1170, the Lord Madoc, son to Owen Gwynedd, prince of North Wales, led a colony and inhabited Terra Florida or thereabouts."

Walter's interest sharpened as the debate continued. Through Wales, England might indeed hope to lay claim to the land to the west. The queen would be pleased, and none too soon. She had sent word after Calthorpe's death to say that, even short one academic, she expected results by Michaelmas. In reality, Walter suspected she wanted her proof much sooner. The rumors that John Hawkins was treating directly with Spain, trying to negotiate the release of Ingram's shipmates, had reminded her of all her old grudges against King Philip. She hungered to have England usurp his claim to the Americas.

Owen Merrick cleared his throat. "Madoc's people, if they reached their new homeland at all, must have landed in what is now Spanish territory. I have no doubt that any remaining descendants have long since met the same fate meted out to those unfortunate Frenchmen who attempted to settle in La Florida."

"Do you think Spaniards also killed the crews of John Cabot's lost ships?" Susanna asked.

"Entirely possible." Weller sounded so positive that Walter could not help but wonder if he'd seen more of the Spanish archives than he'd admitted. "They are the real savages. Spanish troops slaughter natives as carelessly as they hunt down and kill wild animals. Until Pope Paul III declared that the Amerindians must be considered human, Spain refused to acknowledge any difference."

"That is my point," Merrick said. "If there *had* been a 'white tribe,' Welsh or otherwise, early Spanish conquistadors would have killed them."

"Or brought them back as wonders."

General laughter greeted Fletcher's remark, though Merrick scowled.

"Is that common?" Susanna asked.

"A few natives have been carried across the Western Sea to be shown off at European courts," Fletcher told her. "English explorers took captives, too."

"What happened to them?"

"They were rewarded."

"Not the explorers, the natives."

"Those brought to the court of Henry VII were dressed up like Englishmen, although none were ever heard to speak our language, not even after they had been in this country for more than a year." Gainsford shook his head. "Poor, dumb creatures. They are incapable of learning."

No one knew anything more of the Amerindian "wonders."

"Died, I expect," Weller said.

"Or were sent back to their homeland on another ship," Speake suggested.

None of the scholars seemed concerned about the fate of a few unnamed heathens. Like Ingram, the savages seemed to have vanished into thin air. Walter supposed that any who'd been alive in the time of Henry VII must be long dead by now. Henry VIII had succeeded his father more than sixty years ago.

"A pity we do not know what happened to them," Susanna murmured. "It might have been useful to question someone who was born in the New World. Men who visit distant shores for a short time only do seem to return with odd and contradictory perceptions of what they have seen. Well, no matter." She straightened her shoulders and left off fruitless speculation in favor of addressing a more pressing concern. "I have reviewed the translations Master Calthorpe completed before his untimely accident and gone on with them."

That had been no easy task, as Walter well knew. Susanna had spent many long hours since Calthorpe's death laboring over the more obscure Italian phrases. She'd consulted with him about a few of them.

Susanna summarized what Calthorpe had translated, then gave an account of the contents of one small volume in particular. "Master Nicolo Zeno of Venice includes a map of his own making," she told them, "but many of the place names he uses, and the name of the great northern prince for whom his ancestor sailed, are not familiar to me. He calls this prince Zichmni."

Fletcher and Gainsford exchanged raised eyebrow looks.

Ignoring their skepticism, Susanna continued. "An unusual name, I admit. I suspect it was transcribed incorrectly. Master Zeno explains that, as a child, he played with some papers stored in an old trunk and, as children will, damaged a number of them. When, as an adult, he attempted to reconstruct what had been lost, he was left with many gaps. Whoever this Zichmni was, he appears to have reached the shores of the New World a hundred years ahead of the Master Columbus, upon whose landfall the Spanish base their claims."

She passed around the small, leather-bound volume so that each scholar could examine the map it contained.

"I have made a list of Zeno's place names," Susanna told them, "in an attempt to equate them with those we have encountered before."

"Engroneland is clear enough," Gainsford said. "Greenland."

"And Estotiland? Drogio?"

"The lands to the south. Norombega and La Florida."

"These large islands, though, in the middle of the ocean," Weller complained, stabbing at the map with one finger. "There are none such."

"Use your head. He made them up. Or based them on other old tales." Merrick took the little book and examined the map with intense interest. "For all we know, Zeno invented everything in this story, Zichmni included."

"When does he claim this voyage took place?" Weller asked.

"Master Zeno's ancestor first encountered Zichmni in 1380 and went on to serve him for many years. That account," she gestured toward the book, which was now in Fletcher's hands, "is compiled from letters written over a period of some two decades to relatives still in Venice."

"I still say he invented the whole," Merrick argued. "As we have already discussed, it is not unheard of to cobble together a tale of adventure in the hope of appealing to a wide public."

"There is some foundation of fact," Susanna insisted. "These letters are also mentioned in one of the books Master Calthorpe translated."

"What more is said of Zichmni?" Walter asked. "Could he have been an Englishman?" Their greatest need was to find proof of an English voyage of discovery, or at the least one made by a Welshman or an Irishman, since England now had dominion over those lands. Only then could they advance a claim to the New World that would nullify any made by Spain.

"I do not recognize the names of the lands he ruled, but it is clear from the context that they are well to the north of Italy. I assume they must have bordered the sea. Zichmni is said to have heard of a new world on its far side from a fisherman who had been shipwrecked many years earlier but had managed to return home. This fisherman's adventures are detailed in one of the Zeno letters."

"Both Zichmni and the fisherman are figments of Zeno's imagination." Merrick spoke with conviction.

"No doubt Zichmni is," Weller agreed, "but fishermen have known about the mainland to the west for centuries. Those from Bristol sailed there long before either Master Columbus or Master John Cabot."

A new debate ensued, but it covered familiar ground. Fishermen of many lands had set foot on that distant shore. No one knew who had gotten there first. They'd all kept quiet about it in order to protect the location of the best fishing grounds.

A pity, Walter thought, *they'd not felt inclined to brag instead.* Some Bristol fisherman's story about the one that got away might have included a location, perhaps even a map to show the site of an onshore fishing camp. If such a thing had existed, it would have established beyond any doubt England's prior claim to all of the New World.

23

Susanna's head was spinning by the time the meeting adjourned. Thank goodness they had a clerk to take everything down. She'd never keep it all straight otherwise. She took the transcript from young Daniel, a pear-shaped lad with incongruous yellow ringlets framing a too-solemn face, gathered her own materials, and ignored the library in favor of retiring to the privacy of her lodgings. She intended to spend the next hour preparing a soothing herbal infusion in her makeshift stillroom, a process she found almost as calming as the resulting remedy. She craved privacy, and solitude, and quiet.

She got none of those things.

The moment Susanna returned to the manor house she heard the din from the upper level. Sounds of breaking crockery, shouts, and wailing led her to the schoolroom, where a scene of devastation met her astonished gaze. The globe had been tipped on its side. Books were scattered everywhere. A bolt of fabric lay where Rosamond appeared to have flung it. Damask, Susanna thought, seeing the light and shade effects that had been woven into it.

Setting her own burdens aside on the small table just inside the schoolroom, she bent to retrieve the cloth. A soft silk and linen blend, it whispered across her fingertips, clear proof of how expensive it must be. Susanna was not much interested in clothing or fabrics, but even she knew it was quality stuff.

"What is going on here?" she demanded.

Although she did not raise her voice, it carried over the noise the others were making. As if in tableau, they froze. Rosamond, mouth open and face red, swallowed an incipient howl of outrage. Her mother, balanced precariously on crutches with Melka hovering at her side, went rigid. Hester paused in the act of wringing her hands, although tears did continue to course down her pale cheeks. She was a plain-faced young woman at her best. Distress made her look haggard.

Jennet stood a little to one side, on the verge of throttling someone. Susanna knew the feeling, having been afflicted with the same urge herself on previous occasions when Eleanor and Rosamond clashed. She'd hoped they'd made progress. They'd begun taking French lessons together. And the three of them—Eleanor, Rosamond, and Susanna—had spent one pleasant afternoon in a stillroom redolent with roses.

"Mama!" Rosamond flung herself the width of the room, catching Susanna around the waist and clinging like a limpet. "Make them listen to me."

"I do not see how any living creature could avoid hearing you, Rosamond." If her hands had been free on the way upstairs, Susanna would have put them over her ears to block out the child's screams of rage. "What on earth is all this fuss about?"

With slow, painful movements, Eleanor turned herself to face Susanna. "This ungrateful creature refuses to have a new kirtle made."

"Rosamond did not like the color of the fabric her mother chose for her," Jennet explained. There was no need to say more. It was plain that while Susanna had been occupied with scholarship, her foster daughter had passed from mere stubborn refusal to be fitted for the garment into a tantrum of monstrous proportions.

Easing the girl away from her, Susanna observed that Rosamond's face, which had been as red as a beetroot when she first arrived, had faded to the color of a ripe apple.

"Do not coddle her," Eleanor snapped.

Swinging around to scowl at her mother, Rosamond stamped her foot. "I will not wear puke!"

"Puke is the name used for a dirty brown shade, Rosamond. The merchants call this horseflesh color."

It *was* an unfortunate shade of brown, but Susanna did not say so. The situation was volatile enough.

Eleanor's anger, the equal of her daughter's, lent remarkable speed to her progress on the crutches. She tottered toward Rosamond and Susanna, nostrils flaring and eyes snapping. A wave of sweet marjoram, applied with a heavy hand, preceded her. "Neither of you knows aught of fashion." She seized the fabric from Susanna. "This cloth is not puke!"

"I do not care what the color is called!" Rosamond shouted. "I will not wear it. I do not like it."

"You will!"

"I will not!"

"Enough!" Outshouting them both, Susanna intervened.

The sudden silence was absolute. She turned first to Hester but swallowed the order she'd been about to give. Hester sat on the floor, awash in her own tears. Gwyn, who had come into the schoolroom unnoticed at some point after Susanna's arrival, doubtless drawn by the noise, stood beside her, wide-eyed and a bit awed, watching the proceedings.

No help there, Susanna decided. That left only one alternative. "Melka," she said, fixing Eleanor's maid with an icy glare that brooked no disobedience, "take Mistress Rosamond to her bedchamber and keep her there."

A quick, pointed look at Eleanor discouraged the other gentlewoman from countermanding the order.

Rosamond's protest died on her lips when Susanna faced her squarely, placing one hand on each of her shoulders. She gave the girl a gentle shake, just enough to secure her attention. When their eyes met and held, Susanna addressed Rosamond in a stern voice.

"Your excess of anger goes too far, Rosamond. Your mother has the right of it. You must learn to control your temper. Go with Melka now, without argument. I will come and speak to you later when you are calm."

Rosamond swallowed hard, sensing that she had indeed surpassed the limits of Susanna's patience. Melka, after a few quiet words from Eleanor, advanced on the girl in a determined manner and spoke to her in Polish.

To Susanna's astonishment, Rosamond answered in the same language. Even more amazing, she followed her new keeper without further fuss.

"Hester, right the globe. Gwyn, pick up the books."

Thrusting the objectionable fabric at Susanna, Eleanor maneuvered herself toward the door. "I need to lie down." A moment later, she was gone, making her slow and painful way back to her own wing.

Susanna set the damask aside and reached for a fallen inkwell, grateful there was no spill to be cleaned. The stopper was still in place.

"Mistress Rosamond should be made to put things to rights herself," Jennet muttered as she helped Susanna restore order to the schoolroom.

"That fabric is an unappealing shade. It does not suit Rosamond's coloring, and she's clever enough to know it."

Jennet sighed. "Will you forever make excuses for her?"

"I am not sure how much longer I will be able to do anything for her. If Eleanor does not permit her to leave Priory House, she will remain here when we return to Leigh Abbey."

From Jennet's expression, that was an outcome devoutly to be hoped for, but she was quick to find the flaw in her mistress's logic. "After this performance, why would anyone want to keep her?"

There did not seem to be more to say on the subject. Susanna sighed and rubbed the bridge of her nose.

Hands on her hips, Jennet glared at her mistress. "You have a headache."

Unable to deny the accusation, Susanna nodded, then wished

she had not. "I was on my way to the stillroom when I heard the uproar."

"Then get you there now and, after, to your bed."

Yielding to Jennet's gentle bullying, Susanna obeyed. She slept through supper. It was late evening, after a tearful interview with Rosamond, during which the child swore to try harder to behave with decorum and control her temper, before Susanna thought again of the morning's meeting and realized that she'd left everything she'd carried away from it in Rosamond's schoolroom. With a candle to light her way, she went to collect the items.

The damask cloth had been neatly folded and placed atop the papers on the little table just inside the schoolroom door. Only when Susanna lifted the soft fabric did she realize something was missing.

Puzzled, she bent to look underneath the table, but the floor was bare of anything but sweet-scented rushes. She lit more candles and searched the entire schoolroom, noting in passing that the globe had suffered a nasty gouge as the result of its mistreatment. Everything else, save for a broken bowl, appeared to be back in its proper place, for the most part undamaged. There had been no additions made to Rosamond's collection of books.

Susanna frowned, certain she had brought Master Zeno's tale with her from the meeting. She went back to the parlor anyway to look in every corner and even beneath the table, but the story of the mysterious Zichmni was nowhere to be found.

24

I s this what you were searching for last night?" Walter asked.

Susanna seized the book from his grasp with an eagerness most women reserved for greeting their lovers. "Where did you find it?"

"Gainsford discovered it beneath the table in the parlor."

That brought her head up with a jerk, her eyes flashing. "Not possible. I looked there myself."

"Nevertheless, that is where it was this morning." He was inclined to believe she had overlooked it, but it was plain Susanna did not think so.

"Why?"

Her question, he thought, was rhetorical. Why would someone take the book? Why, having taken it, return it, attempting to make it look as if it had merely been misplaced?

A frown wrinkling her brow, Susanna sank back into her chair and leafed through the small volume, no doubt to reassure herself that no pages had been removed. When at last she was satisfied, she placed it atop the writing table in front of her and again met his eyes, her expression mystified.

"It may mean nothing at all," Walter suggested. "Mayhap Master Gainsford picked it up and only later realized that he should not have taken it with him."

"Then why not return it to me direct? What need for a story of finding it in the parlor?"

Unable to answer her, still half convinced she was mistaken, Walter propped one hip against the table and stared off into space. He had more important matters on his mind this morning.

After a moment, she seemed to sense his mood. "What troubles you, Walter?"

"Inaction." He'd replied before he thought through the answer, but it was the simple truth.

"There has been no sign of Ingram?"

"No. And Twide is still at sea. And the other man, Browne, appears to have fallen off the face of the earth for all I've been able to discover about him."

"How ironic," Susanna murmured, "that others admire both of us for our patience and deliberation. Little do they know how difficult it is to do naught but sit and wait."

How long, Walter wondered, would he have to wait for Eleanor to die and Susanna to lose interest in Nick Baldwin?

Banishing that unproductive thought, he levered himself upright, feeling every bit his age on this chilly summer morning, and forced a bleak smile. "We've much with which to occupy ourselves in the meantime. Too much."

The quick grin she sent him made Walter regret even more the barriers that kept them apart. "Indeed. And now that I have this little book again, I suppose I must force myself to reread it, just in case I missed something. Even the part about Persia." She laughed softly. "I have been wanting an excuse to translate that section. I am surpassing curious to know if the sights Nick saw when he visited Shah Tahmasp's kingdom are the same ones Master Zeno recorded in an earlier time."

Walter left with more haste than he'd intended, before he could say what was really on his mind.

The visit to Susanna had not improved his bleak mood. In truth, he felt more downcast now than when he had gone to the library in search of her. Since the last thing he wanted was to encounter anyone else, he circled the manor house, attempting to lose himself in contemplation of the improvements he had yet to undertake.

Much of the early construction had been supervised by letter, since Walter had been in Sweden at the time. He'd missed too much, he decided. When the scholars left, he would resume building and this time oversee every detail. He'd start by improving the main approach, which was at present naught but an unpaved lane winding between sparse hedgerows.

The house looked southwest. From Walter's present vantage point he could see the silver shimmer of the stream that brought fresh water onto the grounds. Turning back to the house, he tried to recapture a small portion of the pleasure planning it had once given him. He'd envisioned an idyllic haven nestled snug within its protective stone walls. When, he wondered, had these buildings begun to acquire the feel of a prison?

The forecourt led to a porch, plain by Eleanor's reckoning but of a design Walter found pleasing. An arched doorway gave entry to his great hall. His disconsolate glance passed over it then returned. He stopped in his tracks. Framed by the portal, Rosamond stared back at him.

"Good day to you, Rosamond."

If she heard the wariness in his voice, she gave no sign of it. Taking the fact he'd spoken to her at all as an invitation for further conversation, she skipped down the steps and joined him in the forecourt. "Priory House is bigger than Leigh Abbey," she said.

"I suppose it is."

"I like it here."

"Do you? Why?"

"There are more open spaces."

"Trees are scarce and it lacks gardens, do you mean?"

"There are too many gardens at Leigh Abbey. Mama spends too much time in them."

He tried to see her life from the child's point of view and supposed there was some merit to her complaint. Susanna's first love had always been her herb garden.

As they walked on, side by side, Rosamond peppered him with questions. Reluctantly at first, Walter answered her. It flattered him that she responded with such enthusiasm to the plans he had for his estate. Bit by bit, his cynicism began to fade.

Rosamond was a good listener. She'd also inherited her father's quick intelligence and her mother's ability to exude admiration. In Rosamond's case, Walter thought the latter might even be genuine. Whether it was or not, by the time they went in to dinner he felt more cheerful than he had in weeks.

25

Seven days after the to-do between Mistress Rosamond and her mother, another uproar erupted. Shouts and screams drew Jennet toward the unfinished section of the manor house. Her expression grim, she stepped through the canvas-draped door into the proposed addition, wondering as she went whether every Monday would bring a new battle.

The walls were up on the ground floor, but held no window-panes and were not roofed in. All building had ceased when the scholars arrived. Sir Walter had not wanted workmen hanging about to spy on what they did here.

Stepping carefully over the rough surface, dodging building stones, Jennet came to a small, enclosed area equipped with a bed of straw and a bolster borrowed from one of the bedchambers. She'd guessed it was Gwyn and Lionel's new trysting place even before she realized that most of the shouting was coming from Master Owen Merrick.

Also drawn by the noise, Fulke came in through the other end of the building. He arrived just in time to see the older man land a vicious blow to Lionel's head. Before Gwyn could draw breath to scream again, Fulke seized Merrick by the back of the collar and heaved, jerking him away from his victim. Gwyn flew to her lover's side, embracing him and unleashing a flood of tears to mingle with the blood already staining his jerkin.

As most of the latter came from Lionel's battered nose, Jennet decided there was nothing to be concerned about and fixed her attention on Fulke and Master Merrick. Frantic to get at his daughter, the scholar put up a fierce struggle, but he was powerless in Fulke's grip.

Jennet wondered what language he was swearing in. Certes, it was not English! "Calm yourself, Master Merrick!" The command, snapped out in the hope of shocking him into compliance, might have been more effective had Hester not chosen that moment to join the fray.

"Lionel!" She rushed toward him. "You are hurt!"

Jennet stepped in front of her, blocking her way. "Return to the house. You've no business here."

"I must help him." So fierce was Hester's voice that Jennet backed up a step. It was as if a hare had suddenly turned on the hunter. Hester pushed Jennet aside, determined to reach the fallen man, but she'd taken only a few steps when Fulke lost his grip on Owen Merrick. The scholar seized his daughter's arm before anyone could stop him and dragged her away from Lionel.

That young man staggered to his feet, still bleeding, bleating a protest, but he was too weak and dazed to do more than lunge awkwardly at the two of them. Fulke came after Merrick from the other side; but when Hester screamed, distracting him, Jennet once more stepped in. There had been enough violence.

"Take your daughter back to your lodgings, Master Merrick." She wrinkled her nose at the smells in the air—freshly spilled blood and that indefinable scent she'd learned, early in life, to associate with brawling men.

Gwyn added her voice to Jennet's. "Please, no more fighting."

Breathing heavily, Merrick met his daughter's eyes. After a moment, he nodded. His hold on her loosened, but he did not release her. When he tugged, she went with him without further protest, but she looked back over her shoulder at Jennet. "You will look after him?"

Lionel was swaying where he stood, fists still raised. Slowly, he let his arms fall to his sides. "Gwyn?"

"I must talk to my father," she told Lionel, "in private."

Jennet's gaze shifted to the older man. His skin was an unhealthy gray and his spectacles, which had been knocked askew, perched at a drunken angle on the bridge of his nose.

Gwyn noticed that, too, and reached up to straighten them. "You must take greater care," she told him in a soft voice. "If you break this pair, you will no longer be able to work." Easing his arm around her shoulder to support him, she led him away.

When they had left, Jennet turned on the other three. As they were all members of Lady Appleton's household, it fell to Jennet, as housekeeper, to take them in hand. "What happened here?" she demanded. She already had a good idea how Merrick had discovered what his daughter and Lionel were up to. Rosamond's former nursemaid had spent the week since Lady Appleton committed the girl to Melka's care in feeling sorry for herself and jealous of Gwyn.

"Master Merrick, he flew at Lionel like a mad thing, he did." Hester tried again to reach the young man's side, but Fulke continued to restrain her.

Oblivious to Hester's sobs, Lionel stared after Gwyn. He looked more like a lost little boy than a man full grown.

Jennet crossed her arms in front of her chest, tapped her foot in annoyance, and glared at Hester. "The evils of idleness must be shaken off by hard work." Lady Appleton had said that to her once upon a time. No doubt the sentiment had been translated from some lofty Latin or Greek proverb, but it sounded well in plain English and worked even better in practice.

"She'll cause no more trouble," Fulke promised, tightening his grip on Hester's arm.

He was angrier than she'd first thought, Jennet realized; but before she could say more to either of them, a rustle of sound drew her attention back to Lionel. Staggering, still dazed by that blow to the head, he had set off in pursuit of Gwyn. Exasperated, Jennet went after him and smacked him on the shoulder with the heel of her hand. It was enough to send him reeling backward. A moment later he fell, landing hard on his buttocks.

"What did you do that for, Jennet?" The face that looked up at her was all wounded innocence. A lock of hair drooped over an eye that was purpling at a rapid pace, but his nose had stopped bleeding.

"You have no more sense than a turnip," she told him. "Let Gwyn deal with her father. When his temper has cooled, you can both talk to him."

"I love her," Lionel declared. "I mean to marry Gwyn Merrick."

Hester's shriek, from forty paces distant, was still loud enough to make both Lionel and Jennet jump.

"Why can you not see what is right in front of you?" she wailed.

Fulke turned her around with sudden roughness and placed his big hands on her shoulders, forcing her to meet his eyes. "You suffer from the same shortsightedness."

Perplexed, she stared at him.

Jennet watched, riveted by the intensity of Fulke's declaration, as realization dawned on Hester. She started to speak, but before anyone could tell whether she meant to protest, or deride Fulke, or declare a sudden change of heart, he stopped her mouth with a kiss so potent it made Jennet's knees weak.

26

Sir Walter Pendennis's journey from Priory House to Boscastle consumed the best part of a morning. Someone familiar with the byways between could have reached the same destination with greater speed, but Walter took his time. He had no desire to take a wrong turning and end up lost. Nor was he in any great hurry to meet with Alexander Trewinard.

He followed the course of the River Valency to approach the village, coming in from the southeast. He was obliged to ford streams twice and passed through an unexpected copse of oak, a rarity so close to the exposed, north-facing coast of Cornwall. A stretch of enclosed, arable ground warned him he was close to his destination. Past the weir, he could glimpse the harbor ahead, a narrow, twisting inlet with cliffs on both sides. Nevertheless, it offered the best landing place for sailing vessels along some forty miles of rugged coastline.

The road to the village curved off to his left, near where the River Jordan joined the Valency. Boscastle proper, he recalled, clung to the sides of a sheltered, steep-sided valley. North of the village, from a promontory, it was possible to see more than three miles in every direction. He had a sudden vivid memory of climbing up there as a boy, with his brothers, to pick out the ruins of Tintagel Castle to the southwest and, to the northeast, the silhouette of Cambeak, an outcropping above the beach men called the Strangles.

He would end up strangled, or otherwise disposed of, Walter thought with a rueful grimace, if he did not keep his mind on the present. He was here to meet a man who supposedly wanted him dead. This was no time for reminiscing.

He urged his horse over a small bridge and past a watermill to stop before a sturdy, slate-roofed stone tower with the sign of a hand, made of wood, suspended from the end of a wand hanging out a window—a variant on the alestakes alehouses commonly used to show brewing had taken place. A traditional ale bench sat outside the front door, since ale and beer sold out of doors cost less than they did by the fire. At present it was unoccupied.

Trewinard had done well for himself, just as Walter's spies had reported.

Tamesin's brother had the look of her—tall, fair-skinned, red-haired, and long-limbed—but his features were more rough hewn. He and Walter assessed each other across the length of the common room with the wariness of two wolves meeting at a watering hole.

"I am told you plan to kill me," Walter said to the alehouse keeper.

Trewinard's deep, rich chuckle bounced off the beamed ceiling. Three men gambling in a corner glanced up from their dice.

"You are misinformed, Sir Walter."

"Did you not leave hearth and home, vowing revenge, when you heard I'd returned to Cornwall? My brother was certain you had."

"If I'd meant to kill a Pendennis, he'd have been the first." Trewinard plunked down two beakers of ale and settled himself across from Walter at a small table.

Walter eyed him warily. "Is it money you want?" He was aware he'd taken a risk by coming here alone. Trewinard could kill him, or hold him for ransom, but the information Walter's intelligence

145

gatherers had provided made him think the fellow would find him of more value in other ways.

Trewinard smiled, but he drank deep before he answered with a question of his own. "How much is your guilt worth?"

"Guilt does not come into it, Trewinard. Had your sister told me she was with child, I'd have defied my father and married her. I am the youngest son. I had no inheritance, but neither did I have obligations. I was free to make my own choice." He sipped the ale, found it well brewed, and swallowed another mouthful. "My age might have caused difficulties, but I suspect I could have found a willing preacher."

Under Trewinard's intense scrutiny, Walter drained the beaker. He waited, using silence to prod the other man into a response.

"If you'd not been sent away so fast after, I might have killed you. The desire for revenge burns hot in youth." Trewinard drank again. "It fades slow, but in time . . ." He shrugged and put his beaker down, still half full. "I am a . . . businessman, Sir Walter. You, I'm told, are now one of the justices for these parts. I believe we can help each other."

"You are a smuggler, Master Trewinard."

Again a hearty guffaw reverberated through the common room. "I keep a kiddlywink with a few rooms above for travelers." He waved a hand to encompass their surroundings. "I am also a free trader, and I trade in information as well as goods." His gaze sharpened. "So, 'tis said, do you."

"I have been known to."

"You seek a man, a sailor."

Walter nodded. "A sailor. And a murderer, mayhap. A man was killed. Ingram ran away. Why else would he leave but because he'd had a hand in it?"

"Well," said Trewinard, "if you are willing to use your influence to protect free trade in Boscastle, I will tell you the answer to that question."

Gaining information about Ingram in return for turning a blind eye to smuggling seemed a fair bargain to Walter. In truth, he had often found smugglers useful allies. With a minimum of haggling, they came to terms.

"Now, tell me about Ingram," Walter said, when Trewinard had refilled their beakers.

"He came here after leaving Priory House, but the tide was wrong and the wind. He had to wait for a ship. In his cups, his tongue loosened, and your name caught my attention." Trewinard grinned. "When I heard how he had been treated, the grievous wrongs he'd suffered as your guest, how could I not help him when the searchers came?" The grin widened. "The news that he was a wanted man frightened Ingram even more than the attack on him at Priory House."

"What attack?" Abandoning his ale, Walter fixed Trewinard with a hard stare.

"He claimed he was assaulted the night he left. A narrow escape, to hear him tell it. He was on his way back to his lodgings from a convivial evening gathering, somewhat befuddled by drink, when he heard a sound behind him. He turned just in time to see a knife blade descending. Had he not had a stout walking stick with him, with which to deflect the blow, he'd have been stabbed in the back. His attacker ran off; but since Ingram did not get a look at his face and had no idea who his enemy might be, he decided it was time for him to leave. He gathered his belongings and set out at once."

"In the middle of the night?"

"Just so. When dawn broke, he found his way here."

Walter suspected there was more to the story. For Ingram to stumble, by chance, upon the only decent harbor for miles around defied logic. "Had he been here before? Had he had other dealings with you?"

A spy for Spain might well court local smugglers.

"He might have heard about my . . . business ventures. I took him with me on the last expedition."

"Where is he now?"

But Trewinard was not prepared to share all his secrets with one of the queen's justices. He'd left home, as Tris had reported, but only to run contraband. "You might inquire of Ingram's family," he suggested.

Walter's eyes narrowed. He hadn't known the fellow had a family. He waited.

"Barking. In Essex, I believe. He's not seen them since his return from that remarkable journey to the New World."

Walter unclenched his jaw. Intelligence gatherers were not what they had been in his day. He should already have had that information. He wondered what else they'd missed. "A pity the fellow did not get a good look at his attacker," he said with false casualness.

"Ah, but he did." Trewinard's grin had begun to grate on Walter. "He got a glimpse of a dark figure in a long, black robe. The second time he told the tale, it was the ghost of one of the monks who once inhabited the priory. By the third telling, the creature also had horns and a tail."

Walter drained his beaker without comment. *Not a demon,* he thought, *nor a ghostly monk. Just a man in an academic gown.*

27

"*Repetez, s'il vous plait,*" Sir Gregory Speake said, and launched into another long phrase in French.

Eleanor and Rosamond echoed his words.

They had established a wary truce since they'd begun sharing both a tutor and a maid. *Patience*, Eleanor counseled herself. She'd had it once, years ago. She could learn to pretend to it again.

Feigning absorption in Sir Gregory's lessons did not take a great deal of effort. For a clergyman he was more amusing than she'd expected. The reading material he selected, however, held Rosamond's interest far better than it did Eleanor's. She could not understand the appeal of letters written from the New World or her daughter's enthusiasm for anything to do with the place called Norombega. The subject bored Eleanor, an opinion that apparently put her in the minority at Priory House.

She had managed to piece together what was really going on here. No one told her much outright, but she knew her husband was not happy at the invasion of his rural retreat. These scholarly intruders had interfered with his building, since he could not have workers in and out and still maintain security. Eleanor had also gathered that Walter had been ordered to achieve results by an entirely arbitrary date and was now being pressured to produce them even sooner.

In the meantime, he was obliged to put up with the antics of

149

five men who were, each in his own way, as difficult to deal with as Rosamond. One could not work without a certain consistency of ink. Another had to have his own chair sent from Cambridge. Petty complaints and demands, all of them, but combined they very nearly drove poor Walter to distraction.

Eleanor smiled to herself. That worked to her advantage. Since her arrival at Priory House, she'd considered her choices, settled on the most tolerable, and was now determined to make her husband depend upon her: for sexual congress; for sympathy; and for, in Eleanor's own good time, the son he so desired. She'd set herself the task of soothing him as only a wife could. After dealing with the scholars all day, he found solace in her bed at night. No doubt his original intention had been to share no more than a cold act of procreation, but she'd soon made him change his tune. Their marriage was not ideal, but it was far more satisfactory than it might have been.

"Were you able to translate Master Verrazzano's letter?" Sir Gregory asked.

Eleanor pulled her thoughts out of the bedchamber and concentrated on the schoolroom.

Rosamond giggled. "Those savages were passing rude."

Sir Gregory gave his habitual little cough and reached for the book he'd left in the schoolroom the previous day. It included several letters written from the New World by explorers in the pay of France.

Another giggle escaped Rosamond. She clapped her hand over her mouth, but her eyes still laughed. Robert Appleton's eyes.

Eleanor spoke more sharply than she'd intended. "Explain yourself, Rosamond. What did the savages do that was so rude?"

Melka, sitting on a stool in the corner, was content with her embroidery and paid them no mind; but Gwyn Merrick, who often stopped by to listen in, leaned forward with increased interest. She had slipped into the schoolroom at the start of the lesson and ensconced herself on the window seat. She'd been so quiet for so long that Eleanor had almost forgotten she was there.

To everyone's surprise, Master Merrick had proven reasonable in the matter of his daughter's honor. Instead of insisting upon sending her away or, worse, going with her and leaving Walter's precious project even more short-handed, Owen Merrick had allowed himself to be convinced to let Lionel court Gwyn. Susanna had promised that the young woman would be well chaperoned at all times and sweetened the pot by hinting that if they eventually married, she would be generous with her wedding gifts. The trouble-making Hester had been sent back to Leigh Abbey in disgrace, with Fulke as her escort.

"The letter calls them animals," Rosamond said. "Its author did not approve of what they did."

As Sir Gregory translated the letter in question for himself, his face went pink with embarrassment. "They, er, showed considerable disrespect as the white men sailed away." Disconcerted, he coughed, shrugged, cleared his throat again, and ended the performance with a sheepish grin.

Rosamond could contain herself no longer. She hooted with laughter. "They bared their buttocks at the French ships!"

For some inexplicable reason, the combination of Rosamond's delight and Sir Gregory's milder, but no less unmistakable mirth amused Eleanor. She knew she ought to lecture her daughter on propriety, and she should pretend to be shocked. Instead, she chuckled.

The laughter proved contagious. After a startled second, Gwyn joined in. Even Melka smiled. By the time Eleanor managed to stop, she felt lighthearted and a bit light-headed, as well. When Rosamond bounced up off her stool and flung her arms around her mother's neck to plant a quick kiss on her cheek, tears welled up at the backs of Eleanor's eyes and she felt a suspicious tightness in the region of her heart.

Unaware of just how deeply her impulsive, affectionate gesture had touched her mother, Rosamond danced away, crossing to Sir Gregory. "Do you suppose those rude natives came from the city of Norombega?" she asked him.

"There is no city of Norombega." This was familiar territory. He regularly denied its existence, and Rosamond just as readily argued the point.

"It is on the map." She trotted over to the globe and set it whirling by batting it with one hand.

"It is naught but a legend," Sir Gregory insisted.

"But legends are always based on something real. Mama says so."

"In this case, Mistress Rosamond, I cite the testimony of Master Andre Thevet, whose writings I read only this morning. A dozen years ago, Master Thevet visited the area where the city of Norombega is supposed to be located. He found no trace of any such thing."

Another slight movement at the window drew Eleanor's attention back to Gwyn. Once again she leaned forward in order to hear better, but this time her body was tense, her expression deeply troubled. Eleanor wondered if Gwyn thought Sir Gregory had stolen a march on her father by finding some new information. These scholars competed over the oddest things!

"Thevet says very plain that there is no city at the place on the river where mapmakers have insisted upon placing it," Sir Gregory said. "He found nothing there but the long-abandoned remains of a fishing camp."

"Fishermen?" The girl looked intrigued. Gwyn's consternation increased. "Where did they come from?"

"He did not say." Sir Gregory coughed. "The settlement could have been occupied by anyone, native or visitor."

"Even an Englishman?" When Rosamond followed the question with a little cough, Eleanor sent a sharp glance her way. The child looked innocent enough, but with Rosamond it was always wise to be suspicious. She did have a wicked flair for mimicking others.

"Even a Frenchman," Sir Gregory joked.

"Even a Welshman?" Gwyn's question was no more than a murmur of sound, but Sir Gregory heard her.

"Not Madoc's descendants, if that is what you are hoping."

Eleanor had no idea who Madoc was, but she thought Gwyn

looked as if she regretted having called attention to herself.

Rosamond, giggling, tugged on Sir Gregory's sleeve. "Even a Basque? Even an Irishman?"

He cleared his throat and tried to look stern. *"Parlez en français, s'il vous plait."*

Rosamond ignored the request. "What if the fishermen were Spaniards? What if they were Scots? Or Flemings?"

Gwyn's sharp intake of breath was so quiet that neither Rosamond or Sir Gregory heard, and if Eleanor had not been looking at the young woman, she'd have missed it herself. Fascinated, she watched Gwyn's mouth flatten into a thin line. Tense and expectant as a misbehaving child braced for a blow, her hands clenched a cushion from the window seat as she waited for Sir Gregory's answer.

Abandoning his effort to resume the French lesson, the scholar replied in plain English. "Early visitors to the New World might have come from any of those places. All fishermen are alike in one thing—they keep the location of the best fishing grounds a close-guarded secret. Had they been willing to share their discoveries, many colonies would have been established in the New World by now, and I have no doubt that some of them would have been English."

28

Sebastian Cabot's papers arrived at Priory House while Walter was in Boscastle. Eager to delve into this treasure, Susanna never even considered waiting for his return.

There were a great many documents inside the chest, many of them hand-drawn charts and maps, but it was a deposition that caught and held Susanna's attention. It began with the words "an account of the death of John Cabot."

Fascinated and repulsed, she read it twice through, becoming so engrossed in piecing together the remarkable story that she was only peripherally aware of it when Rosamond joined her in the library. She did not notice that the girl had picked up and read, one by one, the pages she'd set aside, until Rosamond spoke.

"Do you suppose this was the same tribe that showed their bare buttocks to Master Verrazzano?"

For a moment, Susanna did not know how to answer. She studied Rosamond through narrowed eyes, but her foster daughter did not seem disturbed by the gruesome details of Cabot's demise. The only emotion Susanna could detect in Rosamond's expression was curiosity.

"It is unclear where the massacre of John Cabot and his crew took place," she said at last.

"But it could have been at Norombega."

"Yes, it could have been."

Certainly it had occurred somewhere in the large geographical area marked with that name, if not near the precise location of the mythical city. The only other thing Susanna was sure of was that Sebastian Cabot had deliberately kept secret the circumstances of his father's murder. He'd had good reason to do so. Speaking out would have cost him the patronage of the king of Spain.

Apparently satisfied, Rosamond wandered off to study one of the wall maps. Susanna gathered up the scattered pages. There were many more papers in the chest, all of which would have to be catalogued and studied, but she had learned enough for now. More than she'd wanted to know, if the truth be told.

In 1498, John Cabot had set out from Bristol with five ships. One had turned back. The others, along with Cabot himself, had vanished. Lost in a storm, it was said. But it seemed the truth was otherwise.

Two ships had reached the mainland of the New World, somewhere to the north of La Florida. Cabot's flagship, the *Mattea,* had been wrecked on that rocky coast. A few crewmen had made it to shore, but there they had been slain by natives, all except one man who'd managed to hide among the trees.

If not for that single seaman, no one would ever have known what happened to John Cabot. Escaping detection, he'd made his way south along the shore. By sheer chance, he'd been picked up by the second ship. Soon after, however, it had been captured by Spaniards. They'd interrogated the survivors, stolen the portolan charts the captain had made of the coastline, and then, when they had learned all they could from the English crew, including the story of the massacre, had executed every one of them.

Sebastian Cabot had apparently stumbled across this account of his father's last expedition many years later, when he was in the employ of Spain himself. He'd prudently said nothing, but he had kept this record and left it with his executor when he died. But why, she wondered, had he remained silent after his return to England? She did not suppose she'd ever know the answer to that question.

"Mama?"

"Yes, Rosamond?"

"Can you guess who I am?" A fierce glower on her face, Rosamond bounced up and down.

It was such an excellent imitation of Master Gainsford that Susanna had to suppress a chuckle. "It is not polite to make fun of people, Rosamond."

"But they are all so odd." Rosamond cleared her throat and coughed and looked expectant.

"Sir Gregory's affectation is not something he can control." Susanna meant to sound reproving but did not succeed.

She found it difficult to discipline Rosamond, especially when she so often saw matters from the little girl's perspective. Of late she had begun to wonder if Rosamond would not be better off were she raised by Walter and Eleanor. Neither of them would make the mistake of spoiling her.

Rosamond's shambling walk was Owen Merrick to the life, and when she steepled her fingers and began to mutter in a monotone, Susanna instantly recognized Bartholomew Fletcher.

"Enough, Rosamond."

"But I am not done with Master Fletcher. Do you not want to see the way he scuttles along when he creeps out of Priory House late at night?"

29

The wall that surrounded Priory House appeared solid from what passed for a main road in this part of Cornwall. The little Walter could glimpse of his manor house gleamed in the late afternoon sun, looking prosperous and well built. Clouds scudded across the sky behind it, the shapes of mythological creatures chasing each other.

All was illusion, he thought. Oddly reluctant to return home, he reined in before he reached the gatehouse to stare at his estate. The bleakness of his thoughts matched the heavy weight that had settled in the region of his heart.

A few years ago, he'd planned to retire here, to rusticate. He'd told himself, and Eleanor, that he was no longer interested in a career in courtiership. That had been before his discovery that he was married to a woman who cared more for her own comfort than for building a new life together with him. Being saddled with a stepdaughter who bore a startling resemblance to Robert Appleton did not help matters. The friend of his youth had betrayed them all—Walter, Susanna, Eleanor, and Rosamond.

The dream of returning to Cornwall to become a gentleman farmer like his brothers was tarnished. Walter no longer knew what he wanted, other than things he could not have.

Material wealth was his, but it had not brought happiness. Worse, he now questioned whether he'd lost his instincts. Famous for making quick, shrewd assessments of all manner of men and situations, always able to choose the sensible course, he'd dealt well enough with Trewinard; but when they'd concluded their business and Walter had been about to take his leave, the free trader had given him a bit of advice: "Next time you travel alone, Sir Walter, try to look less like a pigeon ready for plucking. Leave your fine feathers at home."

Walter shifted in his saddle, uncomfortable with the memory. Once he'd been accounted the most skilled of intelligence gatherers. He'd possessed a talent for diplomacy as well as espionage and had exhibited a flair for uncovering and thwarting plots against the queen. Had he lost his edge? Until Trewinard made that comment, Walter had thought himself suitably attired for their meeting.

It appeared he was out of touch with the common man. Leaving off jewelry and fancy trim had not been sufficient to disguise feathers that were not just fine but foreign to the residents of Boscastle. Overweening pride had led him to a misjudgment. He'd been unwilling to ape the fashions worn by his neighbors. Instead, his trunk-hose were precisely tailored to show the shape of his legs to advantage. His shirt was cambric, his doublet made of the fine, thin silk called taffeta in the rich reddish violet color called gingerline. Even the buff jerkin he wore over it and the buskins that came to his knees were of the best quality leather, and his ruff was the latest style, fan-shaped and made almost entirely of lace, designed to sit higher at the back of the neck than in the front and follow the line of his jaw to frame his face and show off the shape of his skull.

He might choose to remain in Cornwall and pursue life as a simple county JP, but Walter had no intention of giving up his luxuries. Not that he'd have much choice about staying after this assignment. The queen had no tolerance for failure.

He had served the Crown well for many years, but that would not be enough to pacify the demanding woman who sat on England's throne. Walter had often told himself he had no interest in being elevated to the peerage, that such honors were too expensive to maintain; but now that he knew he no longer had any chance of being offered such a thing, he'd discovered he did much resent the lost opportunity.

He felt his mouth twist into a wry smile that was more of a grimace. He should be grateful. It was difficult to hold on to one's fortune in the service of the Crown. But it was humbling just the same to realize that unless he could find a way to salvage their mission, his days as a trusted advisor to queen and country were over forever. If he failed, he might not even be welcome to visit the royal court.

He was neither fish nor fowl, not courtier nor country gentleman, and soon—very soon—he would have to make some attempt to reconcile with his family here in Cornwall. Aside from Tris, he'd seen only one of his siblings since leaving home as a young man, and he'd blundered badly during that encounter. Worse, his own cowardice was his only reason for avoiding them. Simply put, he was afraid they'd find him wanting.

Disgusted with himself for indulging in this lengthy bout of self-pity, Walter urged his mount forward, stopping at the gatehouse only long enough for the guard to identify him. He turned the horse over to one of the grooms and went straight to his private study, located at the north end of the east wing of his new house. When the addition was complete, the house would form the shape of a giant E, in honor of Queen Elizabeth, and this room would project from its very center.

It had a pleasant aspect even now, with three glazed windows to look out to the west, north, and east. The western view took in the main approach from gatehouse to porch, the route he himself had just traveled. Once the new stable was complete, he would seal off the south gate, the one through which Eleanor had arrived, the one that led directly to the present stableyard, and be left with a view guaranteed to give him early warning of any visitors.

"Welcome back, Sir Walter," Jacob greeted him. "You've messages waiting."

They covered the surface of his writing table. A letter from John Dee and, enclosed within it, another nagging missive from the queen. A dispatch from his agent in London. Reports from various henchmen. Some information he already had, but it would all have to be gone over again. There would be more to sort out, too, because of his talk with Trewinard. He must order further investigation into the background of each of the remaining scholars and send a man to Essex.

Without being asked, Jacob fetched food and drink, fortification for the task ahead. Walter settled himself in his favorite chair, resigned to dealing with the correspondence, but he'd scarce begun to reread the queen's demands before Susanna interrupted him.

"There's something you should know," she said.

Walter listened in silence as Susanna told him what Rosamond had seen. It galled him to hear how easily the secrecy and security of his project could be thwarted. Bartholomew Fletcher had repeatedly flaunted Walter's authority. Exiting by way of a ruined section of wall, he'd made at least two unauthorized nocturnal forays besides the one on the night Piers had caught him.

Fletcher, he thought, turning the name over in his mind, picturing the pink cheeks, the pleasant smile, the plump, pampered hands. Fletcher did not fit anyone's image of a Spanish spy, let alone a cold-blooded killer, but he supposed that made the scholar an all-the-more-likely suspect.

"There may be an innocent reason why he'd want to slip out without being noticed. Rosamond did not follow him, thank the stars, and has no idea where he went or how long he was gone, but it did occur to me that he could have gone to meet a woman."

Fletcher playing the beast with two backs with some local wench was also difficult for Walter to imagine. "Any absence is a breach of the compact the scholars accepted when they came here."

Susanna nodded. "All of us agreed at the outset to lead a cloistered existence for the duration of the project, not unlike that led by the monks who lived here before us—only minimal contact with the outside world." She sent a faint smile in Walter's direction. "Jennet tells me that some wit among us here said the only difference is that, this time, the monks are ruled by an abbess."

Walter kept his expression carefully blank and hoped Susanna never found out that the term was thieves' cant for the keeper of a brothel.

"Will you question Fletcher?" she asked.

"I think not. Rather I will put him under surveillance. Now that we know where his bolt-hole is, we will watch and wait for him to make his next move." He paused to take a sweetmeat from the tray Jacob had brought and send a thoughtful look in Susanna's direction. "How is it that Rosamond was awake and out of the house to see him leave?"

Susanna grimaced. "She has been paying midnight visits to Courtier."

"What courtier?"

"Courtier is her horse. She is very fond of the beast."

Another way in which she resembles her father, Walter thought. Robert had been devoted to a stallion named Vanguard. "Where was the child's nursemaid?"

"We sent Hester away," Susanna reminded him, "and Melka has other duties. It is her custom to leave Rosamond alone once the child has been put to bed. That is what Rosamond says, at any rate. I cannot ask Melka, since we do not speak the same language, and I was reluctant to explain the reason for my interest to Eleanor."

Walter drummed his fingers on the arm of his chair, thinking of Eleanor, watching Susanna. Once, his wife had seemed the perfect mate. She appreciated the same things he did—fine wines and well-prepared food, lush fabrics in vibrant colors, intricately executed tapestries, and skillfully created, richly decorated furniture.

The woman roaming his study, too restless to sit, must have been in the library when she heard of his return. Ink-stained fingers jabbed at the caul she wore to contain her hair, shoving a stray strand that had slipped loose from confinement back up inside a bag-shaped net made of silk thread. The caul showed evidence of having been pulled at and prodded repeatedly since she'd dressed that morning.

Susanna passed an arras showing *The Judgment of Paris* without glancing at it and likewise ignored a valuable carved and painted panel taken from a church during the Dissolution. When she reached Walter's chair on her next circuit of the room, she stopped. "What will happen if Fletcher compromised our mission?"

"Ask rather what will happen if we find proof he killed Calthorpe and attempted to silence Ingram." Assured of her complete attention, he gave her a brief account of what he had learned in Boscastle.

"This makes no sense. None of the scholars had reason to kill Calthorpe, and of them all I can least imagine Bartholomew Fletcher wielding a knife and attempting to dispatch Ingram."

"Academic rivalry may account for Calthorpe's murder."

"You were quick to discount that motive when I suggested it."

"Back then I believed David Ingram was the guilty party. I have been forced to reconsider. Scholarly matters alone do seem inadequate to provoke murder, and as you say, there could be some other reason for Fletcher to creep out of Priory House at night; but now that we know Ingram was attacked by someone in an academic gown, all the scholars are prime suspects, in particular Master Fletcher and Master Gainsford. Gainsford and Calthorpe were rivals at university, but they also had a personal enmity between them. Years ago, both loved the same woman. Gainsford married her."

Wandering to one of the windows, Susanna stared out. She breathed deeply of the late afternoon air, as if she sought to draw strength from the smell of the land. July was well upon them now. The day had turned hot and sticky.

"Gainsford is the one who claimed he found the Zeno narrative in the parlor when I know I took it into the schoolroom with me. But why would he, or any of them, try to kill Ingram?"

Walter joined her to watch a jackdaw circle in the sky. "Mayhap the killer thought Ingram witnessed what happened to Calthorpe. Or Ingram could have seen the murderer leaving Calthorpe's study."

"Can we rule out Weller, Merrick, and Sir Gregory?"

"No, although I've found nothing suspect about any of them or their families—so far. Weller has no kin. Speake's relatives appear to be above reproach. John Dee himself vouched for them."

"And Merrick's relations?"

"Aside from his daughter, there is only an eccentric old man in Bristol, his grandfather."

"Eccentric in what way?"

"He suffers from the delusion that he is some sort of merchant prince." Walter managed a faint smile. "I am told the old man insists the servants call him 'Lord John.' "

"So we must wait for Fletcher to sneak out again and hope that leads us to proof he is our murderer." She sighed. "I cannot help but feel discouraged."

"We must be prepared for further disappointments," Walter warned. "Even before Calthorpe's murder, we had small hope of success in the great endeavor that brought us here. The queen did not want much—only proof of her right to settle in the New World and an accurate map to the wealth of Cathay. Now she wants both by Saint Bartholomew's Day."

"The twenty-fourth day of August instead of the twenty-ninth of September?"

"Aye. Although she may well change her mind again and want answers sooner or decide she has no interest in the New World at all." A queen's decisions, whether what prince to marry or what voyage to invest in, could be altered in an instant by military or political considerations. And Walter was no longer privy to the undercurrents at court.

"I had best return to my work before time runs out." Determination to meet this new challenge shining in her bright blue eyes, Susanna left Walter to his brooding.

30

Two days before the special meeting Walter had scheduled to inform the scholars they must present their final report much earlier than they'd first been told, Susanna sat alone in the library. The research progressed steadily but showed no sign of yielding the results Queen Elizabeth wanted. More troubling still, they were no closer to discovering the identity of Calthorpe's murderer.

Rosamond's growing ease with her mother should, Susanna supposed, have cheered her; but the more comfortable the two of them grew with each other, the less Susanna saw of the girl who was, and always would be, the closest thing she'd ever have to a child of her own. It was official now. Rosamond would stay in Cornwall when Susanna returned to Leigh Abbey. Eleanor said it was Walter's wish that she do so. Susanna was not certain she believed this, but it made no difference. It was best for Rosamond so.

Stop feeling sorry for yourself!
Think of something positive.

But the only true success she had enjoyed of late had been in convincing Owen Merrick to allow Lionel to court his daughter. Although they were now under close supervision at all times, the two showed every evidence of devotion to one another. It seemed only a matter of time before Merrick gave permission for their marriage. He had stopped trying to put obstacles in their way, save to say that Lionel would also have to be approved by the head of the Merrick family, that elderly eccentric living in Bristol.

Should she be more suspicious of Owen Merrick? Tapping the quill against her teeth, Susanna reminded herself that Merrick was the one Martin Calthorpe had suspected of wanting to steal his research. Calthorpe had implied that Gwyn had been sent by her father to pilfer the transcript of Richard Twide's testimony.

Susanna found Gwyn's story about the brazier suspicious, but nothing the other scholars had remembered of the interview with Twide pointed to any reason for Merrick to have killed Calthorpe.

Indeed, it made no sense for any of the scholars to have murdered their colleague, and yet one of them must have done so. Although Walter still considered Ingram a suspect, and a possible spy, she deemed that solution improbable.

Only five names were inscribed on the paper before her on the writing table: Fletcher. Gainsford. Merrick. Speake. Weller. All men with a mission. All dedicated scholars. But one of them had a motive for murder.

Resolved to discover it, resigned to another long evening of intense study, Susanna reached for the stack of documents she'd gathered together that afternoon. Each packet consisted of a number of pages, all inscribed in Daniel's neat italic hand. The top sheet of every one began with the same words: "Proceedings of the monthly meeting at Priory House."

31

I have found proof that King Arthur sent settlers to the New World," Bartholomew Fletcher declared.

Only moments earlier, he and the other scholars had listened in growing consternation to the announcement that they must produce results five weeks earlier than they'd planned. None of them had reacted well to the change in schedule; but when the grumbling died down, Fletcher had risen to his feet.

"What proof?" Gainsford demanded.

"A garden that contains plants found only in the New World. There is no way they could be there unless they were brought back by early colonists." Ill-concealed elation gave Fletcher's voice more inflection and greater volume. For once he did not mutter.

Walter's gaze sharpened. Fletcher had not tried to leave the compound since he'd ordered the fellow watched, but Walter had received a disturbing report from his agent in London. In light of the earlier nocturnal wanderings, Fletcher's activities on his last visit to that city made him a solid suspect in Calthorpe's death.

Reaction from the other scholars varied from outright disbelief to guarded enthusiasm. Walter waited for the furor to die down before he spoke.

"How did you come to discover this, Master Fletcher?"

"My men have been digging at the site for weeks."

"Your men?" Soft-spoken and deadly calm, Walter's words provoked a wary exchange of glances around the table. Fletcher alone seemed oblivious. Too intent, too excited to care if he'd upset their host, he readily confessed to hiring workers, even told Walter where to find them.

"Tell me, Master Fletcher, how is it that you have men I did not know of? What was so important that you would break the vow of secrecy concerning our work here?"

"Truth!" Fletcher cried.

"You have placed the entire project in jeopardy."

"I've found proof, I tell you, proof! You've only to come with me to see—"

"No one will go anywhere. Not until—"

"They must!"

For a man everyone had thought mild and pleasant natured, Fletcher's metamorphosis was startling. His eyes blazed. His face colored. His breath came in great gulps and puffed out through his nostrils in the manner of a bull about to charge.

"Calm yourself, Bart." Weller laid a hand on his colleague's arm.

Fletcher shook him off. "You mock me. You have all mocked me. But the last laugh will be mine. I have proof, I tell you." From beneath his scholar's robe he produced what at first appeared to be a small, smooth stone.

"*Batata,*" Weller murmured, giving it a name. "The Spanish brought these back from Peru." After he examined the peculiar object, he passed it to Susanna.

"I have read about *batatas,*" she said. "They are said to grow well in Spanish soil, but I have never heard of one imported into England."

The rock, it seemed, was edible.

"There! You see!" Triumph glittered in Fletcher's eyes. "How could it have come here except as I have said? Early colonists brought the plants back with them."

Walter could think of several explanations. The most obvious was that Fletcher was an agent of Spain and had procured the *batata* from that country.

"I have found the remains of an ancient garden on the coast near here," Fletcher said. "I sent one of these *batatas* to Mathias L'Obel, the great herbalist, for confirmation. Just before he left London, he sent me this." With a flourish, he produced a letter. "He confirms that the plant came, without a doubt, from the New World."

"You contacted a foreigner!" Gainsford bounced out of his seat, looking as if he wanted to throttle Fletcher.

Walter sympathized. With none the wiser, Fletcher had managed to come and go from Priory House at will. He had hired men without verifying their loyalty to England and had gone on to consult with someone who might already have spread word of their work to England's enemies. More unconscionable still, according to the report Walter had received from his agent there, Fletcher had met in London with the Spanish ambassador just before coming to Priory House.

"You stand accused of treason, Master Fletcher," Walter said.

"L'Obel dedicated his recent book on herbs to Her Sovereign Majesty, Queen Elizabeth."

"That does not change the fact that he is French!" Balanced on his toes, Gainsford thrust his face into Fletcher's.

Fletcher blinked at him. "L'Obel is Belgian."

"The man's a Catholic. They're all in league against us."

The sound of a throat clearing drew Walter's attention to Sir Gregory. "If L'Obel did no more than identify these as *batatas*, then he knows nothing of any importance."

Seizing the letter as it was passed from hand to hand, Walter skimmed its contents. The herbalist did not seem to have any notion where this particular specimen had come from or why Fletcher had asked him to identify it. Walter hoped the workmen would prove just as ignorant. "Master Fletcher," he said, in a steel-tipped tone that silenced everyone else, "you must make no more unauthorized jaunts about the countryside. You jeopardized our entire undertaking every time you left the grounds."

"You dare, sir, to stand in the way of research?"

"I dare that and more for the preservation of the realm."

Livid, Fletcher began to sputter.

"But if he has found something—"

A slashing movement of one hand cut Weller's objection short. Walter glared at each scholar in turn. "Before anyone goes anywhere, I must secure the site, verify the loyalty of the diggers, and swear them to silence, all without arousing undue speculation in the countryside. It is imperative we do not attract attention. The safety of the nation may depend upon it."

No one dared object, not when speaking against Walter's dictates could provoke an accusation of treason. Grudgingly, Fletcher provided the location of his find. He had been digging in the ruins at Tintagel.

When the meeting adjourned a short time later, the reports from the other scholars having proved anticlimactic after Fletcher's overwrought announcement, Walter stayed behind to help Susanna gather her notes and papers. He pocketed the letter from L'Obel to Fletcher.

"I vow I feel dazed and a bit light-headed after hearing Fletcher's passionate defense of his actions," Susanna said.

"Walk with me then," Walter suggested. "Some fresh air will help us both." He led the way past the unfinished addition to the manor house and along the path that led to the orchard.

"When we've gone, you will be able to resume building here at Priory House," she remarked. "Will you put fish ponds here, close to the house?"

"I have considered small tanks with carp and tench." In his imagination he replaced the ten-gallon barrels that currently held live fish with a chain of small ponds linked by a canal to a reservoir. Properly maintained, drained every few years and so forth, the fish there could be fattened and cleansed of any muddy flavor. "In time, I'll build larger fish ponds—five or six acres in size—and stock them with less amiable fish."

That won a smile. They both knew that trout were not to be trusted in small ponds. Perch were worse, eating even their own spawn, and likewise pike, which had earned the appellation "fresh-water sharks." Only in larger bodies of water would there be room for such predators.

"You might want to add plants to the larger ponds," Susanna suggested, "then harvest them with the fish to add flavor in the cooking: watercress for perch; thyme for moorland trout and grayling."

They had wandered some distance from the house, past a row of cornelian cherry trees and into the apple orchard. Reluctantly, Walter returned to the subject of Bartholomew Fletcher. "Could any plant survive for a thousand years?"

"It is not beyond belief. The Crusaders brought back many herbs and flowers that thrive in English gardens today."

"But who tended these?"

"Who is at Tintagel? Indeed, *where* is Tintagel? You forget, I am a stranger to Cornwall."

"Tintagel is a parish northwest of here. The place Fletcher has been digging in is the ruin of an abandoned castle high on a cliff overlooking the sea."

"Could the castle date from King Arthur's time?"

"I doubt it. The design resembles others I've seen, and they were built no more than a few hundred years ago, but the site is said to have been the stronghold of the rulers of Cornwall a thousand years past. That much may be true."

"Does anyone live there now?"

"No. And we may hope those in the nearest village, a place called Trevena, take no interest in the place and are unaware of the activities of Fletcher's diggers." There were two, unlettered laborers hired in London.

"Fletcher himself might have planted the *batatas,* then arranged to make the find."

"That was my thought, too, although it seems to surpass belief that he should do so."

"Scholars have done stranger things to prove a theory."

"Would *batatas* be difficult to obtain?"

Susanna considered his question as they continued their walk through the sweet-smelling orchard. "To discover the answer to that question, I would have to consult other herbalists. I am not aware of any in the garden Sir William Cecil planted for his London house, although that one boasts many rare plants. A young fellow named Gerard tends it for him. I met him at the same time I met Master L'Obel, when the latter came to England to study our local flora."

"And in the hope of patronage?"

"No doubt. His book is called *Stirpium Adversaria Nova*. It is a most excellent work, made more interesting by woodcuts by Master Rondelet, L'Obel's teacher at the school of medicine in Montpellier. In it, L'Obel praises our own Hugh Morgan, a well-known English apothecary. It is Morgan who is the true expert on plants from the Indies. He obtained, I have been told, a great many new varieties from Francis Drake after his last voyage."

Walter almost swallowed his tongue. His voice cracked as he asked, "What voyage do you mean?"

"The one last year. A pity Morgan did not obtain the plants until after the publication of L'Obel's—" She broke off when Walter seized her forearm.

"That was supposed to have been a close-kept secret."

"Difficult to accomplish when everyone aboard a fleet of ships is privy to the knowledge."

Her tart comment made him wince. He released her arm, duly chastised. She had the right of it. With so many men involved, he should not be surprised that the news had leaked out.

"L'Obel and Pierre Pena, from Provence, and Charles de l'Escluse, another well-known foreign herbalist now in England, are aware of the voyage, since Morgan shared his findings; but I would not let that worry you overmuch. As I have cause to know, few people have much interest in herbals. Both of my books, to which I dedicated years of research, are now out of print."

"Fletcher visited the Spanish ambassador when he was last in London," Walter said.

"Did he?" She paused to inspect an apple tree, frowning at the size of the fruit. "There's your answer, then. He obtained the *batatas* from Spain."

"But what, I wonder, did he trade for them?" What secrets had he known? *"Batatas!"* Walter's exasperation exploded in the single word. "What was the man thinking to turn traitor for such a little thing?"

"You do not know that he betrayed us. Mayhap he did no more than purchase a few samples of an exotic plant and seed the site with them to prove his contention that King Arthur discovered the New World." She hesitated. "It is what the queen wants from our efforts here, Walter. You could let the evidence stand."

He leaned against one of the trees monks had planted decades before. "He evaded my men, a deliberate act, by sneaking out at night. And those forays were well planned. He could not have walked all the way to Tintagel. It is too far. Nine miles or more. Therefore he must have made arrangements for a horse." A number of people had been involved, all without being noticed by his guards.

They began to walk again, circling among the trees. Walter's thoughts shifted to the other matter preying on his mind—Eleanor. He knew what she was trying to do, weaving her web around him, luring him with her siren's ways.

"I had great hopes once," he said after a lengthy silence, "for this house, for my family."

"Leave off feeling sorry for yourself, Walter. You never used to be one to give up without a fight."

Startled out of his brooding, he glared at her. It was disconcerting to have her all but read his mind. "Is that how you see marriage? A battle? Tell me, then, what tactics did you use to defeat Robert?"

Susanna recoiled as if she'd been slapped. Walter was instantly contrite, but she waved off his apologies.

"No. You have the right of it. Robert and I did but tolerate one another. You want more. You deserve more. And you do have a chance for happiness with Eleanor. Oh, yes, I know what she did.

But have you made any attempt to understand why? What effort have you made to build anew?"

"I will never be able to trust her again. And how can she tolerate me? Eleanor married me in the belief I would rise high at court. That will never happen now."

"You are not thinking clearly. Just as you have been obliged to reassess your life, so, too, has Eleanor. She was sunk deep in despair when she first arrived at Leigh Abbey, and at least part of the cause was that when you came to visit you did not spend any time with her."

Although a snort was his only response, he was listening.

"She did not understand your coldness. I do not believe she could remember the reason for it."

"How could she forget what—?"

"Many learned physicians have noted this tendency to forget events that take place immediately before a serious injury. It occurs most often in patients who have head injuries, which Eleanor did suffer."

"Eleanor is capable of pretense."

"Capable, mayhap, but you did not observe her all those months. I did. She passed from apathy and a refusal to do anything for herself to a period when she was certain no one could understand how greatly she had suffered. I suspect she relived bits and pieces of what happened to her when she slept, for she suffered from nightmares. Because she did not sleep well, she was nervous and high-strung during the day. Her mind tended to wander, and when she was able to focus, it was often to dwell upon how close her brush with death had been. Can you imagine what it was like for her? Is it any wonder frustration bred self-pity?"

"She did not remember confessing to me? She did not realize I knew she'd plotted treason?"

"If she had remembered, I believe she would have spoken of it."

"Aye. She'd have lied about it, attempted to make it seem that her sins were not as great as I supposed."

"Most people see their own actions in a positive light. Eleanor complained of many things but never of being misunderstood."

"I understood very well what had happened."

"But you never talked to her about it, Walter. Since she's been in Cornwall, Eleanor has been trying to rebuild her life. I admire her for that. In spite of the pain she suffers with each attempt, she endeavors to do all she can for herself. She may never walk as she did before, and it is certain she will never dance or run, but she *is* able to get about with the help of crutches. That is the woman you married, Walter. Determined. Fearless. Capable of more than anyone expects."

"Aye." He felt his mouth twitch into just the hint of a sardonic smile. "That is what I fear."

32

They approached Tintagel on horseback from the east by way of a cliff path, having abandoned an easier road because it would have meant passing through the village of Bossiney. To keep her mind off the steep drop at her right hand, Susanna concentrated on the stands of bell heather that grew amid the gorse and ling in the open places. In sheltered spots, she recognized bracken and more gorse, for even on the barest rockface, a few wild flowers bloomed.

She checked at the sight of a familiar fleshy plant lying on the track. "Walter?"

He dismounted to retrieve it, then indicated deep tracks climbing from the cove below. "They use pannier-laden donkeys hereabout to bring sand and seaweed up from the shore."

To spread on the fields, Susanna realized. And she now understood how the rock samphire had gotten to Priory House. Fletcher must have had some caught on his boots the night Piers apprehended him.

They continued on, the only sign of life a profusion of birds. She saw razorbills and shags, guillemots and fulmars. And a colony of puffins on the rocks of a headland jutting out west of Bossiney Cove. Another mile on the steep, uneven, winding cliff path brought the ruins of Tintagel Castle into view. Walter had been correct. Its design did not date to King Arthur's time.

Not that anyone was certain of the precise dates of Arthur's reign. Welsh annals placed him at the very beginning of the sixth century after Christ, the time of Walter's Cornish king, but English writers claimed he and his knights flourished later than that by full fourscore years. None of the documents went back to Arthur's own time. Susanna did not see how Bartholomew Fletcher could ever prove anything about an era so deep in the past. It was difficult enough to discover the truth about events only a hundred years old—the true fate of John Cabot, for example.

"You will see now," Fletcher boasted, as he urged his sturdy little Cornish nag down a breakneck descent into a deep valley. Low of stature, the animals were well suited to the rough, hilly terrain. Susanna, Walter, Owen Merrick, and Walter's two henchmen, similarly mounted, followed, then climbed the precipitous slope on the other side. Susanna had to close her eyes repeatedly during the dizzying trek, but her horse did not balk once.

"What do you expect to find?" Merrick demanded in an irritable voice. He'd been selected to accompany them as the representative of the other scholars. "King Arthur's bones? The Holy Grail? Arthur come back, as he promised? Next thing you'll be looking for Owen Glendower still living in the mountains of Wales."

Glendower, Susanna recalled, had led a rebellion against the English and disappeared without a trace at the beginning of the fifteenth century.

"The Grail is not out of the question. It is said that when the remains of Arthur and his queen were discovered at Glastonbury Abbey in King Richard the Lionheart's time, the great sword Excaliber was found as well."

"What happened to it, then? For that matter, what happened to King Arthur's grave?" Merrick's voice rose as his ire increased. "Your grail is a myth. The Welsh stories never speak of it and with good reason, since Arthur was not a Christian. Arthur and his warriors quested in an Otherworld called Annwn and the object of their search was a magic cauldron."

"Do you doubt the truth of all religious relics?"

176

At once Merrick sobered. "Nay. There are some I would give my life to protect."

Walter intervened before they could resume their quarrel, which had been waged on and off all morning as they rode toward Tintagel. "We must walk the rest of the way from here."

They dismounted near the ruins of the old gatehouse. Piers Ludlow, one of the guards Walter had ordered to accompany them, lifted Susanna from her saddle, making light work of the task. He steadied her while she got her footing on the rough, rocky ground. Together, they picked their way around the ruins of the castle.

A strong wind blew in wet mists from the sea, making Susanna shiver as she straightened her kirtle and the canvas outer skirt she wore for protection against weather and dirt during their journey. She was glad she had on warm clothing, including a wool cloak. Although it was high summer, it was cold and damp here on the cliffs. And noisy.

The murmur of breaking waves had been their constant companion all along the coast, at times closer to a muted roar. Now, as they approached the seaward castle wall, it combined with the howl of the wind and the calling of seabirds to oblige them to shout in order to be heard.

"That is where we must go." Fletcher pointed down.

Susanna's stomach lurched. Far below, a narrow strip of sand was the only relief from sheer cliffs and surging water.

The garden that was Fletcher's goal lay upon a headland all but turned into an island by the encroaching sea. To reach it they must first climb down this escarpment, then cross a makeshift bridge of elm trees, felled and laid across a narrow ridge of land with the sea roiling both to left and right, then scale the opposite promontory.

"That jut of land is rectangular in shape and about a quarter of a mile across," Fletcher said. "The garden is near more ruins."

"Is there no other way than this to reach them?" It would not be an easy descent for any of them, but Susanna would be further encumbered by her skirts and by her game leg, which did not always remain stable beneath her.

Fletcher made a vague gesture to the right. "There is a landing place in a small cove on that side of the island, just out of sight around that curve of land. A narrow path leads upward, making use of rock-cut steps, to an opening in a section of battlemented wall—a postern gate, if you will. I keep a boat in that cove, but in this wind we'd have a hard time of it. It is simpler and more direct to go this way."

"A boat is impractical." Walter agreed. "And even the lowest point on the island rises a goodly height from the sea."

Everywhere Susanna looked, she saw cliffs of forbidding gray, as scarred and jagged as the ruins of the castle in their midst. There was no help for it. She must brave the climb. Pasting a false smile on her face, Susanna groped for her composure and followed the men down the tortuous cliff path.

She held her breath as they teetered across the elm logs in single file, the two guards bringing up the rear. Safe on the far side, as they again began to climb, Susanna thought with real longing of the breeches her friend Catherine wore when she traveled. In the ordinary way of things, she considered this apparel on a woman too unconventional, but just now she'd have given a good deal for such sensible clothing.

They paused, winded, at a small chapel built low to withstand the violent storms that buffeted the coastline. It was still intact but no longer in use save by a flock of little coarse-fleeced Cornish sheep grazing nearby. Susanna wondered how they'd managed the climb.

Fletcher's goal lay some three hundred paces beyond the chapel—a walled garden situated in a fold in the plateau that sheltered it from the prevailing westerly winds. As soon as she'd caught her breath, Susanna's interest quickened. She moved closer to inspect the plot. Startled, a rabbit left off eating clover and bolted for cover.

The garden was much overgrown with weeds, except in one area, the place where Fletcher's men had been digging. With a spade he had brought with him, Fletcher began to turn over clots of earth. Within moments he had dug up another *batata,* somewhat shriveled, and a few shards of yellowish-green glass.

Susanna entered the enclosure through the space where a gate had once hung. She stooped to pick up one of the pieces of glass. It was impossible to say what object it had once been part of, but it was very fine. Some sort of drinking vessel, she decided, and tucked the fragment into her pocket as she bent to examine a bit of redware Fletcher had just unearthed. By its shape, she identified this object as a remnant of a wide, shallow, ceramic bowl.

Fletcher's shout of triumph made her drop the pottery. "Deny this if you can!" he challenged them, holding up a dirt-encrusted lump that caught the light even on this overcast day and reflected it back at them with an intensity that could only come from gold.

Susanna handed the scholar her handkerchief to clean the object he had found. Revealed, it was an ugly little statue, so foreign to Susanna's experience that she had no trouble accepting that it might have come from across the Western Sea.

"Here is proof that colonists went to the New World," Fletcher declared. "They sent this back as trade goods. I have seen descriptions of idols like it. They are found among the tribes the Spaniards encountered."

"Are you now the expert on all things Spanish?" Walter asked in a mild voice.

Susanna's skin prickled. She knew that tone. A crooked smile slipped out from behind Walter's usual mask. His eyes lit with a triumph that equaled the scholar's. He was poised like a cat ready to pounce on its prey, and Fletcher was the mouse.

Unaware that such signs were unusual and potentially dangerous, Fletcher steepled his fingers and launched into a lecture. He sounded as if he knew what he was talking about. Certes, Susanna had heard the names Pizarro and Coronado bandied about ere now. She was prepared to believe that they had seen objects such as this in the New World.

But as he droned on, her cynicism returned. The idea that colonists sent out by King Arthur a thousand years ago should have brought back an artifact, let alone buried it here, was difficult to accept; and it defied common sense that Fletcher should find such a thing just when he needed to produce proof of that colony's existence.

Walter cut short the recitation with a slashing movement of one hand. His voice was just as curt. "This 'proof' you claim to have found at Tintagel today was in your chamber at Priory House weeks ago. I saw it there myself, hidden among your possessions. You buried your own treasure, Fletcher. You are a fraud."

"The cache was King Arthur's."

"And you are a liar."

"I am an antiquary!"

"You are also a murderer, Master Fletcher."

Dead silence fell. Nothing broke it but the rush and rumble of the sea, the moaning of the wind, and the lonely cry of a solitary seabird. Walter could not have bettered the drama of the setting or the impact of his words. Until this moment, neither Fletcher nor Merrick had any reason to think he believed Calthorpe's death had involved foul play.

"Martin Calthorpe found out what you were up to, Fletcher," Walter continued. "When he threatened to reveal your perfidy to the world, you killed him."

Merrick looked planet struck. "But, Sir Walter—you ruled Martin Calthorpe's death an accident."

Fletcher choked and sputtered, then blurted, "Have you gone mad? I am no murderer."

Unmoved by the denial, Walter pushed on, relentless in his accusations. "Calthorpe warned you what he meant to do. He offered to give you time to confess on your own. Instead, you waited for him in his study and attacked him when he returned from talking to Lady Appleton in the library. You took care that the death should appear to be accidental then went calmly out into the stableyard to see what all the noise was about."

"You were with me then." Fletcher turned to Merrick. "Did I have blood on my hands? Did I show any sign of just having killed a man?" Merrick, his expression still blank with shock, did not reply. Fletcher swung back toward Walter. "By the rood, Pendennis. You have taken leave of your senses!"

"It was a senseless crime," Merrick muttered, at last coming out of his trance, "murdering Calthorpe. Foolish to try to hide it."

Walter nodded in agreement. "You'll get no support from your fellow scholars, Fletcher. When they hear the charges against you, none will defend you. You betrayed them and our mission, and you murdered Calthorpe when he discovered what you were up to."

Fletcher's face crumpled. He looked as if he might burst into tears. And then, without warning, he shoved Walter to the ground and bolted, vaulting over the wall of the garden with a leap that belied both age and girth. Once on the other side, he ran, but not toward the descent to the bridge, where Walter's guards blocked his path. He veered northeast instead, toward the postern gate he'd spoken of and the steep cliff path to the landing place far below. He kept a boat there, Susanna remembered.

So, apparently, did Walter. He sprinted after Fletcher on a course that cut off that avenue of escape. Fletcher skidded to a halt, head swiveling, eyes wild. Like game pursued by hunters, panic overcame him. He seemed to lose all reason, all sense of what was safe and what was not, and plunged in yet another direction, this time scrambling over the uneven surface toward higher ground.

Merrick, now closest to him by virtue of Fletcher's zigzag course, set off in pursuit with Susanna trailing after, hampered once again by long skirts and her old injury. The wind whipped her hair free of her hood, blinding her.

When she could see again, Merrick had gained on his quarry. Stretching out both arms, he seized Fletcher's sleeve to jerk the other man to a standstill. Fletcher swung round to face him.

Susanna saw Merrick's lips move, but his words were swept away by the gale. Fletcher said something in reply, then went for Merrick's throat.

Susanna risked one glance over her shoulder as she resumed her climb, looking for Walter and his men. They'd needed a goat's surefootedness to keep from stumbling. Piers had gone down, taking the other henchman with him. They lay in a tangle of arms and legs. Walter made better progress but was still some distance away, approaching at an angle. His speed was checked by the uneven surface and the random appearances of shrubs and boulders as obstacles in his path.

Susanna pushed on, teetering, out of breath, the pain in her leg growing worse with every step. She kept her gaze trained on the two men, to the peril of her own progress, and only prevented a nasty fall by catching herself with both hands. For that one brief moment, she looked away from the struggle between Merrick and Fletcher.

When she'd righted herself, she sought them again. She was just in time to see Merrick's foot slip. Ice condensed in her stomach, and she forgot her stinging palms. An instant later, both men had vanished. The only thing left against the gray sky were dark, ominous clouds and a solitary chough with a bill and feet as red as blood.

Susanna's breath stopped. Her hands, raw and bleeding, trembled as she brought them to her lips. Then her whole body started to shake with the realization of what must have happened.

That high ground ahead was the edge of another cliff.

33

ady Appleton arrived back at Priory House after nightfall and accompanied by only one other rider, one of Sir Walter's guards. Her face haggard, she drew Jennet aside.

"Where is Gwyn?" she asked.

"Faith, madam, what has happened? Were you set upon by robbers?"

"Gwyn—where is she?"

"In the hall, with Lionel and Rosamond and Lady Pendennis."

"Come with me." Lady Appleton led the way to her own chamber, avoiding any contact with the others. "What I tell you now must not be repeated to anyone," she warned. "There is no need for the others to know all the details, not even Gwyn."

Jennet nodded.

"Master Fletcher is dead, killed in an attempt to escape after Sir Walter accused him of murder."

Jennet nodded again and wondered how big her eyes had grown. Master Fletcher? Well, he had behaved strangely that one night.

"Gwyn's father died trying to convince his colleague to see reason. They struggled at a cliff's edge, then fell together from a great height."

"Faith," Jennet said again, and breathed not another word as Lady Appleton went on to explain how Master Fletcher had tried to perpetrate a fraud in order to support his theories about King Arthur. His apparent motive for murdering Master Calthorpe had been to prevent him from exposing the scheme.

"And now I must tell Gwyn her father is dead," she concluded, "but not the rest. Walter, who has stayed behind at Tintagel to recover the bodies, feels it sufficient to say that the ground close to the edge of the escarpment gave way."

"Let me bring Gwyn to you here," Jennet suggested.

"And Lionel with her," Lady Appleton said. "He will help her through this crisis."

When they'd told her, Gwyn buried her face against Lionel's chest. Her shoulders heaved as she sobbed, inconsolably, for a span of a quarter hour. Then, slowly, her tears subsided and she began to speak quietly to Lionel. At that point Lady Appleton withdrew. Jennet did not and was startled when their low-voiced exchange abruptly turned acrimonious. She could not make out any words, but the tone was unmistakable. A moment later, Gwyn sprang to her feet and fled, leaving Lionel staring after her in bewilderment.

Jennet started to follow Gwyn.

Lionel stopped her with a scowl.

"Faith! Do not glower at me. I only want to help."

"*She* wants to elope."

"I thought your greatest desire was to marry Gwyn."

"I'll not have what's between us turned into a hole-and-corner affair."

"You mean to insist on a year of mourning?" Jennet could not quite keep the mockery out of her voice.

"Nay." With a rueful laugh he took off his cap, raked his fingers through already disordered hair, and plopped the bonnet back into place. "I'd not wait that long, but it is only right to ask permission of Lord John."

Puzzled, Jennet stared at him.

"That is what they call him, Gwyn's great-grandfather. He's very old. I think Gwyn is a bit afraid of him."

"Do you mean she fears he'll refuse to let you wed?"

"That is part of it, no doubt. He was one of the most successful merchants in Bristol in his younger days. I suppose he is wealthy. But if he's not found Gwyn a husband ere now, how can he object to me? Master Merrick would have allowed us to wed. In time."

Because Lionel sounded as if he were trying to convince himself, Jennet's heart went out to him. Of a sudden, he seemed very young. "When she takes her father's body to Bristol for burial, we'll all go to support your suit. There will be no chance of refusal then."

"That's what I tried to tell Gwyn, but she said I do not know her family. That's when she ran off."

"She's upset," Jennet reminded him. " 'Tis only the shock of her father's death that makes her so emotional. She'll come around."

She was confident she spoke the truth. Lionel could charm any woman out of her fears. And no one could resist a cause Lady Appleton espoused, not even a stubborn old man with the pretentious title of "Lord John."

34

Walter turned the small gold statue over in his hands, marveling at the workmanship, awed by the pagan power it represented. It felt impossibly smooth to the touch and warmed as he caressed it. *A thing of power,* he thought, *ancient and mysterious.* It was the figure of a warrior, or mayhap a god of war, for its squat, broad-shouldered body was surmounted by a helmeted head. Small, fierce eyes stared back at Walter from beneath the half circle of a headdress that was as high again as the shape of the man who wore it.

The decision to send his prize to the queen came easily. It was too rare and precious to keep for himself and the expensive gift would please her, as would the news that Calthorpe's murder had been solved. She would be less pleased by the results of their research. Now that Fletcher's theory had been shown to be based on fraud, they had no proof to offer of early English claims to the New World. There was little point in waiting until Saint Bartholomew's Day. Saint Lawrence's Day was closer, the tenth of August. They would dedicate their report to him, Walter decided with grim humor; and after it had been dispatched to court, they could celebrate by going to Lawrence Fair at Bodmin.

At least he now had answers to a few of his questions. The names of Fletcher's Spanish connections in London had been waiting for him on his return to Priory House. No doubt one of them had supplied the scholar with this statue, as well as with the *batatas*, in spite of standing orders in Spanish territory to melt down all such pagan treasures into ingots. In the name of their church, the Spanish conquistadors were determined to stamp out every vestige of any religion but their own.

"Your pardon, Sir Walter." Jacob hesitated in the doorway of Walter's private study.

"Yes? What is it?"

"A package just arrived from London, for Master Merrick."

"Give it to his daughter, then."

Jacob fidgeted.

"What?"

"You left orders that you wished to examine any item sent to anyone at Priory House." Walter had given that command when he'd first learned of Fletcher's correspondence with the herbalist, L'Obel.

"Very well. Give it here."

This packet was small and oblong and heavily padded. When Walter opened it, he found a note wrapped around yet another layer of packing that concealed the nature of its contents. Expecting nothing out of the ordinary, he unrolled it and read. A low whistle escaped him as he absorbed the implications.

"Fetch Lady Appleton," he ordered.

35

Susanna was winded by the time she reached Walter's study. Spurred on by the urgency in Jacob's voice, she'd rushed down the stairs from Rosamond's schoolroom in the west wing and across the straight but as yet uncobbled alley that led from the road to the porch of the manor house.

"What do you make of this?" Walter passed her first a note, then a pair of bone-framed spectacles with tinted lenses.

Taking both, she drew in several deep breaths, filling her nose with the scent of bayberry candles. Trust Walter to have every luxury!

"It seems clear enough," she said, after she read the short message. "This letter comes from a spectacle maker in London who undertook repairs at Master Merrick's request." She glanced again at the date of that request and felt a chill race along her spine. "These were broken at about the same time Martin Calthorpe was murdered."

"The very day, I do think. What happened to that shard of tinted glass you found on the writing table in his study?"

"I put it in my pocket." Reaching through the placket in her kirtle, she found the pocket, a separate item of clothing tied to her waist. Inside were a candle stub, flint and steel, needle and thread, and a number of small bits and pieces—lost buttons and the like—that she did not want to risk losing. Her searching fingers touched glass but the bit she withdrew first was the one she'd found at Tintagel. Setting it aside, she foraged again, this time with better success.

Walter took the shard of tinted glass and placed it next to the spectacles. The match in color was too close to be coincidence.

"It wasn't Fletcher who killed Martin Calthorpe." Susanna could scarce believe what she was saying. "Owen Merrick murdered him."

"The original lenses must have been broken during Merrick's attack on Calthorpe. He'd have picked up as many of the pieces as he could find, but this one he left behind."

"He could not see very well once his spectacles were broken."

"The next day he sent these away to be repaired and wore the gold-rimmed pair, the ones with clear glass. No one noticed anything odd in that."

Susanna pictured the day of Calthorpe's death in her mind. In the stableyard, Merrick had held his spectacles in one hand. She'd thought nothing of it at the time. Many scholars used them only for reading. "How can Merrick be guilty? Fletcher was the one who fled. Were they allied in some foul plot?" They had been together right after Calthorpe's death.

Walter's frown told her he did not like the suggestion.

"You are thinking they were both spies," she said.

"In truth, I was considering that, by running away, Fletcher provided Merrick with a perfect scapegoat. I'd accused him. He bolted. Merrick reached him first. He must have been trying to push Fletcher off the cliff in the hope we would think his death an accident. Certes, Merrick did not intend to fall with him." Walter's sudden bark of laughter held no humor. "What irony if Merrick perished because of eyesight too impaired to judge his distance from the edge, for other than plunging to his own death, his plan worked just as he hoped it would."

Susanna thought of Tintagel. An exchange of words. Merrick's hand on Fletcher's sleeve. Fletcher's grab for Merrick's throat. What Walter suggested made a terrible kind of sense . . . but only up to a point.

"Fletcher had a motive, to keep Calthorpe silent about the fraud. Why should Merrick kill him? When we considered him before, the only thing we could fix on was his academic rivalry with Calthorpe."

"It no longer matters." Walter looked no happier than she felt, but he seemed resigned to the inevitable. "Further questions will do naught but displease the queen. I have carelessly lost half our scholars. There is no profit in continuing our research. What few conclusions we have reached will be written up and submitted as soon as may be. All the papers and books we've gathered together can be sent to Mortlake to John Dee. Sir Gregory Speake can take charge of that, with young Daniel to accompany him. As for Weller and Gainsford, I feel certain they will be happy enough to retire to Reading."

It took Susanna a moment to think why they would want to go there. Then she remembered the outbreak of plague. To escape infection, all lectures at Oxford had been canceled and the scholars sent to university-owned properties in the country. The rest of the world had gone on its merry way while they'd been here in Cornwall, unaware of and unaffected by matters that had turned into an obsession for those at Priory House.

"If you will collect the materials you have been translating, I will send them on with the rest," Walter added.

"I do not like to abandon a task half done." Nor was she content to leave questions about murder unanswered. Three men were dead, and she did not know why they'd died.

"We have no choice."

"We know who was responsible now. Surely we can determine why. Murder—"

He cut her off with an impatient gesture. "We know all that is necessary. The killer is dead. What need to ask more questions? I do not believe Merrick had any connection to Spain. Fletcher, who did, possessed no damaging information to pass on. His discoveries were all in his own mind, as I am certain his Spanish contacts were aware."

He could not be moved to reconsider.

Susanna left Walter's private study a short time later, discouragement dogging her footsteps. At the least, she'd hoped to find some definitive answer in their research. With a heavy heart, she headed for the library. Walter was right. There was no reason to delay the task of packing up books and papers.

She entered the parlor through one door just in time to glimpse Gwyn Merrick leaving by another. Puzzled, for she could think of no reason for that young woman to be in this area, Susanna crossed the room to look out a window. Gwyn had already vanished into the rabbit warren of old priory buildings beyond.

Frowning, Susanna entered the library. The smell of smoke was still strong enough there to send her into a momentary panic. Then she realized that the fire had been confined to the hearth, where burning paper had already turned to ashes.

Only one item appeared to have been destroyed. Susanna poked at the charred remains of a document or letter, but there was not enough left to identify.

With leaden steps, she walked to her writing table. The materials from the estate of Sebastian Cabot appeared to be as she had left them, neatly stacked, but she did not trust the evidence of her eyes. From a locked casket, she retrieved the inventory she had made, since one had not been sent with Cabot's chest, and in less than a quarter of an hour knew what it was that Gwyn had burned. The story of John Cabot's death at the hands of Amerindians was missing.

Setting aside her list, Susanna buried her head in her arms. Why would Gwyn do such a thing? Heartsick, she accepted that there was no innocent explanation for Gwyn's behavior. Whatever Owen Merrick had been up to, his daughter had been in his confidence. An accomplice, perhaps even an accessory, to murder.

36

They were leaving Priory House. Eleanor's elation knew no bounds. They were all going—Susanna, Jennet, Gwyn, and the scholars. She'd promote Melka to housekeeper, she decided, hire new maidservants . . . and mayhap employ a congenial companion.

For an instant, Eleanor saw herself in the role her cousin, Lady Quarles, had played in her own life—lording it over a household, resented by her underlings, growing ever more bitter and petty as the years passed. Blinking hard, she banished the image. It did not have to be that way. She could recapture Walter's affection, strengthen her bond with Rosamond, find new friends. There were other great houses in the neighborhood. She would host house parties for gentry from Launceston and Bodmin and whatever other towns existed in this godforsaken wasteland.

Rosamond's wail of protest interrupted her thoughts. "You cannot go! Mama, you cannot leave me here!"

"I cannot take you with me, Rosamond. I must accompany Gwyn to Bristol to return her to the bosom of her family."

Eleanor frowned, wondering why. What had remained of Gwyn's father and Master Fletcher had been buried at Priory House in the same monks' cemetery where Master Calthorpe was interred. It would have been sheer folly to transport a body any distance in the heat of summer. Furthermore, Eleanor had been under the impression Lionel meant to take Gwyn to Leigh Abbey as his bride.

"When will you come back?" Rosamond demanded.

"I do not know," Susanna said.

Rosamond's voice rose to a howl. "You mean to abandon me!"

"Listen to me, Rosamond." Susanna knelt in front of the girl in order to tell her the truth face-to-face. "For now, it is best that you remain with your mother and stepfather."

Eleanor was certain Susanna did not want to leave Rosamond behind, but for some reason known only to herself, she had decided that this course was in the best interests of the child.

"Nooooooo," Rosamond wailed—no pretense this time, but real distress.

Seizing her shoulders, Susanna forced Rosamond to meet her gaze. "Do you like Sir Walter, Rosamond?"

Although her eyes swam with unshed tears, Rosamond's answer was unequivocal. "Yes."

Eleanor noted that Susanna did not risk asking Rosamond if she had any liking for her mother.

"Sir Walter Pendennis is your papa now," Susanna said. "He needs you to stay here and help him learn how to be that. You must do your best to please both him and your mother. In that way, all three of you will find happiness."

"You put too much burden on the child," Eleanor objected.

Two heads whipped around to stare at her. Susanna blinked in surprise, as if she'd been so absorbed in her exchange with Rosamond that she'd forgotten there was anyone else in the schoolroom. Rosamond just seemed puzzled.

"Do *you* wish me to stay, Mother?"

Eleanor hesitated. The girl had potential. And there had been times, a few, when she'd even sparked a flash of maternal feeling in Eleanor's bosom. More important, though, Walter wanted her here. "Yes, Rosamond," she said, "I would like your company at Priory House."

37

Rain fell in sheets, turning Priory House dark and gloomy. Brooding, Sir Walter Pendennis sifted a half dozen glittering stones through his fingers. They were variously called Bristol crystals, Cornish diamonds, and Saint Vincent's rocks—pretty things found in zinc mines and passed off to the unwary as real diamonds.

Since he was the local justice of the peace, a recent attempt to do just that had come to his attention. In the course of dealing with it, he'd acquired the baubles. Toying with them, he found, helped him think.

He missed Susanna, although she'd been gone less than a day. That was one thing bothering him. The other was Eleanor's attitude. She'd undergone a change these last few weeks, becoming more biddable and less brittle.

Or was that wishful thinking on his part, an attempt to fill the void left by Susanna's departure? He felt as if he'd had an arm amputated, but at the same time there was a nagging sense that, having rid himself of an infected limb, he might now hope to survive.

He could still build a new life here just as he'd once planned, repair the rift with Tris and the rest of his family, sire sons. All he had to do was focus on the dreams he'd had before Eleanor's betrayal.

That was the part that worried him. Trust came hard. It seemed a great leap of faith to accept that her desires and his should once more be aligned.

A small sound from the doorway had him reaching for the knife sheathed at his waist. He swung his head around then froze as he caught sight of Rosamond.

"Why did you look so sad?" she asked.

Without waiting for answer or invitation, she entered his private study. Like a curious young bird, she twisted her head this way and that, taking stock of her surroundings. She lifted each book he'd left atop the flat-topped traveling chest. The illustrated edition of Vitruvius, published sixty years ago. One of the volumes of Sebastiano Serlio. Vredeman de Vries's *Architectura.* And John Shute's thin volume, the *First and Chief Grounds of Architecture*, the book Walter had helped Shute research on a long-ago trip to Italy.

When she'd completed the survey, Rosamond's intelligent brown eyes regarded Walter, full of unasked questions. He found them less disconcerting today, although they still reminded him of her father. Walter fought an uncharacteristic urge to fidget under that steady stare.

"I have a great deal of work to do, Rosamond. What do you want of me?"

Her face crumpled and she blinked at him, as if she might be about to burst into tears. "Why are people always too busy to spend time with me?"

Guilt swamped Walter. There was no excuse for taking out his ill humor on a child. "Your pardon, Rosamond. I am out of sorts."

"Do you miss Mama, too?"

"Yes, Rosamond, I do. She has been my very dear friend for a long time."

"Just before Mama left, she said I should ask you to be our new French tutor, since Sir Gregory is no longer here to teach us."

"Our? I did not realize you had anyone to share your lessons."

"Mother does." Rosamond sent a tentative smile his way, disarming him further. "Mama said you speak French very well because you lived in Paris. She said my father once visited you there."

Poignant memories brought an unexpected lump to Walter's throat. "I suppose," he said, after a moment, "that if you would like to continue your lessons, I can guide you."

"Mother, too? She is very quick."

"Your mother, too. If she'll have me."

"I had to share lessons with Kate and Susan at Leigh Abbey," Rosamond confided. "They are older than I am."

"Would you prefer companions your own age?" He wondered if his brothers had likely offspring. It disturbed him that he did not already know the answer to that question. He, who knew the secrets of princes and noblemen, had not troubled to uncover the most basic facts about his siblings and their families.

"I think I should like to be the oldest. If I had brothers and sisters, I could tutor them."

"Siblings for you will be as God disposes," Walter said, thinking of the sons he'd like to have. Then he looked again at Rosamond. Her unique heritage, carefully honed, could make her a woman to be reckoned with. Was that why Susanna had entrusted him with the girl's upbringing?

He'd kept her here to lure Susanna back, Walter reminded himself. And he did not trust Eleanor. But he felt a smile creep over his countenance as he held out one hand. "Let us go and find your mother," he suggested, "and discover how she feels about having me as a French teacher."

A short time later, when Rosamond had gone off to pick apples, chattering happily in Polish with Melka, Walter sat alone with his wife in the pleasant retreat she had created for herself, her solar.

He tried to imagine Susanna in Eleanor's place, sitting quietly, hands busy with embroidery. The image was jarring. Susanna, as he'd last seen her, had been clad all in bombazine, a plain, twilled fabric blend of cotton and wool. Her face had been somber, as befitted the escort of a young woman griefstricken over the death of her father. That the father had been a murderer was irrelevant, as was Susanna's contention that Gwyn must have known what Owen Merrick was plotting. None of that mattered now. Walter had washed his hands of the whole affair . . . which left him here—with Eleanor.

On impulse, he extracted the pouch he'd tucked into the front of his doublet and showered the Bristol crystals across his wife's lap. "A gift for you, my dear."

"Diamonds?"

"Alas, no." As he summarized the inquest he'd conducted in his capacity as justice of the peace, he expected to see disappointment replace the bright light of interest in her eyes, but she surprised him.

"You enjoy the role of judge." Eleanor stirred the stones with one idle finger. They glittered against the sea green sussapine of her skirt. "Will it be enough for you?"

"I do not know," he admitted. He plucked up one of the crystals, his hand brushing the costly silk upon which it had been resting, and held it up to the light. It was not what it first appeared to be, but it had a certain beauty of its own.

She handed him another stone. "Cornwall was your home once. It can be again."

"I've fences to mend first. Not just with Tris, but also with my oldest sister, Grace. She is a widow, her children grown. When I first came here in the spring, to make sure everything was in order for the arrival of the scholars, she heard of my presence in the neighborhood and arrived, uninvited, determined to lend a hand." He grimaced. "Moved in, without a by-your-leave, taking the bedchamber you now use, and set about putting the place to rights. I was grateful for her help, up to a point, but I could not tell her of our mission here at Priory House or explain why she must leave before my guests took up residence. She departed in a huff, vowing not to speak to me again until she'd had an abject apology."

"She left a few items behind, I believe." Eleanor's smile was the brightest he'd seen from her since before her accident. She almost seemed . . . relieved. "I would like to meet all your brothers and sisters."

Walter sighed. "I suppose I will have to grovel."

Eleanor chuckled. "Think of it as a novel experience."

"Oh, no. I've had much practice—at court."

"An older sister, I am certain, outranks a queen."

Her teasing made him smile and coaxed him into regaling her with stories about the rest of his siblings. They were laughing together over an incident from his childhood—a rooster had chased him onto the top of a hayrick, obliging his brother Armigal to rescue him—when Jacob interrupted them.

"Courier's come, Sir Walter." He handed over a packet.

"Naught but a letter from Nick Baldwin to Susanna," Walter said when he'd pulled off the outer wrapping. "This arrived from London?"

"Falmouth," Jacob said.

"A ship from Hamburg must be in port there." He turned the missive over in his hands. He could open it and read its contents on the grounds that it might relate to their work here. But the Priory House project was officially over. The scholars were gone. The papers and books and maps had already been dispatched to Mortlake.

And Susanna was on her way to Bristol.

"Send a rider after Lady Appleton," he told Jacob. "With luck he'll catch their party in Boscastle before they take ship. If not, have him go on by land. That route is longer, but he should still reach Bristol before she leaves there for Kent."

"Why should Master Baldwin write to Susanna?" Eleanor asked.

"Because he is her lover." At her start of surprise, he frowned. "You did not know?"

Walter thought back. Eleanor had stayed in Baldwin's house in Hamburg after she was injured, but he had been in England then and she had been in no condition to gossip with his servants. By the time she'd recovered enough to travel to Leigh Abbey, Baldwin had returned to the Continent. She'd never seen Susanna with her lover, never had reason to think of them together. Had she come to believe that Walter, who had once asked Susanna to marry him, was Susanna's lover? Eleanor's jealousy of Susanna had long been apparent to him, but until now he'd never considered that he might have misjudged the reasons behind it.

"Were you not curious about what Nick Baldwin said?" Eleanor asked a short time later, when Jacob had left with the still unopened letter.

"No," he said, and was pleased by the knowledge that he spoke nothing but the truth. "That part of my life is over."

38

Susanna had argued against a journey by sea. She had a long-standing aversion to travel by water, but the land route would have taken much longer, especially with a party that included pack horses and women. They'd have had to ride southeast to Launceston, the only reliable way across the Tamar into Devon, then through two rural counties in which it would be far too easy to lose one's way.

Local lanes were distinguishable only to those who knew them, and most people went no farther from their homes than the nearest market town. Walter had warned that they'd be fortunate to cover ten miles a day if they insisted upon crossing Exmoor to the hill country of Somersetshire. Roads that might seem to be a direct route to their goal would turn out to be lanes wandering through fields to woods and pastures and uplands that ran past enclosed fields bounded by hedges and stone walls.

On the day after their departure from Priory House, Susanna had time to ponder those facts. High winds and torrents of rain had stranded them in Boscastle.

Roads would have been just as impassable in such a downpour, but she chafed at any delay. Waiting gave her too much time to worry about the coming voyage and to have second thoughts concerning the real reason she'd insisted upon accompanying Gwyn to Bristol. In spite of Lionel's love for that young woman and hers

for him, Susanna meant to uncover the truth about Martin Calthorpe's murder.

But when she succeeded, what then? And would Lionel regard
her quest for answers as justified or see it as a personal betrayal?

"Do you think the old man will give his permission?" Jennet
asked in a low voice. She, too, had been watching Gwyn and Lionel and knew that Lionel was set upon asking Gwyn's only surviving relative, the elderly great-grandfather, for Gwyn's hand in
marriage.

"I can think of no reason for him to refuse," Susanna said.
"Owen Merrick was ready to agree before he died."

The best that could be said for this poor excuse for an inn was
that it was warm and dry and they were out of the elements, but
they were crowded into a tiny common room cheek by jowl, even
though Susanna had paid for the privilege of dining alone with
her party. Lionel and Gwyn sat close together on a window seat,
their noses all but touching as they gazed into each other's eyes.

"That old man sounds an odd duck, for all he was a successful
merchant. Gwyn says he calls himself 'Lord John' and puts on airs
to match."

Gwyn, Susanna thought, said a great many things, not all of
them true. She'd destroyed two documents, Twide's testimony and
the account of John Cabot's death. Why? What did the two things
have in common? Only Norombega, a land far away across the
Western Sea. Why should a young woman from Bristol care about
that?

The obvious answer was that she did not, that she'd done
naught but her father's bidding.

In the distance, a horse nickered. Susanna had paid the red-
haired innkeeper a shilling each to feed the horses, to assure
they'd be in good condition when Piers returned them to Walter
at Priory House.

She was less certain her resources would keep the people she
most cared about safe from harm. It was not that she thought
Gwyn had helped kill Martin Calthorpe. Gwyn might not even
realize what her father had done, although she must suspect. But

she had to know why those papers needed to be destroyed. That meant she knew why Calthorpe had been a threat to Merrick.

The last thing Susanna wanted was to wreck the happiness of two young people, but she could not in good conscience sanction Lionel's marriage until she had heard a logical explanation for recent events. She hoped a glimpse of Gwyn's home and family might give her some hint of how to proceed.

The door to the common room slammed open, admitting a man dressed for riding. Dripping onto the rushes, he came straight to Susanna. "Message sent on from Priory House," he said.

Susanna's spirits lifted when she recognized Nick Baldwin's familiar seal. His letter was in answer to the one she had sent him weeks earlier. He'd put it aboard a ship leaving Hamburg for Falmouth just as he, too, departed that city. Smiling, she ordered a hot meal for the messenger. Nick was on his way home.

But when she read on, her smile faded. There was a reason for his early return. His mother was ill, perhaps dying. Nick feared it was the plague. Susanna glanced at the date on the letter and frowned. Nick must already be in London, and by now Winifred Baldwin would no longer be ailing, she'd have recovered or be in her grave.

Powerless to do more to help Nick than plan to stop in London on her way back to Leigh Abbey, Susanna sat down on an uncomfortable wooden bench to read the rest of the letter. Bless him! In spite of his concern over his mother's health, Nick had taken the time to search his memory and the extensive records he kept and write down everything his friend Lorenzo Zeno had ever told him about the Zeno family.

"Nicolo Zeno was a wealthy man of Venice," he wrote, "captain of a galley that fought at Chioggia in a great battle there in the year 1380 and of the same family as Lorenzo Zeno, the man who befriended me in Persia. The Venetians in general are great explorers. Long ago they acquired mathematical methods of navigation from the Levant. In the time of Nicolo, they carried on overland trade with Germany, Lombardy, and the Baltic. Nicolo sailed into the Atlantic, mayhap all the way to Greenland, and visited many islands north of England. Both Nicolo and his brother Antonio sailed for the lord of the Orkneys, whose family name was de Sancto Claro in the Latin form. It is more commonly written Zinclo, in Italian, and Sinclair, in English."

Zichmni?

Susanna wondered if the vagaries of handwriting and spelling might account for the difference, especially in documents that had been damaged by time and careless handling. Then, too, Master Zeno might have had some complex political reason of his own for deliberately disguising the identity of his northern lord.

She left the inn's private parlor for the small bedchamber she shared with Jennet and Gwyn and unearthed a list of dates she had compiled during her research at Priory House. What she already knew fit well with what Nick's friend had told him.

"The Orkneys," she murmured. Had they been claimed by Scotland by 1380? Or had they still belonged to Norway? She had some vague recollection of a great queen who'd ruled all the lands in the Baltic at about that time.

"Where are these Orkneys everyone keeps mentioning?" Jennet asked in an irritated voice. She'd come into the chamber, unnoticed, while Susanna was studying the list of dates.

"Everyone?" Susanna gave her a sharp look. Jennet was known to exaggerate.

"Aye. Well, you and Gwyn Merrick."

"What did Gwyn say about the Orkneys?"

Jennet obliged with a story about Gwyn's ancestors. As she told the tale, Susanna continued to stare at the list in her hand.

The pieces fit together. Twide's statement. The Zeno narrative, borrowed and then returned. The story of Cabot's death. All three concerned events in a place most mapmakers called Norombega.

"Gwyn's ancestors," she mused aloud, "had ties to the Orkneys in the reign of Henry IV, and that reign began just after one Zichmni, a great northern lord, made a voyage to the New World."

Her gaze shifted to the little pile of Gwyn's possessions and her eyes narrowed. Walter had mentioned seeing an old account book, written in Latin, when he searched Gwyn's bedchamber at Priory

House. How old? she wondered. And did it hold more clues to this strange business?

"Watch the door," she ordered Jennet.

It did not take long to find the book, which was very old indeed. Holding it close to a candle, Susanna began to read.

Most of the entries were records of payments for household goods. A few were recipes for herbal remedies. But the last pages contained a list of supplies. The amounts were sufficient to sustain a large party of travelers on a long voyage.

39

Gwyn's behavior as they approached Bristol puzzled Jennet. She seemed nervous, as if she were afraid she would be blamed in some way for her father's death. Or mayhap for her failure to bring his body home for burial. Or did it have something to do with the book Lady Appleton had found? Jennet had watched her mistress read it and been curious about what it contained, but Lady Appleton had not explained. She'd just looked disturbed afterward and asked Jennet if she thought Gwyn's love for Lionel was real. Then she'd returned the book to Gwyn's cap-case before that young woman retired to their shared bedchamber for the night.

The next morning they'd set sail. Once aboard ship, Jennet had known better than to ask Lady Appleton questions. She had never been comfortable aboard any ship, and on this journey, brief though it was to be, they'd already had to contend with all manner of hazards. Even the beginning of the voyage had been fraught with peril. For safety, sailing vessels had to be towed in and out of Boscastle Harbor. Ropes tied to hobbler boats, each manned by eight rowers, as well as those controlled by men on shore, had been required to keep their small ship in the middle of the chan-nel. An island standing off the harbor entrance had presented another obstacle, and then, in open water, they'd still had to face fast tidal currents and the possibility of sudden, fierce, northwesterly gales.

After they entered the winding, seven-mile stretch of river that led direct to Bristol, the way was bordered on both sides by shallows, mud flats, and outcroppings of rock, and, at the last, the high sides of a narrow gorge, where near vertical cliffs rose more than three hundred feet above the waters below. The river pilot who'd come aboard at an anchorage called Hung Road brought them through a channel cut hundreds of years before in order to create a harbor for large ships in the very heart of Bristol, a fortified city built on hills and connected by bridges.

Secure on land again, relieved to be out of danger, Lady Appleton paused to look back out over the mast-dotted harbor and spoke for the first time since they'd left Boscastle. "From here brave Englishmen first set out to find the riches of the New World." A note of awe suffused the comment.

Startled, Gwyn followed Lady Appleton's gaze, but her voice sounded grim. "At low tide the water recedes, leaving those ships still in port to squat on the mud for nine hours out of every twelve, waiting for the tide to come in and lift them free."

She turned away from the sight and led them at a brisk pace up narrow, twisting streets, some no wider than a man's shoulders. Shops and houses opened directly onto these lanes, their upper stories jutting out above, each projecting over the one below and blocking out the sun, just as they did in London. In a matter of minutes they'd left the worst of the tenements behind, along with the stink of marsh and encroaching low tide and come into an area filled with large, timber-framed houses.

"There are only two Merricks left," Gwyn said, as she stopped before a substantial dwelling. "I am the youngest, the last."

"And the other is your great-grandfather—he must be ancient indeed," Lady Appleton said.

"Five and eighty," Gwyn replied.

"She is in awe of him," Jennet said in a soft voice as Gwyn opened the thick, oaken door and went in ahead of them.

"And a little afraid," Lady Appleton whispered back.

Inside it was cool and dark. The only light that filtered in came through windows glazed with tinted glass. A thronelike chair placed near an ornate hearth dominated the hall. At first Jennet thought it was empty; then she saw movement. A frail white head lifted to reveal dark eyes burning in sunken sockets. In spite of age and apparent ill-health, the skeletal figure had a presence about it. Jennet no longer wondered why they called him Lord John.

40

Susanna looked up as Jennet entered the bedchamber she'd been given as an honored guest in Lord John's house. "Did you complete the tasks I gave you?"

"Aye. If I do not return before tomorrow afternoon, the goldsmith will follow your instructions. But why take such precautions, madam? Are we in danger?"

"I am . . . uneasy." There did not seem to be any servants about, but she lowered her voice as she drew Jennet down beside her on the bed. "Owen Merrick killed both Martin Calthorpe and Bartholomew Fletcher."

Jennet gasped. "Does Gwyn know?"

"She must suspect, and it follows that Lord John does, too. I believe Merrick and his daughter came to Priory House not to advance our knowledge of the New World, but to keep us from discovering certain details about one part of it."

Why they'd done this was still unclear to her. As near as she could reckon, Lord John had no direct connection with events in the documents Gwyn had destroyed, although he would have been a young boy in Bristol when John Cabot sailed away on his last voyage.

"Oh, madam, I do not like this at all."

"Nor do I, Jennet; but for Master Calthorpe's sake, and for Lionel's, we must try to learn more."

"What do you intend to do?"

"Beard the lion in his den. What else?"

She led the way to the hall, where Gwyn's great-grandfather still sat in his thronelike chair. Gwyn and Lionel had drawn stools close to his right side.

Lionel hopped up as soon as he caught sight of Susanna. "Excellent news, madam. Lord John has agreed to my marriage to Gwyn."

"Has he, indeed?"

"Do you disapprove, Lady Appleton?" Lord John's voice was not strong, but his eyes glittered with an intensity that made her wary.

If he'd been ten years younger, she'd never have risked this confrontation. She suspected he still had a volatile temper. But he had already lived well beyond the life span of an ordinary man. He leaned heavily on a stick, even seated, and if he could walk unaided, she'd yet to see him do so.

"I have questions, Lord John. If Lionel still wants to marry Gwyn after I have heard your answers, I will not stand in his way; but I am responsible for the members of my household, and I cannot let him enter your family blind to its . . . history."

Lord John's smile was not pleasant. "Questions, madam? Or accusations?"

"I do not intend to make public anything you tell me. Why should I? Those responsible for murder are no longer alive to be held accountable."

Gwyn's gasp confirmed part of what Susanna had guessed, but she kept her eyes on the old man.

"What is it you think you know, Lady Appleton?"

"That there was a colony sent to the area we now call Norombega shortly after the year fourteen hundred, the year the earl of Orkney returned from that place. Preparations for the journey are recorded in an old account book kept by one Alison Dunnett. Your ancestor, I believe."

Gwyn, eyes wide, clenched Lionel's hand so tight that he winced.

"England and Scotland were at war at the time, reason enough to keep the venture secret. But what happened afterward? Were they forgotten? Or did they deliberately cut themselves off? Either way, I believe this settlement gave rise to rumors of a 'white tribe' in the New World, rumors that began to circulate almost as soon as the Spanish made their first landfall."

No one reacted to this claim, so she continued.

"A few years after Spain's early voyages of discovery, an English ship was wrecked in Norombega. The survivors, including John Cabot of Bristol, were killed to keep them from spreading word of the colony's existence. But one man escaped the slaughter. He does not seem to have realized what really happened. He assumed the hostile natives were Amerindians, but they were not, were they?"

The old man hesitated, then shrugged. "No, Lady Appleton, they were not. My father gave the order for that massacre."

Susanna blinked. She had not expected that revelation. At her side, she felt Jennet tense. Lionel just looked confused.

"I do not pretend I understand all the connections and relationships, Lord John, but I have recorded my thoughts and suspicions in a letter. Should anything happen to me, it will be sent at once to Sir Walter Pendennis."

"Given what my great-granddaughter has told me of you, Lady Appleton, I expected no less. Pray, continue."

"There is not much more for me to tell. Why are you determined to keep the existence of the colony secret? Cabot's murderers are long dead."

"I am still among the living, Lady Appleton." His smile, however, made her think of a death's head. "Let me tell you a story. In the year of our Lord 1403, a group of colonists, including Sir Gavin Dunnett and his wife, set out from Scotland. As you surmised, they used the charts brought back by Henry Sinclair, earl of Orkney, to guide them to the new land. They were also entrusted with the keeping of a sacred object. It was their charge to remove this relic from all danger of being captured by our enemies, the English. It was thought they would either use its terrible power against us or attempt to destroy it. Any such attempt, Lady Appleton, would have unleashed unimaginable evil upon the world."

From the grave expression on Lord John's face, he believed every word of this remarkable tale. Susanna wondered why he should be so forthcoming, but she was loath to interrupt his narration. There would be time enough when he had finished to ask more questions.

"The relic was kept secure in a box made of an unknown metal," Lord John continued. "The colonists' charge was to bury it and conceal its burial place for two hundred years. If it remains unseen by man for that length of time, it will be rendered harmless."

Ingram's treasure, Susanna thought. Aloud she asked, "Two hundred years?"

"Until the year of our Lord 1603. When the ship made landfall, those aboard buried the box on an island."

Twide's island. "A dangerous object with supernatural powers," she murmured.

"A sacred trust," Gwyn corrected her.

Susanna had been taught not to put much stock in "holy" relics. Along with the monasteries, Henry VIII had done away with popish idols and the possibility of miracles procured by visiting the shrines of the saints. But faith was a powerful force, and the same men who advocated the strictest tenets of the New Religion and denied the healing power of a holy well were the first to accept that a witch might dwell among them able to harness occult powers to do harm. Susanna had learned not to reject any possibility out of hand.

"Is it the Holy Grail?" Jennet whispered.

Gwyn's great-grandfather gave a dry cackle that sent chills down Susanna's spine. "It is forbidden to describe our sacred trust or the precise powers it possesses, but I will tell you that it is most ancient, older than any church in existence today."

"Generation after generation, our family has renewed its pledge to guard this secret," Gwyn said.

"There was little difficulty for the first hundred years." Lord

John seemed to be looking into the past, his eyes out of focus, his voice growing more thready with every word. "What you call our 'white tribe' intermarried with Amerindians. We adopted many of their ways. But we stayed close to the island to guard our sacred trust."

"Then Cabot came."

"Aye. And three years later, another Bristol ship appeared." Gwyn's great-grandfather paused, as if to gather his thoughts. When he went on, his voice seemed stronger. Pride lifted shoulders stooped with age. "I was born John Dunnett, a prince in that new land. I stood on a promontory in what you call Norombega and watched that second ship anchor in our bay. A few days later, following my father's orders, I allowed myself to be captured and taken across the Western Sea. My mission was to learn how matters stood here. I was still a lad, although I was big and looked older than my years." His laugh reminded Susanna of the cackle of a raven. "Any older and I'd never have passed for a native. Real Amerindians do not have much body hair. A beard would have given me away."

"You were one of the 'wonders' brought back to England and taken to the court of Henry VII," Susanna said. "Did you plan to return to Norombega?"

"That was to be my decision. Making sure the colony remained a secret was my primary goal. After a few years, when king and courtiers had lost interest in me, I was able to leave London and start a new life. I had learned a great deal by listening. I had mastered the English language. Since there did not seem to be any immediate danger to my people, I traveled to Scotland. That is where I found the account book."

He cast his fulminating gaze on his great-granddaughter, who hung her head. "You failed to keep it safe from discovery, girl. I am disappointed in you." With a glare that promised a suitable punishment would be forthcoming, he resumed the telling of his tale.

"I settled in Bristol, where I created a new identity for myself. I became John Merrick, of Welsh descent. I married and bred up progeny to continue what I'd crossed the Western Sea to do—use any means necessary to eliminate threats to our sacred trust."

A little silence fell while Susanna considered what she'd just been told. Even if this relic had no real power, word of its existence would cause an uproar. Radical reformers in England and Scotland would be as eager as any representative of the Inquisition to destroy such a thing. It would be best for everyone concerned to leave it buried, but that begged the question of why Lord John should of a sudden have revealed its existence to her. If, for the seventy years he'd spent in England, he'd kept this secret, it did not make sense for him to break his silence now.

She glanced at Gwyn. With Owen Merrick gone, Lord John had no one else to carry on his family's obligations. Only Gwyn and any children she and Lionel might have.

The old man was feeble. He needed help from outsiders. And Susanna wanted to help him, but she needed one more answer first. "Tell me, Lord John," she asked, "did your grandson go to Priory House with the intent to do murder?"

41

Gwyn looked so horrified by Lady Appleton's suggestion that Jennet took a step toward her, compelled to offer reassurance and comfort. No matter what her father had done, Gwyn must not blame herself.

Lionel warned her off with a glare. His arms wrapped around his beloved, he appeared ready to defend her against anyone, even Lady Appleton and Jennet.

"His mission was to misdirect any discoveries that might threaten our sacred trust," Lord John replied. "No more."

"And no less. Why was Calthorpe killed?"

"Tell her, Gwyn," Lord John ordered.

Lionel spoke first. He faced Gwyn, hands on her shoulders, eyes locked with hers. "Nothing you say can change what is between us. Remember that. I love you and I mean to marry you, no matter what you or any of your family have done."

Jennet shifted so she could see Gwyn's expression. Tears streamed down the young woman's cheeks, but she seemed to take strength from Lionel's words. After a moment, she managed a tremulous smile and spoke to him, ignoring not only Jennet and Lady Appleton but also Lord John.

"My father meant to search Master Calthorpe's study. He did not plan to kill anyone. When Master Calthorpe came in and caught him, Father tried to flee and the two of them collided.

Master Calthorpe fell to his knees. Father's spectacles flew off."
Gwyn sniffled. "That threw him into a panic. He struck Master
Calthorpe. After that, it seemed to him that he had no choice. If
Calthorpe lived, he would ask questions. Father could not risk
what might come out."

She scrubbed at her eyes and sniffed again, but Lionel never
faltered in his devotion. Although Jennet could sense his distress,
he continued to stroke Gwyn's arms with gentle, soothing caresses.

"When I left you that day," Gwyn said to Lionel, "I saw Father
come out of Master Calthorpe's study. I did not know what he
had done, but I noticed that he held his spectacles, broken, in one
hand. I caught up with him, meaning to accompany him into the
stable yard. Lady Pendennis had just arrived. But he sent me to
our lodgings to fetch his spare spectacles and before I could return
with them, he joined me there. He said I was needed in the house,
that guests had arrived. It was not until much later that I learned
Master Calthorpe was dead."

"What prompted your father to search Calthorpe's study?" Lady
Appleton asked.

"He'd overheard Master Calthorpe's questions to Master Alday
and was concerned that there might be more documents contain-
ing information about John Cabot's voyages. Lady Pendennis's arrival should have provided a diversion, but Master Calthorpe did
not go out into the stable yard. Instead he returned to his study
and found my father already there."

"*More* documents? So you did steal Twide's statement?"

"Yes, Lady Appleton, I did. Father read it, then burned it.
Twide mentioned a sacred island and also his discovery of a broken and rusted sword."

"Did your father find additional documents in Calthorpe's
study?"

"One. A letter from the same Mantuan gentleman whose account Calthorpe had come across in one of the Italian books. It
gave a slightly different version of what Master Sebastian Cabot
had told the Mantuan about John Cabot's death. It came close to
being the truth."

"So your father destroyed that, too."

Gwyn nodded.

"Why did your father leave the book by Master Zeno behind?" Lady Appleton asked. "I would have thought that far more dangerous."

"He did not realize what it was. It appeared to deal with Persia."

"I see," said Lady Appleton. "But once I revealed what else it contained, he decided to translate it for himself to be certain it held no further surprises."

"He told me to steal it," Gwyn admitted. "I did so while you were distracted by the quarrel between Lady Pendennis and her daughter."

So, Jennet thought, Gwyn had taken the book to her father. He had read it, reassured himself there was nothing in it to cause him more trouble, and convinced himself that if he left it in the parlor, Lady Appleton would believe she'd dropped it there herself. Since she'd already read it, unwelcome attention would have been focused on the idea of a Scots settlement had he not returned the book. He must have thought he'd gotten away with the trick when she made no fuss, just as he believed he'd gotten away with murder.

"And Ingram?" Lady Appleton was as persistent as Jennet had ever seen her. She meant to tie up every loose end. "I suppose it was your father who tried to kill him?"

Startled, Gwyn at last looked away from Lionel to stare at Lady Appleton. "I know nothing about any attack on Davy Ingram."

"Ingram saw and heard the same things Twide did. When it seemed he might tell me about them, your father tried to stop him. He came at Ingram with a knife, but Ingram used his walking stick to defend himself."

That must have been why Master Merrick had been rubbing his ribs the day she and Gwyn inspected the brewhouse, Jennet thought.

Gwyn buried her face in Lionel's doublet. He patted her back, no less supportive than before, but his complexion had gone a sickly color and his eyes were dull.

"It was pure luck that Twide shipped out before Owen Merrick realized what was in his statement," Lady Appleton continued. "He must have lived in fear of Twide's return." She left Gwyn to Lionel and addressed Lord John. "Or were you, mayhap, keeping watch for him here in Bristol?"

She did not wait for an answer.

"On the cliffs at Tintagel, Master Merrick was not trying to capture Master Fletcher. He meant to push him off the edge. Some might see it as rough justice that he ended up going over with him."

"My grandson is beyond the reach of the law," Lord John said, "and to my mind he sacrificed his life to a greater good. Do you mean to betray us, Lady Appleton? That letter you wrote will do untold harm if it falls into the wrong hands."

Jennet held her breath as Lady Appleton weighed what they had been told. She did not need long to make her decision. "Retrieve the letter to Sir Walter, Jennet, Now. I will destroy it in Lord John's presence as proof he can trust us never to speak of what has been said in this room."

"Go with her, Lionel," Lord John ordered.

Of a sudden, Jennet felt uneasy leaving Lady Appleton behind. "I do not trust Lord John," she whispered to Lionel as they went out into the streets of Bristol. "Where are all his servants?"

"He's an old man. What harm can he do?" He sounded testy, but after a moment he began to smile. Without warning, he caught Jennet by the waist and whirled her around.

"What are you so happy about?" she demanded when he put her down.

"That old man," Lionel reminded her, "has given me his permission to marry Gwyn. How can anything be wrong when I am to have her to wife?"

42

Come closer, Lady Appleton," Lord John requested when Jennet and Lionel had left the house. "Sit beside me, that I do not have to strain to hear. I am a feeble old man. None of my abilities are what they once were."

Susanna noted the odd little sound that statement provoked from Gwyn but thought nothing of it. It was only when she came within reach and Lord John bounded to his feet with unexpected agility that she realized his frailty had been a ruse. A moment later his arm wrapped around her throat with strength enough to cut off the flow of air. She was perilous close to blacking out as he hauled her toward his chair and forced her to sit.

Unable to summon sufficient control over her limbs to fight him, she ended up tied hand and foot. By the time she recovered enough breath to protest, she'd been immobilized. Cackling to himself, Lord John left her side to fetch an ornate wooden box from a shelf in a nearby cupboard. Within, two wheel-lock pistols nestled in purpose-built, velvet-lined compartments.

As Susanna watched in increasing alarm, Lord John ran loving fingers over the brass barrel and wooden stock of one of them, then poured in powder from a powder flask and rammed it firmly home. He added a ball, again applied the ramrod, then reached for a second, smaller flask. His dexterity in putting the fine priming powder into the pan located atop the wheel and alongside the vent of the barrel told Susanna he knew how to use the weapon. He repeated the entire complicated process with the other pistol, smiling all the while. The expression made his face look even more like a death's head.

"Why kill me?" Susanna heard no betraying tremor in her voice, but her throat felt raw from rough handling.

"You are an outsider," Lord John said. "You cannot be trusted." His calm voice left her in no doubt that his mind was set upon protecting his sacred trust.

Susanna did not dare look at Gwyn. She was too afraid she would see the same determination, the same fanatic gleam, in that young woman's eyes.

"We await your servant's return with the letter." Lord John held one pistol in each hand. "I must be certain to leave no evidence behind."

Once again a small sound of distress escaped Gwyn.

"Do you mean to kill Lionel, too?" Susanna asked.

He started to deny it, then fixed his great-granddaughter with a speculative stare. "Are you breeding, girl?"

Eyes wide and terrified, she shook her head.

"A pity. If you were already with child, we could do without him."

Gwyn loved Lionel, but she feared Lord John. Evaluating her chances of getting out of this predicament alive, Susanna found little in that to encourage her. She did not doubt Lionel's loyalty to her, but if he walked into this situation unprepared, that would only get him killed.

She was very much afraid that all their lives—her own, Jennet's, and Lionel's—depended upon Gwyn Merrick; and given the way that young woman was trembling, tears once more streaming down her face, it did not appear she would be much use. She was terrified of her great-grandfather, as well she should be. His obsession with this "sacred trust" had turned him into the same sort of zealot responsible for the worst excesses of the Spanish Inquisition.

Guns, Susanna knew, were notorious for misfiring, but she had

219

to assume the old man was expert with his pistols. Each fired only one shot, and he would have no time to reload; but if his aim were true, two shots would be sufficient to dispose of both Jennet and Lionel, assuming Lionel refused to go along with Lord John's plans. Lord John could then take all the time he needed to deal with Susanna. She tugged at her bonds, but the knots held tight, biting into the tender flesh at her wrists.

"How many have you murdered to keep your secret over the years?" she asked.

Lord John did not answer, but Gwyn stifled her sobs and dried her tears with the backs of her hands.

How many generations, Susanna wondered, had this one old man trained as killers?

After what seemed an endless wait, Jennet and Lionel returned. They were met by Lord John and his pistols. "Stand still," he ordered. "Take the letter, Gwyn. Make sure it is the right one."

Susanna's heart sank when Gwyn obeyed. She took little comfort in knowing a copy existed, already dispatched to Nick with instructions that it be read in the event of her death.

"It is the letter," Gwyn said.

"Gwyn?" From the devastation in Lionel's voice, he had guessed what Lord John intended.

"Bind the woman," the old man told his great-granddaughter. The pistol aimed at Lionel's head never wavered.

Meekness was not part of Jennet's nature. She fought her younger, stronger opponent until Gwyn wrestled her to her knees. Their struggles took them over half the hall and ended on the far side of a trestle table. Wrenching Jennet's arms behind her, Gwyn pushed her flat on the floor. Sir John tossed a length of rope in their direction, setting one of the pistols down in order to do so. He kept his eyes and the other gun trained on Lionel.

"Now, then," he said to the young man, "you have a choice to make. My only son died many years ago. You know what happened to my grandson. My great-granddaughter is my only remaining kin, sole heiress to a considerable fortune, but whatever man marries her must also pledge to take up the responsibility of our sacred trust."

Lionel stared at him in horrified fascination. "No one here will betray you, Lord John. Why have you bound Lady Appleton? She will not—"

"Only family can be relied upon, Lionel. You will soon be family, will you not?"

"I mean to marry Gwyn, yes. But—"

"Anyone who is not with us is against us. The deaths of Lady Appleton and her companion will be blamed on robbers. You need not worry that any will suspect you of complicity."

"But there is no need to harm her," Lionel argued. "She has already sworn to keep your secret. She never breaks her word. Never."

"These two women must die," the old man insisted. "It is the only way. And if you do not help me dispose of them, then you will die, too." He hefted the pistol to emphasize his point.

Lionel sent an agonized look in Gwyn's direction.

Susanna jerked at the ropes that bound her. They were so tight and unyielding that she no longer had any sensation in her hands.

"I am no murderer, Lord John," Lionel said. "I will not kill for any man—or woman." He avoided looking at Gwyn, but his voice shook on that last word. Then it came out strong and steady once more as he added, "Nor will I cover up such a crime."

Susanna could not hold back a groan. If only Lionel had pretended to go along with Lord John's plan, the old man might have lowered his guard, allowing Lionel to seize his weapon. Now it was too late.

Eyes fixed on the mechanism as Lord John pressed the trigger, releasing the wheel-lock, Susanna felt as if time slowed to a crawl. She saw the pan-cover open, knocking the stone onto the spinning wheel and causing a shower of sparks.

At the same instant the priming powder ignited, Gwyn flung herself at her great-grandfather, knocking his arm aside. The explosion of the pistol filled the room with the smell of gunpowder and a haze of smoke. The ball landed, harmlessly, in the ceiling, sending a shower of plaster down upon the combatants.

For a stunned second, no one moved. Then Lord John dove for the other pistol, abandoned atop the trestle table. Distracted by Lionel's rush to Gwyn's side, Susanna did not see what happened next, but somehow the second gun ended up in Jennet's hands. As Lord John grappled with her, trying to regain possession of the weapon, it went off with a muffled report.

The old man sagged. Jennet squirmed free of his encircling arms, flailing at him until he crumpled to the floor. He landed on his back and, with a groan of pain, turned his head to glare at his great-granddaughter.

"Traitor," he rasped.

Blood poured from a gaping wound in his chest.

Lionel pulled Gwyn into his arms, holding her so that she did not have to watch the old man die.

Jennet backed away from the grisly sight, feeling behind her for Susanna's chair. Only when she bumped against her mistress's legs could she stop looking at what she had wrought. She shuddered once, convulsively, then knelt and began to saw through Susanna's ropes with a knife.

"Where did that come from? How did you get free?" Belatedly, Susanna added, "My thanks to you, Jennet. You saved our lives."

"No, Gwyn did that. She only pretended to bind me. And she gave me the knife."

Rubbing her wrists, stumbling a little as the blood rushed back into her feet, Susanna made her way to Lord John's side. It was far too late to offer any herbal remedies, even if she'd been inclined to save him, but his eyes were open and glazed and if he could still hear her, she felt compelled to speak.

"No one will betray your sacred trust, Lord John. I do swear it."

Over the top of Gwyn's head, Lionel's somber gaze met Susanna's. "I love her," he said. "I do not care what her family has done."

And she loves you, Susanna thought, *more than her own kin or their sacred trust.* It was not the most auspicious beginning for a marriage, but with love and good fortune, and Lord John's fortune, too, these two had every hope of making a success of their union.

"He must have been mad," Lionel murmured.

"Madness is as good an explanation as any." Susanna gently pried Gwyn free of Lionel's embrace and indicated that he should remove the body. "Did you ever see any proof that his story was true?" she asked.

The young woman blanched. "Could it all have been a delusion?" she whispered. "The white tribe? The relic? The sacred trust?" At first appalled by the notion, when Gwyn had considered it for a few minutes she seemed to find comfort in Susanna's suggestion.

"He was an old man. His wits had wandered." So saying, Susanna set her mind to organizing what must be done. She had no difficulty convincing the local coroner and justice of the peace that Lord John had been the unfortunate victim of a tragic accident with a pistol. He was buried the next day with all due pomp and ceremony.

Three weeks later, Lionel and Gwyn were married. By then they had convinced themselves that Lord John had invented the whole fantastic tale.

Susanna did nothing to disabuse them of this belief. There was no harm and much good, she had decided, in letting the two young people think they had been deceived.

"Was any of Lord John's story true?" Jennet asked, as they watched the happy couple exchange their vows.

"We will never know for certain," Susanna admitted, "but if there is a sacred relic, I can think of no better way to keep it safe for another thirty-two years than to dismiss it as a fabrication."

A Note from the Author

Far-fetched, you say?

Not really.

First of all, "plantations" in America were much earlier than most people think. Plantation simply meant settlement. The Spanish started planting permanent colonies almost as soon as Columbus found land in the New World. In 1563, a group of French Huguenots attempted to settle in Spanish territory. By the time their leader returned home for supplies, wars of religion raged in France. He fled to England, hoping for financial support from Queen Elizabeth; but when he refused to swear allegiance to her, then tried to sneak out of the country, she had him imprisoned. At the same time, she was considering a proposal to send English Catholics to colonize La Florida. This plan fell through, but a few determined Englishmen sailed to the New World on one of John Hawkins's ships, intending to join the French colony. The Spanish ended the hopes of both French and English settlers when they slaughtered every non-Spaniard in the area.

The next attempt made by England was not until some twenty years later, with the Roanoke colony; but throughout the 1570s Englishmen continued to be interested in exploration, discovery, and settlement. Although the search for a northwest passage took precedence, the idea of establishing "plantations" was never abandoned. It might have received even more support had there not been an attempt in progress at the same time to plant English colonies in Ireland.

Many of the places my fictional scholars accept as real—Saint Brendan's Fortunate Isles, Prince Madoc's lost colony, and the lands named in the Zeno narrative, are probably sections of present-day North America. Certainly there is no doubt that fishermen from several seafaring nations crossed the Western Sea well before Columbus.

David Ingram really existed. He returned to England in 1569, the same year in which he walked from the Gulf of Mexico to present-day Nova Scotia, but his story was not published until much later. By then he'd embellished the tale to such an extent that he was not even believed in his own time. The captain under whom he served, the same John Hawkins mentioned above, spent much of 1571 treating with Spain for the release of the other survivors. Because of this, some of Queen Elizabeth's advisors suspected him of plotting treason.

Legends of Templar treasures hidden in the New World during the Middle Ages abound, including one that credits Henry Sinclair, earl of Orkney, with building the Newport Tower in present-day Rhode Island as a hiding place for the Holy Grail. The sixteenth century was a time when people still believed in the supernatural and the concept of a holy cause.

Most of the documents, maps, and books to which I refer are real, although some are no longer extant. The Zeno narrative, which was discredited in the eighteenth and nineteenth centuries, was shown in the twentieth to be completely plausible. On the other hand, although surely his son had some ideas on the subject, no one today knows for certain what happened to John Cabot. The "maps and discourses" Sebastian Cabot left with his executor had vanished by the 1580s.

It is possible they were destroyed, along with many other records housed at the headquarters of the Muscovy Company, during the Great Fire of London. Or they might have been casualties of the sack of John Dee's library at Mortlake in 1583. Dee acquired a great deal of information on exploration and discovery. He accepted as fact most of the theories I have my fictional scholars advance, including the possibility that King Arthur sent colonists to America. Dee preferred the name Atlantis.

I've tried to be consistent in spelling place names, although the mapmakers of the period most assuredly were not. I chose Norombega, generally spelled with a *u* nowadays, because that was the most common spelling in Susanna's time. There might have been a "white tribe" in Norombega, but both its origins and its fate have long since vanished into the mists. The mythical city of Norombega is believed by many to have been located on the Penobscot River at the present site of Bangor, Maine.

The wonderful thing about writing fiction is that one can speculate about history's mysteries without the need to uncover absolute proof. Anything is within the realm of possibility. If you are interested in my sources, the complete bibliography is at *www.kathylynnemerson.com,* but my primary goal in writing this book has been to tell a good story. Enjoy!